THE
BODY
AT
BLACKWELL
LAKE

ALSO BY A.M. CAPLAN

Echoes
Reverberation
Dead Quiet

THE
BODY
AT
BLACKWELL
LAKE

A.M. CAPLAN

THE BODY AT BLACKWELL LAKE

Printed in the United States of America

First Printing, January 2022

Cover design by Best Page Forward
Typeset in Palatino by Chapter One Book Production, UK
Printed in the United States

FOR HEATHER

There's no one I'd trust more to help me cover up a homicide

PART 1

FINDERS KEEPERS

Some things were better lost than found.

—Stephen King

1

Cora reached overhead and caught the small silver bell that hung above the door. She trapped the clapper between her thumb and forefinger, keeping all but a quiet, tinny *ching* from escaping. But Harold had ears like a bat. From somewhere inside the dim interior of the pawnshop, he called out, "We don't open 'til nine."

The bank of fluorescent tubes overhead spit and flickered, then stayed on. Harold came out of the back room in a hurry, then slowed to a shuffle when he recognized her.

"Oh, it's just you, Cora." Harold swiped his hands across the legs of his brown polyester pants. They left streaks of dust like ghostly handprints on his thighs. "Maybe you should dust that off for me while you've got a hold of it. God knows I can't reach."

"Dust it? I'd like to kick it across the street. Bells are supposed to make nice, tinkly noises. This one sounds like a root canal." She let go of it, wincing at the shrill jangle, and let the door fall shut behind her. The thing *was* dusty, and she scrubbed her hand against her faded t-shirt. "Why do you unlock the door so early if you aren't ready to open?"

Harold reached past her and turned the red and white open sign. "Why do I unlock so early?" He pulled a rag out of his back pocket and rubbed a fingerprint from the glass beside the sign, then swiped at the dusty prints on his pant legs. "Don't want to miss the chance of being robbed bright and early. I'm too old for those nighttime stickups." Harold moved on to the closest display case, running his rag across the glass top, then carefully over a neat pyramid of baseballs in clear acrylic cases. When he was finished, he turned to really look at her for the first time and shook his head. "You okay, kiddo? You're white as a sheet."

"I'm always white as a sheet, Harold. I'm fine." Cora wasn't exactly fine. Her vision was blurry, like she was wearing glasses with the wrong prescription. She shook her head to clear it, and the blur receded to her peripheral vision. It was annoying, but bearable. "Just tired," she lied. "The rain last night kept me up."

Harold looked at her for a moment longer, then nodded. "If you say so." He bent over and gave a pair of guitars on stands a swipe with his rag and stuffed it back into his pocket. "Where the hell you been, anyway? Ain't seen you in a month. I was starting to think you skipped town."

"I've been around," Cora said. "I just didn't have anything for you. Pickings have been a little slim."

"The lady has nothing for me. God forbid she stop by just to say hello?" Harold tsk-tsked and went behind the glass case that served as his counter, turning on the blocky electric cash register with his key. While it beeped and chirruped, he looked sideways out the display window to the sidewalk. A large black dog sat on its haunches, tied with a leash to the parking meter. "You can bring him in, you know. I'd make an exception for Rocky."

"What, and have him miss the chance to slobber all over every kid that walks by?" Cora gave a dismissive wave in the direction of the dog and pulled the bag from her shoulder. Plunking it down on the counter, she flipped open the worn leather flap and began to dig.

Harold crossed his arms over his high, round belly. "You know, Cora, it's probably not so bad you haven't come by to see me so often. Things have been pretty slow. I'm not really looking to buy any—"

"Good story," Cora said, hiding a smile. She found what she was looking for in the bottom of her bag, jumbled in with the loose change and pens lifted from the bank. "You always say that, and you always buy." She pulled a small chamois pouch from her bag and held it up.

Harold shook his head and sighed. "I always buy because at heart I'm a giant marshmallow."

"You always buy because I never bring you junk." After a moment of fiddling with the tiny ties, Cora opened the mouth of the pouch and turned it over onto the counter. The contents slithered out and landed on the glass in a waterfall of metallic clinks.

Harold uncrossed his arms and reached under the counter for a jewelry tray. He picked up the bracelet, laying it out over the black velvet and nudging it into a straight line, then fished a jeweler's loupe out of his shirt pocket. Putting it to his eye, he bent over the tray. "Sapphires and diamonds, huh? Real ones." Harold lowered the loupe and winked at her. "But you knew that, right?" He raised the loupe again and turned the bracelet over, examining the markings on the back of the clasp. "Eighteen karat. Little dinged up from being worn, but that don't make no matter."

The loupe went back into Harold's breast pocket, and his hands came down on either side of the tray. He leaned toward Cora. "Two hundred."

Cora tried to keep a straight face, but she was pretty sure one side of her lips twitched before she could catch it. "Two hundred, Harold? This bracelet cost somebody four, five grand, easy." It was probably closer to three, but he knew that as well as he knew two hundred was an outright insult. "I'll give it to you for two *thousand.*"

"Maybe it cost somebody two grand brand-new out of a jewelry store in New York, but in case you haven't noticed, this ain't New York." Harold waved a hand around the pawnshop, past the old watches and newish TVs and baseball cards and hunting rifles. "And it's not worth anything if I can't move it and make a profit. Some of this stuff sits here forever, just reminding me I'm too soft when it comes to pretty ladies."

She rolled her eyes and pointed down into the display case. "We both know half the business you do here is jewelry, Harold. Maybe two grand is asking a *little* much," she conceded. "I'll take a thousand, because I'm a sucker, but only if you don't give me any more crap about not being able to sell it. I don't recognize a single thing in this case. I definitely don't see a single thing *I* sold you." She crossed her arms and stared him down. "The only thing in this case you haven't moved since last time I was here is that ugly parrot necklace." She uncrossed her arms and pointed at it, a bright, flashy mess of enamel and paste stones on a fat, fake gold chain. "I sure as hell didn't sell you *that*. Those are not real rubies, you know."

Harold's eyes flicked to the necklace, and he shrugged. "Eh, sometimes real don't matter. If it's showy enough, people don't care. I'll give you three hundred."

"Eight hundred."

"Four hundred." Harold's eyes narrowed. "That's if it's clean, goes without sayin'. Nobody's going to come looking for it, are they? Cops ain't gonna stop by searching for stuff from a robbery or something like that, take it and leave me with a piece of paper and a bad taste in my mouth?" Harold picked up the bracelet and closed the clasp, weighing the shining circlet in his palm.

It was Cora's turn to narrow her eyes. "Have I ever once brought you anything hot, Harold? I got it the same way I get everything." She cocked her head toward the window. "Rocky nosed it out while we were taking a walk. I went through all the proper channels trying to find who lost it, and now it's mine, fair and legal."

Harold tilted the bracelet back and forth in his hand, letting the overhead lights glitter off the blue and white stones, following it with his eyes while he considered.

"You know what, Harold?" Cora closed the flap of her bag and slung it back over her shoulder. "I think maybe I'll see if I can get rid of it online. Takes longer, but I know I can get more for it. I only came by because I was hoping to get a little cash in hand. But I'm sure I can get by." She held out her hand, palm open.

"Six hundred. Final offer." Harold curled his fingers a little more closely around the sapphires and diamonds, cutting off her view of the shimmering stones. "That's as high as I can go." He sighed. "Hope to hell I can turn it around right away, else I don't know how I'll manage to keep the lights on this month."

She didn't buy his sob story about six hundred dollars pushing him into the poorhouse any more than Harold believed she was going to walk back out of the pawnshop with the bracelet. Cora closed the hand she'd been holding open. Harold slipped the bracelet into his shirt pocket where it settled against the jeweler's loupe with a click. Then he opened the register and started to count out crisp hundred-dollar bills.

2

Stuffing the fold of bills into the front pocket of her jeans, Cora let the bell jangle to its irritating heart's content when she opened the door to leave. Outside the pawnshop, she found a little knot of people gathered around the big black dog tied to the parking meter.

"Hey there, boy. You're a good boy, aren't ya?" The dog clearly thought so. He leaned in to let the little boy scratch behind his ear, almost knocking him over in the process. Rocky looked like he was half mastiff, half mountain gorilla, but his size didn't seem to bother the child a bit. He waved over an even smaller boy, and a moment later Rocky was getting both ears scratched at the same time. The dog's eyes rolled back in indecent-looking enjoyment.

Cora started toward them when her vision suddenly clouded again. The fog she'd passed off as lack of sleep to Harold returned, and with it, a prickle in the tips of her fingers, like ants crawling just beneath the surface of her skin. She reached back blindly, and when her hand found the brick wall, she sagged against it. Cora closed her eyes and took a deep breath, then another and another. When she opened her eyes again her vision was still blurry, but it was better, clear enough to get her home.

She wobbled like a daytime drunk to the curb and was reaching out to untie Rocky's leash from the parking meter when a woman stepped in front of her. "Is this your dog?" she asked. "He's the one that saved those little kids, isn't he?" The boys stopped scratching Rocky's head and stared at Cora. "I saw him on the news. He's quite the hero, isn't he? Can I get a quick picture of him with my boys?" Not waiting for an answer, the woman pulled out her phone and turned toward the dog.

"Knock yourself out," Cora muttered to the woman's back. "Could you do it quick though?" she added. "Rocky's got to go … ah … to the vet. Shots and …" She trailed off, not bothering to keep making things up, since no one was listening. The phone clicked and clicked and clicked, the woman pausing only to turn the screen to a different angle every few seconds. Rocky tipped his head to the side and let his tongue loll out, hamming it up for the camera.

The woman took about a million pictures while Cora shifted uncomfortably in the background, curling and uncurling her fingers against the spidery tingle in their tips. When it looked like the snapping was slowing down, Cora swooped in and grabbed Rocky's leash.

"Gotta go." Cora dragged the dog down the sidewalk without looking back. She got to the end of the street as fast as she could manage with a giant, unwilling dog digging in his heels behind her. Cora stopped pulling when they turned the corner onto Union Street.

"You can drop the act now, furball," Cora said. "Hero, my ass. If I took this leash off, you wouldn't be able to find your way home, let alone a couple lost kids."

Rocky was ignoring her, more interested in the thin line of oily rainwater trickling down the edge of the street. She pulled him away. "Don't drink that. Come on, you can have some without a layer of motor oil at home. And if you don't give me a hard time between here and there, I won't tell everybody you're a total fraud. Must be nice, getting all the credit, doing none of the work."

Looking up, she would have sworn the dog rolled his eyes at her. Then he shot forward, this time dragging Cora along behind.

She had to jog to keep up with him, but that was fine. By the time they reached the end of Union Street the annoying fuzziness in her vision had cleared. When they turned onto Maple and she could see her house in the distance, the prickle in her fingertips had died away to the faintest numbness. She let Rocky slurp up a bowlful of water and then loaded him into the truck.

"Okay, dog, time to go to work."

3

The previous May, a small girl and boy squeezed past a loose board in the playground fence and wandered away from Little Sprouts Daycare in Pine Gap. Two days, two cases of dehydration and poison oak, and one broken collarbone later, neither five-year-old Harper Culwick nor four-year-old Jackson Raupers could remember where they'd been headed when they decided to make their escape.

For a couple of kids with no destination in mind, they'd managed to cover an impressive amount of ground, most of it uphill through a heavily wooded corner of section twelve of the Pennsylvania game lands. They'd wandered so far afield that when Jackson lost a shoe and tumbled down a streambank, snapping his collarbone like a twig, the search party looking for the missing kids was six miles off.

Cora had been much closer to the missing children, doing the same then that she was doing today, hiking from the outskirts of Pine Gap toward Blackwell Lake.

"No, Rocky. Put it down. That's disgusting." Rocky didn't listen; he never listened to Cora. The dog kept the cloudy plastic Pepsi bottle full of something that wasn't Pepsi clamped firmly in his jaws and carried it a few hundred yards up the narrow trail. Cora sped up, trying to get close enough to catch him, but he shot ahead, staying just out of reach. Whatever was inside the bottle slopped nastily back and forth when he swung his head back to look at her.

"Come on, dog. You can't be thirsty enough to drink that. Put it down."

The dog stopped and dropped the bottle to the ground. "Good boy," she said. Rocky looked up at her, then stepped over the bottle toward a mound of deer droppings and started nosing at the pile of black shotgun pellets.

"No, Rocky. Don't do it. Don't you dare."

He dared. Cora just sighed and walked around him, not wanting to watch as he went into a full-body roll on top of the pile. *Enjoy yourself now, dog,* she thought, *because you're looking at a ride home in the back of the truck and a bath with a cold garden hose later.*

She left him behind, not concerned when she rounded the bend and he fell out of sight. Rocky would catch up, and it wasn't like she needed him for what she was after. The dog could find a pile of poop like it was his job, but he hadn't found the lost children any more than he'd found the bracelet she'd turned into a roll of bills this morning.

Damn it, the money. It was still in her front pocket, not the best place unless she wanted to be picking it out of the blackberry brambles later. Cora fished the roll out of her pants and was tucking the money into the bag slung across her chest when the haze once again crossed her eyes. The tingle in her fingers returned as well, an uneasy crawling that threatened to worm its way up through her fingers and into her hands. This time, she didn't try to push it away. Cora let it come.

Standing still, Cora kept her eyes open and slowly turned her head from side to side. Ahead of her, slightly to her left, a round tunnel cleared in her vision, so vivid it seemed to be magnified, though fuzzy around the edges like greasy fingerprints around the border of a windowpane.

Cora turned her body slowly, knowing that if she looked away from that small clear place, her vision would cloud again. The tingle in her fingers was now in her toes as well, running like the low voltage hum of an electric fence. She took a step forward. Toward what, she didn't know. She couldn't explain it this time any more than she could the thousands and thousands of times it had happened before, but she knew what it meant. Somewhere not too far away was something someone had lost.

Walking forward robotically, Cora held on to the clear spot. When her legs carried her off the packed dirt of the trail, she stumbled, going down hard on both knees, her vision turning to static again. Rocky came up and nosed at her side. "Shh. Don't move," she hissed.

Ignoring the dig of stones into her knees, she turned her head slowly back and forth. To the east, everything came into laser focus again. Cora stood slowly and dusted the pine needles off her hands. "Never mind," she told the dog. "Move. Please move. Jesus Christ, dog. You stink."

Cora took one cautious step forward at a time. It was like walking while looking through a pair of binoculars that constantly needed to be adjusted. As she went, the sensation in her limbs grew, snaking inward from the tips of her fingers and toes into her arms and legs. It grew in severity as it progressed, ramping up into a stinging, burning current.

"Come on, Rocky." Cora was led back onto the same trail she'd left only a hundred yards earlier. "And do not roll in any more poop." She paused to orient herself again and stomp some feeling back into her feet. "I'll put you on the leash. You hear me?" He heard her, because he darted on ahead before she could make good on her threat.

A few yards up and she was forced off the trail again. "Rocky, get over here," she called out, getting no response. She worked her way through scraggly, orange-skinned pines, their fallen needles making a soundless, rust-colored cushion underfoot. It was harder going now, where every turn she made to avoid a tree left her temporarily blind, forcing her to feel her way around it, then stop and reorient herself. But she knew she was getting closer; the sensation in her hands and feet had grown almost unbearable. A warm, damp trickle made its way down her spine.

"Woof." Out of nowhere, Rocky barreled into the back of her knees. Cora landed on her tailbone, watching his rump disappear as he blazed past, the upturned tail of a deer bobbing ahead of him. She wasted a minute trying to untangle a cluster of burdocks from her hair, but ended up yanking them out, taking a knot of long dark hair with them.

"Rocky, come back here!" she yelled. The only thing that came back was the echo of her voice. She got to her feet and dusted off the seat of her jeans. Finding her direction again, Cora took a step forward.

All at once the tingling fell away. It vanished so quickly it was like she'd been stripped naked, and Cora shivered.

She could see clearly again, no matter which way she turned her head. Looking down, she reached out with the toe of her boot and brushed away the layer of pine needles that covered the ground. In a ray of sun that cut its way through the cover of the trees, something glinted.

4

Cora rubbed it against her pantleg to clean off the dirt, then slid a fingernail under the silver catch and flipped it up. A tiny hinge, filled with grit, ground silently when she lifted the cover.

The face of the small round compass was covered with scratched, milky glass. The needle was hung up pointing north-northwest, caught on the edge of the waterlogged face.

"Well, crap." Cora snapped it shut again, then scraped a little more of the clotted dirt off the back. There was an inscription etched shallowly on the metal, though time had rubbed it so faint it was impossible to read. The casing felt like it might be silver, unless the weight was coming from the water that had seeped in and spoiled the dial. It might be worth a little something, cleaned up. Not much, but it was better than nothing. Cora slipped it into her bag.

That was the problem—well, one of them—with the unexplainable pull that led Cora to lost things. There was no telling what she was going to find. There didn't seem to be any rhyme or reason as to why some things called to her and others didn't, which meant there was no way to know if it was going to be worth the effort. Sometimes it was the bracelet—by now shined up and in the case at Harold's Pawn with a hefty price tag on it—sometimes it was a pair of kids who wandered away from daycare. Today it was an old compass, fallen from a hunter's pocket God knew how long ago.

Rocky had trundled his way out of the thicket and sidled up next to her, making sure to rub whatever he'd been rolling in onto her pants.

"Give me some room, pup. You reek," Cora said. He moved away, but only to nose at the little divot in the ground she'd pulled the compass out of. "At this rate, it's scraps this month for the both of us." Rocky snuffled indifferently. "Come on. Let's finish the loop. Maybe we'll get lucky and find a pair of earrings to match that bracelet."

Rocky took off, kicking up a spume of pine needles in his wake. Cora headed back for the trail and started to slog upward, her calves complaining about the incline. Fortunately, the path would turn soon and level off, cutting along the southeast edge of the game lands before swinging down again, back toward the dirt lot where she'd left her truck.

She found Rocky waiting for her at the turn of the trail, nose to the ground. At least he looked like he was searching for something. That was the only reason she had a dog at all. Until a couple years ago Cora simply told people whatever she thought they would believe when she found something and needed an explanation, blaming luck or good eyesight or a metal detector. She might have gone on like that indefinitely, if the strange pull hadn't pulled her right up to a body in a shallow grave.

Something had begun tugging at her almost the minute she stepped out of her truck that morning, but Cora hadn't really been that bothered. It was an annoyance, to toss her book and brown-bagged sandwich back in the cab and go take care of the blurred vison and tingle in her hands, but it was early, and there wasn't a soul nearby to see her stumbling around. *I'll go find whatever it is,* she remembered telling herself, *then I can spend the rest of the morning by the creek with my book and a peanut butter and jelly. Could be worse.* It had been.

Falls Creek was broad and shallow, and as she'd waded through the cool, knee-high water, it had been a relief against the burning tingle in her toes. On the opposite bank, at the base of a gnarled willow, the feeling had fallen away. Like so many other times, there was nothing visible on the surface, so Cora knelt and dug at the loose soil. A few inches down her fingers sank into an empty eye socket.

Cora stood for a long time looking back and forth between Falls Creek and the skull and ribcage she'd uncovered. If she called the police, how could she explain why she'd chosen to dig a hole right here? No one would believe she'd just stumbled on it buried in the ground. Worse, someone might think Cora had put it there. She could go home and make an anonymous call or send a note, but how sure was she it wouldn't come back to her, making her an even greater object of suspicion?

More than once she'd started to walk away. But she couldn't bring herself to wade back across the creek and pretend it hadn't happened, that there wasn't a human being—what was left of them, at least— abandoned under a piddling three inches of dirt.

She'd stood there, wavering, trying to decide what to do, until the bark of a distant dog had reached her from somewhere far away and given her an idea. The next day Cora called the police from the same place to report that her dog Rocky, fresh from the shelter, had smelled something and taken off. She tried to work some amazement into her voice when she told the police officer how she'd found him digging up a bunch of bones next to Falls Creek.

Thankfully there hadn't been a repeat of that sort of find, and she had to admit it was convenient, being able to blame the dog for whatever she turned up. Cora watched him trot ahead, following more slowly behind, until the trail began to flatten, skating across the upper limit of the game lands. The path was narrower here, and darker too, tightly bordered with close-grown maples and white pines that reached to the sky like church spires. Only weak, filtered sun made it through the intertwined branches, starving the seedlings below into spindly, shrunken things that cowered close to the ground. The trail ahead wove in gentle curves along the boundary between state land and the private property around Blackwell Lake.

The lake was spoon-shaped and deep, with black water and blacker history. The current owners had tried to dress it up, stringing a chain of identical white chalets around its edge like an expensive pearl necklace. At least that's what they looked like to Cora in the glimpses she'd gotten in late fall when there were fewer leaves to block the view. To get a closer look would have meant going beyond the no-trespassing signs. Cora could see three of the bright orange squares nailed to trees from where she was standing. From what she'd heard, Blackwell Lake enforced the part that read *Violators will be Prosecuted.*

She didn't have any need to cross onto the property, anyway, because plenty of the rich guests found their way off the resort. They pedaled high-end mountain bikes up and down the trails, hiked to the old mine entrances or the abandoned cemetery perched on the hill above the lake. Sometimes while they hiked and biked, they lost things. Expensive things.

Cora stopped when the path began to run downhill again. "Rocky," she called. He'd wandered off into the brush, uninterested in staying on the path. Listening for him, she heard nothing except the chitter of squirrels and wind whistling through branches. "You better show up before I get back to the truck, or I'll leave you here," she muttered. Taking a last look around, she could see everything and feel nothing; it was both a relief and a disappointment. It didn't look like there was going to be any more tripping around blindly, crashing headlong into trees today. But she wouldn't go home with anything in her pocket she might be able to turn into a wad of cash, either.

There was a rustle in the underbrush, and a fall of feet like drumbeats. Rocky burst out of the woods behind her, then shot past, racing down the path ahead of her. "Rocky, wait!" she yelled, but he was gone as quickly as he'd appeared. She started after him, when it hit her like a train.

It happened so forcefully Cora's knees locked up and her boots skidded on the dirt. Her vision was swallowed up in a burst of bright white. What usually started as a buzz and hum in her extremities was a brush fire in her veins.

She felt Rocky come back, brush against her legs, but she couldn't see him. Leaning down, she put her hand on his back and used him to keep her balance while she made a slow, careful turn. Cora spun until she found her vision again.

When the clear tunnel of sight was in front of her, she followed it. It took her off the trail and uphill, forcing her to scramble up a crumbling embankment, using exposed roots for hand holds. When she made it to the top, she could see which way she was being taken. Cora was being pulled away from the east side of the lake, away from the showy chalets, up the steep rise that overlooked it. Cora didn't know of anything that lay that way except the old Blackwell Cemetery.

She held out a little hope the path would veer off, but it narrowed as she neared the falling stone fence that marked the edge of the cemetery. When she passed it, the burning increased, like a friction fire raging under her skin, and the tunnel of clear space she could see through shrank to a pinprick. The pull was so strong Cora thought if someone were to pick her up and bodily remove her from her path, her heart might burst. Rocky must have sensed something stranger than usual was happening, because he came up beside her and pressed against her leg.

"I want to go home, Rocky." Her voice was a quiet, child's whimper, but it still sounded too loud in the small clearing that was empty of even the chatter of birds. It was too much, painful and disorienting, so intense that it frightened her. "I want to—"

She jerked forward involuntarily, moving before her mind sent the message to her body. It pulled her in. Cora was so close now that a strange hot glow like a ring of fire ran around the edge of her vision, creating a halo around the grave marker ahead of her, framing the dark stone in a circle of red.

When her foot next hit the ground, the feeling of emptying and release was so sudden and complete that, for a moment, Cora thought maybe her heart *had* stopped. All the unwelcome sensations disappeared, leaving her washed out and empty and cold.

Rocky saw it before she did. He sat down on his haunches in front of the tipsy gravestone and let out a pained whine. There was the sound of a whip crack when Cora clapped her hand across her mouth. Draped over the top of the gravestone, as bright as copper, was a long, thick braid of human hair. It was attached to the head of the woman propped up against the other side, one bloody hand thrown out beside her, reaching desperately for nothing.

5

"It's a rock or something, Bill. Just let him have it."

"What if it's evidence, Sam?" The paunchy man bent over, his Game Commission uniform pants stretching dangerously across the seat. He reached an arm toward Rocky one more time, but the dog scooted backward, staying just beyond the outstretched hand. Bill gave up and groaned his way up to his feet, then pulled off his cap and swiped at the sweaty ring it had pressed into his hair.

"It's nothing, Bill. Just keep him from getting close to the body and hold your water until the state police get here. Let them decide what's evidence. Besides, I don't think he's gonna let it go without a fight, whatever it is." Sam Cooper gave Rocky and the small brown object between his teeth a last look and pulled the radio from his belt. "Bill, head back out to the pull off and bring the staties in when they get here. Radio me when you're on your way."

He waited until Bill had crammed his hat back on and made it to the tree line before turning to Cora. Unlike Bill, Sam Cooper didn't look to be suffering from the heat, despite the rugged forest-green pants and long-sleeved shirt that made up his uniform. He was cool and reserved and examining Cora in a way that made her even more self-conscious of the spatter of vomit down the front of her shirt. He reached a hand up absently to pat his chest pocket, dropping it back to his side before he spoke. Cora adjusted her bag, fiddling with the flap that closed it.

"Sorry, what?" Cora had missed whatever it was Sam said,

momentarily distracted, staring past him to where the pale, outstretched hand was visible around the weathered gravestone.

"I said you're probably going to have to tell them everything you told me three more times. We've had bodies turn up in the game lands before—never quite like this—but anyway, seems like the people who found them had to repeat themselves to every new uniform that shows up. Could take a while. I'll have Bill run you and Rocky back to town, after. He's parked on the outside, off Mountain Run."

"I'm parked in the north side lot. I can go back the way I came. It's fine."

"You sure? It's a long way." Sam turned back toward the body and shook his head. He hadn't gotten sick like Cora had, and later Bill when he'd gotten there. The two men had been the closest thing to law enforcement in the area when she called 911. "Got to be four, five miles if you hiked up from the Pine Gap side. What were you doing up here, anyway?"

She shrugged and looked over at the dog. Now that Bill was out of sight, Rocky put down the brown bundle he'd been so unwilling to let go of, letting it drop between his front paws. "Just hiking. Rocky's big. He needs a lot of exercise. We were headed back down, but he must have smelled it … er, her. He just took off. Once he finds something …" Rocky nosed at the thing between his feet. It looked like a fallen walnut still wearing its blackening outer husk, or a burl knocked off one of the pine trees that bordered the cemetery. God knew what the dog found so irresistible about it. Then again, he'd been known to eat roadkill.

"And you don't have any idea who this is," Sam said, "or how she got here?"

Cora's eyebrows shot up. "It's a dead body. Of course I don't know how the hell it got here."

"And you didn't touch anything?" he said, cocking his head sideways. The shadow from his hat brim disappeared, his dark eyes fixed on hers. She had a sudden urge to look away, but resisted, thinking it might make her look guilty. She wasn't guilty; there was just something unnerving about his stare. He was looking at her so intently she could see her own pale eyes reflected like little points of light in his.

"Nothing," Cora said, breaking the uncomfortable eye contact to nod toward the limp, outstretched hand. "I was going to, to see if she had a pulse but ..."

"But what?"

"Look at her damn head," Cora said. Her stomach lurched again.

Sam nodded. "How long do you think it was, before you called for help?"

"As long as it took me to walk back out to the trail so I could get a signal. Then I came back and sat over there." She pointed toward a tree that had fallen across a cluster of graves, propped up like a bench across the broken stones. "The only time I got up was to get Rocky away, because he was nosing around by the ... by her."

That was when the vomiting had happened. When Cora went to get the dog, she got her first good look at the head propped up against the stone. The woman's skull was misshapen, flattened in the back. It looked deflated, like a balloon losing air.

"Another one of Rocky's finds, huh? This one's a damn doozy." Sam looked over at the dog. Rocky was currently rolling around on the ground, paws in the air, grinding every pine needle he could into his thick black fur. Sam reached up again to pat absently at his breast pocket. Without realizing it, Cora reached for her bag again.

"Are you okay?" Cora asked. "You keep grabbing your chest." He looked too young and fit to be having a heart attack, but one dead person a day was more than enough.

"I'm fine." He slid his hand back down to his side. "Lost something. Funny, now I can't tell whether I used to reach for it all the time while it was there and never thought about it, or if I'm doing it now because it isn't there."

"What was it?"

"A compass. My granddad gave it to me." He shrugged. "Maybe it'll turn up."

Cora slid her hand down into her bag and rummaged around. "Does it look anything like this?"

Taking the compass from her outstretched hand, he turned it over in his palm. Rubbing a thumb across the surface where dirt covered the inscription, he looked up at her with confusion. "Where did you get this?"

"I, uh, Rocky nosed it out of the brush on the way up here." She looked away, using the dog as an excuse to not meet his eyes. "I think it's ruined, though," she said. "I opened it. The dial inside got wet."

Looking back at him, she saw him shaking his head. "It didn't work when I lost it. I got it wet when I was a kid, about two days after my granddad gave to me. Never could bring myself to tell him I ruined it."

"You carry a compass that doesn't work?"

"I don't need one around here," he said. "Guess it's more a good luck charm or something. Thank you." He slid it back into his pocket, buttoning the flap carefully over it. "I feel like I need a good luck charm out here. This place always gives me the screaming meemies."

"Because it's a cemetery?"

He shook his head. "Nope. I don't have a problem with cemeteries, I mean, not beyond the usual." He pointed toward the lip of the hill, where it rolled away toward Blackwell Lake. From up here, a sliver of water could be seen between the trunks of the trees. "You live here, so you've heard all the stories. There's as many bodies under that lake as under this ground. Maybe more." A burst of static came from the radio in his hand. Bill was on his way back, labored breathing coming through loud and clear. "State investigator's on his way with the ME," Sam said. "We'll get them to ask their questions before they do anything else, so Bill can run you back."

"I told you, I can walk." Cora was eager to be out of here, but not enough to subject someone to the smell of her vomit-covered self and her equally stinky dog in a closed car.

"Well, it's a free country." Sam shrugged, taking off his hat and running a hand through the dark blond hair before putting it precisely back on. "But thing is, when I got here, I *did* touch that woman. Had to see if she had a pulse. She didn't, but she did have a temperature. It was pretty close to mine. I can't imagine you think she tripped and did that to her own head. Makes you wonder how far away whoever did that to her is, doesn't it?"

6

"Rocky, come." Cora stood on the porch and held the screen door open. The dog was nearly invisible inside the cloud of flying dirt he was kicking up, digging a hole for the lump of brown something he'd stubbornly carted all the way home from the cemetery. "Fine. Ignore me then," she said when he didn't so much as cock an ear in her direction. She stomped across the yard to him, getting a dirt shower in the process. She reached down and unsnapped his collar. "See how you like sleeping on the porch tonight," she added, leaving him to destroy the yard.

When the door fell shut behind her, the old spring closer squalled like a tortured cat. Cora had been meaning to fix it for weeks, but the can of WD-40 was all the way down in the basement, and she didn't have enough energy left to make Rocky stop digging up the yard, let alone worry about a rusted spring.

She toed her boots off onto the patch of faded linoleum inside the door and crossed the tiny kitchen. Stopping to plug her dead cell phone in on the counter, she went into the living room, turning on the old fringe-shaded lamp on the table by the couch as she went. It broke through the late afternoon dimness enough to indicate the way to the narrow hallway off the living room. The door to the smaller of the two bedrooms was partly open, the bed visible through the crack, neatly tucked and covered with a faded quilt. The second bedroom door was closed tight. All the doorknobs in the house were the same—old porcelain, crackled with age and stained the color of tea from years of being turned by grubby hands—except the one on the door to the second bedroom. It had a shiny stainless steel lever lock with a keyhole and a deadbolt above. She used the key attached to the ring on Rocky's collar to unlock the door.

Glimpses of the room in its previous life were still visible here and there; scattered tack holes and faded outlines from movie posters scavenged from the old Rialto on her side, the remnants of a border of flowers and butterflies on her sister's. The same carpet covered the floor as had for as long as Cora could remember, once blue but now so unevenly worn and faded it looked like spoiled cottage cheese.

Not that too much of the carpet showed, anyhow. Cheap metal shelving lined every wall, blocking the window she'd covered with brown paper. Big plastic tubs were stacked two high in front of the shelves. In the small space left in the center of the room, an old desk sat.

Pulling out the chair, Cora knelt in front of the desk's kneehole and slid out a gray, fire-proof lockbox. Opening it with the combination, she reached into her bag and fished out the roll of hundreds from that morning—which now seemed like exactly five years ago—and added them to the tidy stack of bills inside. She admired it for a second before relocking the box and shoving it back out of sight.

Crawling out from under the desk, Cora sat back in the desk chair and looked around. Here, in Cora and Kimmy's old bedroom, the metal shelves and plastic tubs were crowded with neatly arranged items, every one of them a lost thing the strange, unexplainable pull had led Cora to find.

A hundred different earrings were laid out on one shelf: hoops and balls of gold and silver, a cluster of diamonds in the shape of a daisy, a tiny dangling teardrop emerald, a silver owl with ruby eyes; not one had a mate. On the shelf below them, an ivory comb and two silver-backed hairbrushes were lined up like soldiers next to a pearl-handled switchblade and a straight razor with a bald eagle engraved on the blade. The shelf below held rings: gold bands worn thin from years of marriage, thick silver rings set with tiny diamonds, school rings and college rings and fraternal order rings, a man's ring so large and patinaed she wasn't sure it was really a ring at all but possibly a nut fallen off a bolt the size of a giant's thumb. Old quarters and buffalo nickels were on the shelf next to them, and pennies: wheat pennies and white pennies and bronze pennies, all laid out in concentric circles around a trio of jade animals, soft green and perfect save for the tip of one elephant's tiny tusk. There were silver spoons and eyeglasses and money clips with bills in them as brown and decayed as last fall's leaves with tiny pale mushrooms growing between their folds.

The plastic tubs held items too big or heavy for the shelves; hand tools and thick leather-bound books, a set of Dresden ware only two dinner plates short of complete, dug up from under a foot of silt in the bed of Falls Creek, a cloisonné jewelry box with nothing inside but a lock of white-blond hair tied with a ribbon that had crumbled to dust when Cora picked it up. There were odd pieces from ten different silver coffee services in one tub. Another held toy cars: a Dinky Triumph, a Corgi Saloon, and a bright red pedal car with a slick white racing stripe and pedals that turned as smoothly as if it had been made yesterday rather than in 1945.

These were the things Cora kept after she found them. There were far more she didn't. Broken bicycles and plastic barrettes and single blown-out tennis shoes. Handguns (those went in the river), wooden legs, broken eyeglasses, and innumerable pornographic pictures (those were in the river with the guns).

Over the years, Cora had found countless things. Some of them were awful, some of them were just interesting. When she was lucky, they were valuable. Those items, the ones that might be worth something, were in this room waiting to be sent back out into the world for what Cora thought were very competitive prices.

Opening her laptop, Cora found the spreadsheet where all the items in her motley collection were listed. Scrolling down to the bracelet Harold bought that morning, Cora marked it sold. She saved the change, then took a moment to look down through the list. Her livelihood was a never-ending game of hurry up and wait. Hurry up and find something of value, then wait and hope no one claimed it before she could legally resell it.

Looking through her list, Cora found only one item that had reached that point since last she'd checked: a Yuma hunting knife, the handle ringed with a band of turquoise. Opening her browser, Cora went to the Game Commission website. On the left side, at the very bottom, she clicked the link for Lost and Found.

Finding things on the game lands had its benefits. For starters, it was away from town. In town there were more people. More people meant more lost things and therefore a whole lot more discomfort for Cora. Even when she managed not to injure herself falling over, the embarrassment burned as badly as her fingers and toes. There might not be as many things to find on the trails, but at least no one had to see her glassy eyed and stumbling numbly around. And laws about found objects were tricky and differed from place to place. When she found things on state property and posted a notice showing she'd made a good-faith attempt to return it to its owner, anything unclaimed after six months was hers.

On the Game Commission Lost and Found page, the listing for the turquoise-trimmed knife had disappeared. That brought a smile to her face. Cora found the knife on a shelf in the back of the room and put it on the desk to be introduced to the fine folks on eBay.

Her cell phone rang in the kitchen, but Cora ignored it. There were a dozen messages in her email inbox that needed attention. Eleven of them turned out to be junk, but the last message let her know an item she had listed online was sold.

It wasn't the most exciting sale, amounting to a whopping thirty-five dollars before selling fees and shipping. But a buck was a buck. Cora got a padded envelope out of the desk drawer and took the 1933 Chicago World's Fair collectible spoon down from its shelf. She'd found it wedged behind a bench in the municipal park bandstand downtown nearly two years ago. Holding it in her hand now, Cora wondered again how long it had been there and who the hell had been carrying around a tiny spoon with *A Century of Progress* etched on the handle.

Cora dropped the spoon into the envelope and was taping on the shipping label when the phone rang again. This time it set Rocky barking.

"Hold your water, mutt." Cora pushed back from the desk and headed for the kitchen. She let the dog in and picked up the phone. "Shit." Cora saw the name on the phone, also getting a look at the time, which had gotten away from her. She put it on speaker while she scrambled into her shoes. "Kimmy, I'm sorry. I'm heading out right now. I totally lost track of time."

"Did you hit your head or something?" Cora's sister said. "Is that why you lost track of time. It must be, because I can't imagine what besides a serious brain injury would make you forget to call your sister and tell her you found a damn dead woman in the woods."

"How did you hear about that?"

"I'm a beautician, Cora. The salon is basically a news station."

"I was going to tell you at dinner." Cora had one foot out the door, then turned and went to the back bedroom to shut and lock it and retrieve Rocky's collar. "And it's not like the lady was going to get any deader between then and now."

"Now?" Kimmy said. "Now as in the time you were supposed to pick me up so we can make it to P.J.'s before half-price happy hour is over?"

"I'm sorry, Kimmy, I'm in the car."

"No, you're not, you big fat liar. I can't believe you forgot all about me, making me wait all alone in a restaurant, getting hit on by every guy that walks in."

"I'll be right there. I—"

Kimmy's laugh cut her off. "I'm just messing with you. I really called to tell you I'm running late as hell. I haven't even left work. Can you guys just pick me up there?"

"You're a jerk. I'll be there in ten." Cora looked down and got a glimpse of the barf-spattered shirt she was still wearing. "Maybe fifteen."

7

"Rocky, stay in the—"

The dog managed to shoot all hundred and thirty fluffy pounds of himself over her lap and out the driver's side door of the truck, one of his back paws getting her squarely in the crotch as he went. Rocky barreled across the empty parking lot and around the building toward the back door. Cora limped slowly after him, not bothering to try to call him back.

She didn't yell because it wouldn't do a bit of good, and because Mourning Glory was a funeral home and yelling didn't seem appropriate, even when the place was closed.

"I'm back here," Kimmy called as soon as Cora pulled open the door. Rocky pushed by her and trotted inside.

"You should lock this when you're here alone at night, sis."

"I only just unlocked it a minute ago for you guys," Kimmy said. "Besides, who the hell is going to wander into a funeral home at night?" Cora's sister looked up and grinned, then gave the figure lying on the preparation table one last swipe across the cheek with her powder brush.

"Is that Mrs. Beauchamp?" Cora asked. Kimmy nodded. "Her hair looks amazing. Good job."

"I know, right?" Kimmy peeled off her nitrile gloves and reached down to scratch behind Rocky's ears. "It makes me sad, though." Dropping her brushes into the cleaning solution, Kimmy started to pack up her supplies. "Her daughter dropped off about five hundred dollars' worth of hair so I could do her up real nice. I've been doing

Belva Beauchamp's hair over at Mane Event for like three years now, and she's been nursing the same weave the whole time. It would've been nice if they'd thought to buy her something decent while she was alive to enjoy it."

Snapping her makeup case shut, Kimmy gave her own hair a swing for emphasis, the braids fanning out and falling back to her waist. "Speaking of," Cora said, "those look good."

"Right? There was a ton left from when I did Regina Hemmerly last week. Now that one, she always had good hair. Bought her own last year when they found out the radiation wasn't doing any good, told me exactly how she wanted it done up for her viewing. I called her son to tell him there was about twice as much as she needed, and he told me to keep the extra. I had Monae do me yesterday after close." Kimmy carefully draped a paper sheet over Mrs. Beauchamp. "Just let me put her away and then we can go."

Cora waited for Kimmy to wheel the body into the refrigerated room. Coming back out through the haze of white mist in her white smock, Kimmy looked like a ghost.

"What?" Kimmy said, taking off the smock and hanging it on a hook by the door, then snapping the room light off behind them.

"Nothing. I don't know how you can work here during the day, let alone by yourself at night. It's creepy, being around all these dead bodies."

"Says the person who found one in a cemetery this morning." Kimmy waited for Cora and Rocky to go out, then locked the back door with her key, testing it to make sure the lock had engaged. "To be honest, I like it here better than Mane Event most of the time. No rent on the chair, and I've never had a single client complain."

⟫◆⟪

P.J.'s was small and dim and at its best, clean-ish. But it was the only bar in Pine Gap, and the only place in town that served food between seven p.m. and six a.m. when the Divine Diner opened for breakfast. Over a high round table, Cora told Kimmy about finding the woman in the cemetery. She was relating her ride off the mountain with Bill, trying to describe the look on the deputy warden's face when he caught a whiff of her barfed-on shirt and Rocky's cologne of deer dump at the same time, when P.J. came to the table with their order.

"Nachos for the ladies"—he set a tray down in the middle of the table—"and jalapeño poppers for Rocky my boy." P.J. picked up one of the deep-fried balls and tossed it in the air. Rocky caught it and wolfed it down, then pawed the air for another.

"P.J., he threw those up all over my passenger seat last time. The cab still smells like dog barf and peppers."

"Couple won't hurt, will they, Rock? Cause you're such a good smart boy. Ain't ya, boy? Ain't ya?" P.J.—all six feet, three hundred and fifty bald and greasy pounds of him—baby talked to Rocky, who ate it right up, along with a half dozen more poppers. When the basket was empty, P.J. patted the dog on the head and made his way back to the bar, weaving between the close-set tables deftly for a man his size. Rocky watched him go, ears drooping sadly. He'd be even sadder when he found out he was going to be taking yet another ride in the back of the truck today.

"Rocky, lie down," Cora said. He tipped his head her way like he didn't understand, then ducked under the table. It was wobbly, and when he pushed past her legs, the glasses rattled and beer slopped over the top of her glass. "Come on, dog. Stop being such a nuisance."

"Don't listen to her, baby. Come over here. Come see Auntie Kiki." Rocky went to Kimmy and plopped his heavy head on her lap so she could scratch his snout.

"Why the hell does he listen to everybody but me?" Cora mopped up the beer with a napkin, then picked up her glass and took a swallow, wiping the foam off her upper lip with the back of her hand.

"Rocky doesn't listen to you because he knows yours is nothing but a marriage of convenience." Kimmy picked up a nacho, using it like a shovel to plow through the cheese. "He and I, our relationship is built on pure love." There was probably something to that. Cora needed Rocky as cover, so she fed him, housed him, and when she couldn't stand the smell any longer, gave him baths that always ended up with her wetter than him. But Kimmy? Kimmy adored the dog, and the feeling was mutual.

Kimmy froze with a chip in front of her mouth and shuddered. "I still don't know how you're so damn calm right now. You found a dead body a couple hours ago. Why aren't you freaking out?"

"You just spent four hours bent over a dead body, and you're fine."

"Ugh, six. I came right from my morning shift. But it's different," Kimmy said. "There's dead dead, and then there's murdered dead. And then there's murdered in a damn haunted cemetery dead. That's scary as hell."

They worked their way through the tray, and it gave Cora a chance to wonder if she *should* be more shaken up. Maybe it hadn't hit yet. Kimmy saw the change in her expression.

"You good? Outside, you said it was okay in here tonight?" Kimmy swallowed and took a swig from her margarita. Cora's strange quirk was old news to her sister.

"It was. It is," Cora said. "It's not that."

Kimmy cocked her head and gave her a suspicious look, but Cora was telling the truth. P.J.'s was hit or miss; sometimes she could feel the usual faint, distant electricity, telling her if she got up and walked in the right direction, the feeling would bloom. Other times it hit her so hard she didn't even make it through the door. But tonight, thankfully, was one of the former, and Cora sipped her beer gratefully.

"What is it, then?" Kimmy leaned toward her sister.

Cora shook her head and examined the bubbles climbing up and down the sides of her beer glass. "Nothing. I was just thinking about Mom. I wish she was here, but at least she never had to see me running around in the woods tripping over dead people. It weirded her out enough when I was only finding fishing lures and old baseball gloves. She just pretended I had some idiot savant level of observation."

Kimmy snorted and pulled her napkin up in front of her mouth. She had to take a drink and wipe her eyes before she could talk. "Mostly the idiot part. There are blind people more observant than you are, Cora.

I've seen you walk past a twenty on the sidewalk on your way to pick up someone's old nail clippers." Kimmy grew serious. "I think it just scared her. I mean, remember when you found that old silver charm thing in the river? Mom thought you were going to drown. You just couldn't stop until you had it."

Nodding, Cora's hand drifted to her wrist. She remembered perfectly, though she had only been six when it happened. They'd been visiting their mom's Aunt Reva—dead ten years now—where Kimmy and Cora played along the edge of the slow, bottle-green river while their mom and Reva sat in aluminum lawn chairs on the bank and drank sweet tea spiked with brandy. There were crayfish under the rocks beneath the Milltown Bridge, and Kimmy and Cora had been turning up the stones and trying to catch them before they shot away in a backward zip. Cora had a stone tipped up in her hand when her vision went cloudy, and she felt the tingle in her fingers for the first time.

She couldn't swim, but Cora dropped the rock and waded out where the water was over her head. She pushed herself up off the mucky bottom for breath, then sank down into the green water, going up and down three or four times before their mom hauled her to shore. Cora had it in her hand by then, an old, teardrop-shape pendant on a bit of broken silver chain. The terrible fiery feeling had gone as quickly as it had come.

Cora still wore it, the little charm, attached to a silver charm bracelet. She wasn't sure why she'd kept it all these years, except she felt oddly attached to it. Maybe because it was the first thing she ever *found*. It was where it had all started.

8

"**M**an, your dog's huge."

Cora paused with her glass at her lips. A man was standing next to their table, backwards hat and a big smile pulled up above his scraggly brown goatee. Rocky didn't look any more impressed than Cora was, but he wasn't one to turn down attention. He popped out from under the table, rattling it so Kimmy had to shoot out a hand to catch her margarita glass before it tipped over.

"Good catch." Mr. Goatee had seen the quick grab. That was no surprise, since he'd been staring at Kimmy the whole time. "Do you and your friend wanna play pool?" He cocked his head toward the pool table in the rear of the bar.

She'd been jealous when they were teenagers, but at this point Cora wasn't bothered anymore. Her sister just attracted more attention. She was beautiful, with big brown eyes and perfect dark skin and a sweet little dimple on each side of her face. People gravitated toward Kimmy.

"How about it?" he said. "You and your friend want to see if you can beat me? I'm Trevor, by the way." Trevor stuck his hand out to Kimmy. Cora turned her head so she could roll her eyes without being seen.

Kimmy flashed him a brilliant smile, teeth even and white. "Trevor, huh? I'm Kimaya, and this is Cora, my sister."

Trevor gave a look Cora's way and nodded. "Do you and your *sister* want to play?"

Cora gave Kimmy a pleading look, but it was ignored. Cora picked up her beer and took a long swallow. She was just going to have to wait it out.

"I must not have spoken clearly." Kimmy leaned forward slightly, prompting Trevor to do the same. "When I said sister, I meant sister. Did you think that because I'm Black and she's white that we aren't really sisters? Did I misspeak, or did you just assume ..."

Trevor's face went blank for a second, then he scrambled to recover. "I, uh. I didn't mean ... I just thought ..."

There was full, uncomfortable silence. Poor Trevor rocked back and forth on his heels while Cora pretended to be desperately interested in the bottom of her beer glass.

"I uh," he stammered. "Listen—"

Kimmy couldn't keep it up any longer and broke out into laughter. "I'm just messing with you. I mean yeah, she's really my sister. She's adopted, man. You should have seen your face, though. Thanks for the ask, but we're heading out after we finish our drink."

Trevor shuffled off a second later and Cora looked at Kimmy, shaking her head. "You can't really blame people for not knowing."

Kimmy ran her finger around the top of her margarita glass, tipping the remaining salt from the rim to the inside. "I don't blame people for not knowing. I blame them for assuming. It's a bad habit." She reached down and patted Rocky absently under the table. "You could be my friend, my sister, my partner, my next victim, my whatever. He just assumed based on what's most convenient for his little straight, white dude sensibilities. Maybe next time he'll think before he opens his mouth and tries to pick up clearly uninterested women in a bar."

Cora watched her sister scrape the last of the cheese off the nacho tray with her fork and stick it under the table for Rocky to lick. "Gross, Kimmy, people eat off those."

"They wash them. And dog mouths are cleaner than people's. People are nasty."

Rolling her empty beer glass in her hand, Cora contemplated another, but it looked like Kimmy was serious about heading out. She did look tired, shoulders a little more slumped than usual, biting back a yawn. Before her shift at Mane Event, Kimmy worked at Burlington Elms nursing home a couple days a week, blue-rinsing and rolling old ladies' hair. Days like today, when she had a shift at Mourning Glory on top of everything else, didn't leave a lot of time for sleeping in between.

Cora watched Kimmy wipe off the gross, slobbered-on fork with her napkin before setting it on the tray, then reach into her purse for her wallet. "Nope. I got it." Cora waved Kimmy's wallet away and pulled a couple of bills out of her pocket. "Trade. I need a cut and color when you get some time."

Stuffing her wallet back in her bag, Kimmy got out of her seat, then knelt to give Rocky a goodbye rub and a kiss on his nose. She stood up and straightened the front of her silky white shirt. How Kimmy could wear so much white and not destroy it was a mystery to Cora. If it were her standing there, it would look like the nachos had attacked.

"I'm going to walk back to the funeral home. Burn off some of those nachos. I'll call you if I get a cancel at Mane this week. Love you, sis."

"Text me when you get home safe," Cora said. "Love you more."

She watched her sister walk out into the darkness. Then she tucked her money back into her pocket and caught P.J.'s attention, ordering another drink. She wasn't quite ready to go home.

When P.J. delivered the fresh beer, she sipped it thoughtfully. Alcohol was a slippery slope for Cora. A few drinks were fine, helpful even, in taking the edge off the hum lost things put out. Too many, though, and things went haywire. Cora turned into a homing beacon for lost objects far beyond her normal range and with intensified effects. All of that was followed by the immense joy of waking up with a horrible hangover.

Rocky had decided he could sit in judgment of her drinking habits better from Kimmy's chair and had jumped up nimbly onto her vacant seat. Sitting on his haunches, he was tall enough to stare down at her in disapproval.

"Get down, Rocky." His nails needed a trim and were probably digging holes into the seat cushion. She waved a hand to shoo him back to the floor, but he ignored it, looking over her shoulder toward P.J., who was trundling back in their direction.

"Look at him, sitting up like he's people. Ain't you clever, Rock. Who's a smart boy? Who's my best customer?"

"Maybe he can pay the tab, if he's such a good customer," Cora grumbled. "Or did you forget your wallet again, Rocky?"

"Don't listen to her, Rocko." P.J. reached a meaty arm over and gave Rocky a scratch, then picked up Kimmy's margarita glass and the empty nacho tray. Rocky watched it go with doleful eyes. "Don't you mind her, boy. She's just bitter causen you got more friends than she does."

She couldn't argue with that.

"Cora." The voice beside her was unexpected enough that she jumped. A wave of cold beer cascaded over the side of her glass and off the edge of the table. This time she didn't react quickly enough to dodge it, and it flowed in a cold stream directly into her lap.

"Sorry. I don't know how you didn't see me coming." Sam Cooper had come up beside her unnoticed, almost even with her ear when he spoke. It was unusual to see him off duty; the stiff green uniform had been replaced with worn-in jeans and a dark t-shirt. He wasn't as imposing without the added height of his hat. "Rocky, get down," he said.

Rocky instantly jumped to the floor. Sam slid into the empty seat.

Most of the mess was hidden under the table, though Cora could feel a trickle of beer making its uncomfortable way toward her butt crack. Sneaking a look down, Cora saw she'd managed to get a glob of cheese on her shirt as well. She was now down two shirts for the day; her wardrobe couldn't afford too many more casualties.

"Were you looking for me?" Cora asked. "I gave the state police my number and all my information." She looked across to the bar, where P.J. was trying to catch Sam's eye. "How did you even find me?"

Sam shook his head. "I wasn't really looking for you, but I saw your truck sitting in the parking lot when I was on my way home."

"How did you know it was mine?"

"It's pretty recognizable with that Bondo and Rust-Oleum theme you got going. Plus, the lights were on."

"Shit."

"Don't worry. I turned them off. Should start fine, if you haven't been in here that long. You really should lock it, though."

Cora raised an eyebrow. "Why the hell would I do that? I pray to the insurance gods every night someone steals, hits, or torches that piece of crap. I'm not going to lock the doors and make it harder for them."

"Here ya go, boss." P.J. put a glass of beer so dark it looked like chocolate pudding in front of Sam. She saw him slip something to Rocky under the table at the same time, probably more jalapeño poppers. It was going to be a vomit night for sure. She sighed.

"Thanks, P.J.," Sam said.

"No problem. I owe ya one for them bears." P.J. shuffled away and Sam took a drink from his beer. It left a mustache of butterscotch-colored foam on his upper lip. He quickly swiped it away.

"Bears?"

"Bears. P.J. lives ... Hold on." Sam took the coaster out from under his drink and folded the cardboard circle in half. He slid out of his seat and disappeared under the wobbly table. It rocked back and forth for a moment then was steady. Sam popped back up and sat back down. "Sorry. Stuff like that drives me nuts. Anyway, P.J. lives out on Long Valley Road. A black bear and her cubs were tipping over his trash cans and cleaning out the bird feeders. They weren't doing that much damage, but I guess they were scaring the daylights out of his cats. All nine of them."

"Holy shit. Nine?"

"Nine," Sam said. Cora looked over at the bar, trying to picture huge, gruff P.J. at home under a blanket of cats.

"I didn't come intending to track you down," Sam said, "but since I found you, I might as well tell you. It'll be all over the local news by tomorrow anyway." He leaned toward her, lowering his voice. "They already identified your dead lady from the woods."

"She's not my dead lady," Cora said. "Who was she?"

"Name was Avery Benson. Resident of New York City, summer guest at the Blackwell Lake Resort." Sam leaned back and reached for his head like he expected his hat to be there. When it wasn't, he brushed the hair back from his forehead. "It's not exactly public knowledge yet, but it will be as soon as her family is notified. I wouldn't want that job. How do you explain to somebody their wife or daughter had their head caved in on a tombstone?"

"Who do they think did it?"

Drinking off the rest of his beer, Sam watched the foam that was left slide down the side of the glass in a treacly stream. "No clue. It's all on the state police now. What I told you is what I overheard while they were at the scene." He shrugged. Looking down, Sam prodded Rocky gently with his shoe. "I imagine there'll be people pounding at your door to take pictures of Wonder Dog down there pretty quick, once it comes out he found the body. Especially after those bones and the kids last year. He's getting to be quite the celebrity."

Rocky stood, thumping his head on the underside of the table when he got up. This time the table didn't wobble and nothing spilled. "Sure is something, him being able to walk into the woods and right up into something like that, and way out there." He gave Cora a look. When she didn't answer, he got up.

Outside, Sam waited to make sure the old truck started, and when Cora pulled out of the parking lot, she could see him standing there, a lean, dark silhouette in the red wash of her taillights.

9

Her bag felt like it weighed a hundred pounds. Cora dragged herself along the sidewalk, ready to drop it and her clothes the minute she was inside the door and crawl into bed. It had been a bountiful day. And draining as hell.

Cora had avoided her usual route along the border of the game lands in the weeks since finding the dead woman. She wasn't afraid; Rocky might not lift a paw to defend her, but he was big enough to make anyone with bad intentions think twice, and she always carried a can of bear mace in her bag. But she doubted the guests at Blackwell Lake felt as confident. Cora had an idea that having the lady in the next cabin bludgeoned to death had cut down on the off-property excursions.

The problem was, if she didn't get out and find some things of value to build up her inventory before the weather started to turn, it was going to be a lean winter. So, before dawn, she'd gassed up the truck and driven to the fairgrounds in Forksville.

It was drizzly and miserable, and she managed to rip her pants squeezing around the locked gate, but once she was inside, Cora barely remembered anything. Her vision had tunneled, and her hands felt like she'd grabbed an electric eel; it went on that way for hours. Lost things had been scattered like seeds, just waiting for her to find them.

She hitched the bag higher on her shoulder and tugged the flap more tightly over the top. It was overflowing: a woman's watch, rose gold with a shiny black face; a silver eagle in a plastic case, bought from a coin vendor then spun from a pocket on a clanking carnival ride;

two iPhones; an anniversary band with a row of little round diamonds running down the middle; a silver compact mirror so tarnished it might have been lost fifty fairs ago; a gold fountain pen. The cast-iron cat she'd found last sat like a bowling ball in the bottom of her bag. Cora thought about dumping it on the sidewalk to get rid of the ache in her shoulder, but she was almost to her door.

"You got another one there." The voice startled her—it seemed to come straight out of the overgrown boxwood hedge in front of the house before hers.

"Oh, hey, Mr. Debusher." Cora didn't have to tell Rocky to stop. Old Mr. Debusher never left his little gray box of a house without his pilled, cable knit cardigan, the stretched-out pockets filled with treats for Rocky. It had been like that since about two days after Cora brought the dog home from the shelter. He'd barked a lot more then, and she'd been afraid the old man would complain about the noise. Instead, he'd widened the crack between their fences, making it big enough for Rocky to squeeze through. He came back and forth so often for treats that one of these days he was going get his furry ass stuck between the slats.

"Where you been, my boy? Ain't seen you this day, that's the truth."

Rocky sat on his hind legs and raised a paw to put it gently on the old man's thigh, waiting patiently for the arthritic fingers to ferret out a bone-shape biscuit. Mr. Debusher chuckled when Rocky crunched it up and nosed the saggy bottom of his sweater pocket for another.

"No, you don't, you little scamp. You'll spoil your dinner." Mr. Debusher patted the black head that came up to his hip, then turned to Cora. In the disappearing sun, the frizzle of white hair over the shiny brown cap of his skull lit up like a halo, making him look like an elderly, wrinkled angel.

"I said, you've got another one, Cora. He's been standing on your front porch a good while now. I thought at first he were a Jehovah's Witness or summat, but he didn't try and save the rest of the street from hellfire, so I 'magine he's another one of them news fellas." He cocked his head toward her house, where Cora could see the peak of her roof over the top of the fence. Mr. Debusher gave Rocky a gentle rap between the ears with his gnarled hand. "Looks like maybe you're gonna be in the pages again, young man." Mr. Debusher looked back up at Cora. "Got ever' one posted in Elba's scrapbook, you know. Didn't have nothing in it after she passed, anyhow. I figure she'd be fine with me filling it up."

"I was hoping this had all about worn itself out." Cora took a couple steps away from Mr. Debusher's gate and looked around the corner of the fence toward her house. Sure enough, there was a man standing on her front porch. Across the street, a green and tan SUV too new for this neighborhood was squeezed in behind Marla Tiddles's rusted minivan.

"You can come in and wait 'im out, if you want." Mr. Debusher hobbled a step backward to let her pass, but Cora shook her head.

"Thanks, but I guess I'd better get it out of the way. I'll just tell him to leave. Anyway, how good a reporter can he be, if he's just getting here? It's been weeks." She waved to the old man. "Good night, Mr. Debusher. Come on, Rocky."

Cora started down the short stretch of sidewalk toward her house. When Rocky didn't come up beside her, she paused, turning back. He stood on the sidewalk, still as a statue. "Come on, Rocky." He didn't move, just stood there at rigid attention.

"Fine then. Have fun squeezing through the fence, because I'm not leaving the gate open." *Hope you get stuck, chubby little beggar*, she thought. Cora flipped open the latch and opened the gate, stepping onto her sidewalk and heading for the front door.

At the sound of the latch dropping back into place, the stranger stepped out of the darkness under the porch and into the glow of the carriage lamp. He was big enough to throw a shadow down the sidewalk almost to her feet, and it made Cora a little nervous. Her hand shifted toward her bag, where the canister of mace made a comforting lump in the bottom.

"Miss Gilbert," a low clear voice said. "I'm sorry about the time." He looked past her, to where the day was just a cigarette's tip of orange burning along the sway-backed rooftops across the street. "I promise it was a decent hour when I came. I've been waiting since then."

His voice had Cora expecting someone older, but under the yellow light, she saw he wasn't much older than she was. He was tall, head not far from the porch roof, with dark hair cut close to his head and neatly trimmed facial hair outlining his jaw. His dark clothes blended in with the shadows.

"Can I help you?" Cora felt rather than heard Rocky slip through the space in the fence and come up behind her. The man had seen the dog coming and crouched down.

"Hello there. You must be Rocky." He held out his hand, but Rocky didn't approach. The dog was friendly enough, but even he didn't like everyone, and she shrugged when the man lowered his hand and got up.

"Well then." His eyes followed the dog, who was trotting back down off the porch and heading to the edge of the yard to hold court over his burial ground of sticks and rocks and stolen gloves. The man turned back to Cora, his eyes an unidentifiable color in the dimness, but ghostly pale, startlingly light against his darker skin. "Miss Gilbert, my name is Jacob Adler. I was wondering if you would speak to me about the woman you found."

"Mr. Adler, I—"

"Jacob, please."

"Um, Jacob, everything about that has already been on the news." Cora edged around the man, getting between him and the front door she very badly wanted to be behind. "Rocky found her, but that was all we had to do with it. The state police are the ones with all the information. If you want to take a picture of him"—the dog was a black shadow in the corner of the yard—"it's kind of dark, but knock yourself out. You've probably got a deadline or whatever."

Jacob Adler looked at her with confusion for a moment, then shook his head. "I'm not a reporter." His lips pulled up into something like a smile, but smaller and sad. "I'm not here for an interview. I came looking for your help. I need to find out what happened to Avery Benson. I need to find out who killed her. Avery is … Avery *was*, my fiancée."

10

"I'm … sorry for your loss," Cora said. She'd been caught off guard, her words coming out a moment too late and awkwardly. "It's terrible, what happened to her. But I'm not sure what I can help you with. I don't know anything more than you do. Probably a hell of a lot less, honestly." Cora gave up on going inside and went over to the porch swing. The old wooden slats groaned when she put her overloaded bag on the seat and sat down beside it. Jacob Adler turned where he stood on the top step and leaned against the porch post.

"I don't know anything," he said. "That's the problem. I've spoken with the investigator assigned to the case so many times he's started avoiding my calls. I've talked to the medical examiner, the county coroner, and the state forensics lab. I bet I've met every reporter that's come here to bother you and even more that haven't. I've spoken to everyone where she was staying, from the other guests to the guy that does the landscaping. I've talked to Avery's friends, her coworkers, the lady who did her nails, the guy that waxed her car." He took a step forward, coming to stand in front of Cora. He reached out a hand and grasped the chain attached to the porch swing, stopping it swaying. "I have spoken to every person that might have seen or heard anything, and nobody has any answers." His voice faltered. "Someone dragged her into a cemetery and slammed her against a headstone until her skull caved in, and nobody has any God damned idea who did it or why."

Jacob let go of the chain and stepped back abruptly, turning to stare across a yard that was now dark save for the small puddle of light the bulb over the porch made. The air was dense, thickening ahead of a storm that would soon blow down over the mountains and batter the little clump of town at its foot. The rising wind rustled the leaves to an excited whisper, and far away, lightning flickered, backlighting the clouds for a brief second before returning the sky to darkness.

The flash spurred Jacob to move again. He spun back toward Cora. "This was not how it was supposed to happen." He swiped a hand across his eyes. His words were short and concise and didn't match the tearful motion, but Cora couldn't hold that against him. Losing someone was like that. The injured places scabbed over unevenly, and sometimes you had as many hard sharp edges as you did painful tender spots.

"We were having a hard time," he admitted. "Things weren't perfect. Avery was struggling with some stuff. She was pushing me away. I was so wrapped up in my own …" Jacob trailed off and took a breath. When he began again his voice was calm and even. "I thought it was coming back together, though. The longer she was at the lake, the more like herself she started sounding. Last time I talked to her she was excited to come home. The next day—"

Rocky's nails clicked against the wood, making them both look. He circled the swing, stopped to eye Jacob, and then went to lie down on the mat in front of the door.

"I …" Cora trailed off. "I'm sorry. I really am. I just don't know what you think I can help you with. Or Rocky, I mean. Rocky found her." She gave the dog a nod, like it would make the words more true.

"I understand that. I do." Jacob crouched in front of her, eyes level with hers. "I want you to take me there, you and Rocky, to where you found her. That's what I came here to ask. If he found her body, maybe the police missed something, and he can find that. I've got to know what happened to her, who did this." He stared at Cora with large, pale eyes. "I don't know what else to do. The police have nothing, and now, it feels like they aren't even trying. It's the last thing I can think of."

She looked away, using Rocky as an excuse again, though it was just a reason to break his intense gaze. Cora was still looking at the dog when she spoke. "The police tore the area apart pretty good. You know that, if you've talked to them. Rocky isn't going to find anything they didn't, especially after this much time."

"I know, but if there's even a chance." His tone was pleading. She heard the sigh of the porch as he stood in front of her. "It wouldn't take up much of your time. And maybe even if we don't find anything, if I saw where she … where …" He took a deep breath. "Maybe it will give me some closure. Maybe I'll be able to leave it alone and sleep at night, knowing I did everything I could."

Cora shook her head. "I'm sorry. I can't."

He put up his hands, imploring her. "Please, don't say no. I'm not asking for much of your time—"

"I'm sorry. I can give you directions, if you want. It's not that hard to find. You can go there yourself and—"

"I'll pay you," Jacob said. "I'll give you five hundred— No, I'll give you a thousand dollars, just for a trip up and a little time for Rocky to look around."

Hopefully he didn't see the slight flick of her eyes toward the house. If he was looking for the right place to put the hook, that had been it.

When Cora and Kimmy's mother died, there had been enough to pay for the funeral expenses. All that was left after that was the house. It wasn't much, but it was theirs. Now that Kimmy had moved in with her boyfriend, Cora intended to buy her sister out of her half. The box of cash under the desk, the part that didn't come back out for bills and truck repairs and food, was getting to where that might really happen. An unexpected windfall like this, it would get her that much closer.

She looked at Jacob, who was waiting expectantly. Her resolve started to bend. She studied him for a moment, handsome and stone-faced in the half-light of her porch. And unfamiliar. Strange. That pulled her back. He was a stranger. This man had literally shown up on her doorstep, wanting her to go alone with him to an abandoned cemetery in the middle of the woods, one where another young woman had met an especially grisly end.

"Please." His voice was broken and desperate. "What do you say?"

Cora looked at Rocky, who was snoring softly on the door mat. "I say it's late." She stood and reached into her bag for her house keys. "It's late, and I don't know you. I'm sorry, but the answer is no." She unlocked the door, waking Rocky. He stood up between her and Jacob, stretching like a cat before turning to nose the door open. "Good night, Mr. Adler. I hope you find what you're looking for."

11

"He offered you a thousand dollars?" Kimmy paused with a hank of Cora's hair in her hand. She shook her head, then went on brushing the dark brown dye to the tip. "*And* he was hot?"

"Yeah, I mean, I guess. It was pretty dark." Cora shrugged. Neither the money nor the man's appearance was relevant now. She wasn't likely to see a thousand dollars or Jacob Adler any time soon.

"You know," Kimmy grumbled, "I have clients that pay me good money to dye their hair the shade you're covering up." She separated out another length of Cora's hair, then tugged on it. "And if it gets much longer, I'm going to have to start charging you more for product."

Kimmy said the last part a little louder than was necessary, so the woman standing behind the front counter couldn't help but hear. Then she winked at Cora in the mirror. Kimmy didn't charge her anything, so double the going rate for a cut and color would still be a solid deal.

"Seriously, I'll never understand why you don't leave it the color it is." Kimmy gave Cora's roots a couple dabs, then turned to set the plastic bowl of dye on her station. Cora eyed herself in the salon mirror. Above the collar of the nylon cape, her hair was a flat, slicked-down cap. There was a smudge of chocolate-colored dye next to her ear, and she snaked a hand out from under the cape to wipe it off.

Her sister batted her hand away. "I got it. You'll get it on your face, your hands, *and* your pants. I know you." Kimmy wiped the smudge away with a damp towel, then piled the length of Cora's hair on top of her head before stripping off her gloves. "I'm going to get Martha started. I should be able to get her under the dryer by the time you're ready to rinse."

"No hurry." Cora got up and grabbed a ragged magazine from the rack and headed for one of the empty chairs in the waiting area. "I'm fine however long."

"However long is going to be forty-five minutes, max. More than that and I'll be scraping your hair up off the floor and polishing your bald head instead of rinsing you."

Cora heard a snicker and saw the stylist next to Kimmy laughing. "Remember when Monae forgot to set the timer on that lady's rinse?" the woman said. "Head up, Izzy, or this is gonna be crooked." The stylist pulled on the braid she was working on. The girl the braid was attached to lifted her head and moved her phone closer to her face. "She fell asleep in that corner chair, and by the time Monae remembered and rinsed her she looked like that blue-haired fairy from the paper towel commercials."

"She loved it," Monae called from two chairs down. "The old fart she'd had her eye on in church finally noticed her. Took her out for coffee after Bible study."

"I bet he noticed her. He'd have noticed that shade of blue from outer space," Kimmy said. "Maybe that's your thing, Mo. Hair color even the blind can see."

Monae pointed the scissors in her hand at Kimmy and waved them back and forth. "Laugh all you want, Kimaya Gilbert, but you better remember it next time you need done. See what color you come out."

Mane Event wasn't a glamorous place. Dropped like a little concrete box in the lot between the Feed and Seed and Pine Gap Drug, the salon's teal and salmon color scheme was painful to look at. Inside, it was always stiflingly hot and smelled to high heaven from hair color and acrylic nail solution. There was duct tape over the splits in the old waiting room chairs and a big rainbow splotch in the middle of the floor, where someone had dropped a tray of nail polish bottles roughly a hundred years ago. But it was always so cheerful behind the foggy glass door. Someone was always laughing, the stylists ribbing each other or moaning about difficult customers. Over the top of the wrinkled magazine Cora looked around and wondered what her life would be like if she got up every morning and came to work someplace like this.

She hid her face behind the magazine. It would never happen, not here or anywhere. Some days Cora didn't make it to the end of the street without having to detour and find something. And those were the luckier days, not half as interesting as when it happened in the middle of something. She'd lasted three days at the Divine Diner before losing her sight, dropping a full pot of hot coffee and scrabbling around under the tables for a rubber bouncy ball. When she'd stood up, surrounded by broken glass, covered in coffee, every eye in the place had been on her. At the Quick Wash, they'd had to shut down the automatic bay after she got her arm stuck in the drain trying to fish out a set of car keys. No job she'd had ever lasted more than a week. Fat chance one ever would.

Cora closed the magazine she wasn't reading and put it down, running her finger between her neck and the collar of the stifling cape. *Why did the damn things always have to be so tight?* She yanked at it irritably, then got up, suddenly suffocating in the close, fuggy room. "Kimmy, I'm just going to go sit outside until I'm done, okay?"

Kimmy nodded, deftly combing out a section of Martha Jackson's hair and coiling it around a pink foam roller. Heading for the door, Cora heard Monae calling down the row of chairs to Kimmy. "Quick, turn off that timer. If her hair falls out, maybe you can talk her into growing it back her natural color."

The door fell shut, closing off the chemical smell and the laughter. Cora turned back to look at her reflection in the window, at the part down the center of her head, where dark brown dye covered the strip of lighter roots.

At least when Kimmy did it, it looked good. When Cora first colored it herself when she was fourteen, she had turned her hair, a fat ring around her scalp, both palms, and part of the bathroom floor jet black.

Their mother had been furious, scrubbing Cora's hairline red to remove the sloppy ring, standing with her arms crossed in the doorway while Cora scoured the stained linoleum to a faded purple with Comet. But neither her mother's anger nor the manual labor kept Cora from doing it again when a half inch of her roots was showing. There was less mess the second time, at least.

By the third time everyone was used to the color, and her mom had figured out why her daughter was dyeing her long, honey-color hair dark as ink. Cora would never look like her mother or sister with their clear, liquid brown eyes, dark skin, and black hair. This was as close as she could get. And it was as different as possible from anything inherited from the parents who'd abandoned her.

"Cora." Kimmy poked her head out the door. "Hello. Earth to Cora. Come back inside. Time to rinse."

Tipped back in the rinse chair, the water ran down over Cora's ears and away in a muddy-brown swirl. Kimmy hummed quietly to herself, squirting a big dollop of shampoo into her hand and working it into a lather in Cora's hair.

"You didn't forget about tomorrow, right?" Her hand froze on Cora's scalp.

"No. I didn't forget."

The sudsing resumed. "And you have a dress to wear? Or pants. If you wear pants, they've got to be nice pants, the kind that look good with heels. No jeans. You cannot wear jeans, Cora. Promise me."

"Ouch." Cora jerked away from the scalding water.

"Sorry." Kimmy adjusted the temperature and began rinsing.

"Sorry, my ass," Cora grumbled. "You know what, I think I'll just grab something out of that garbage bag of dresses from after Aunt Reva died. I'm sure the mothball smell will come out in the wash." Cora opened her eyes to enjoy the stricken look on her sister's face. She got a shot of water in the eye instead.

"I swear, Cora, I will shave you bald in your sleep. This is import-ant." Kimmy wrapped a towel around Cora's head. She pulled the lever to sit the rinse chair back up with a little more force than necessary and nearly shot Cora across the room.

"Geez, calm down. Don't worry, Kimmy, I won't embarrass you. I promise no one will ever know the biggest city I've ever set foot in is the Dollar City in Canton."

"It's not like that." Kimmy stopped wiping down the rinse sink and twisted the damp towel in her hands. "I didn't mean that. It's just—"

Cora spun around and threw her arms around her sister, cutting her off. "Calm down. I know. It's Dante's big night and his parents and a whole lot of equally out-of-our-league people are going to be there. I'm not going to embarrass you in front of your boyfriend and the world showing up looking like I got my outfit at Citgo." She let go of her sister and leaned back so she could look at her. "I got a dress last week. It was at Salvation Army, but it still had the original tags on it and everything."

Kimmy tilted her head to the side. "What color?"

"Black. Black is always acceptable, right?"

"Long or short?"

"In the middle, like halfway between hooker and kindergarten teacher."

Kimmy didn't smile, but she looked relieved enough to nod her head. Cora followed her back to her chair. "Okay. I trust you," Kimmy said, "but don't even think about bailing at the last minute. I'm leaving early to ride up with Dante, but I swear to God I will drive back here and haul you out of the house if I have to. I need you there for moral support."

"Yeah, yeah. I'll be there. Starts at six, right?"

Nodding, Kimmy pulled the towel off Cora's now evenly mahogany-color hair and began to comb it out. "Six. It takes at least an hour to get to Corning, but give yourself extra time, so you can find it." Kimmy lowered her voice and leaned close to Cora's ear. "And in case you have to, you know." Cora rolled her eyes. She knew. "Be on the road by four thirty." Kimmy put down her comb and picked up her scissors, stopping to lock eyes with her sister in the mirror. "Maybe four would be safer. Be in the truck by four."

"Fine," Cora said. "Just trim my ends quick so I can get out of here.

I left Rocky with Mr. Debusher and if he's there too long he'll have eaten so many treats he'll be farting all night."

Kimmy froze, open scissors in her hand, horrified look on her face. "Oh my God. Don't be late, and damn it, *please* don't say anything like that tomorrow night."

12

Cora left ahead of schedule. She dropped Rocky off at Mr. Debusher's at twenty after three and was opening her driver's side door two minutes later. Four would have given her more than enough time, but she wanted plenty of extra so she could walk to the museum from wherever she had to park. Cora wanted her exhaust-burping Ford F-150 with its leprous skin of Bondo and primer where no one could see it.

Tossing her bag onto the seat, Cora dropped her heels on the floor and hitched her dress up to an unladylike height. She pulled away from the curb and was a hundred yards from the stop sign at the end of the street when the phone rang.

"Are you getting ready?" Kimmy's voice was loud and shrill through the speaker. "You should be at least out of the shower. If you aren't, get in. Right now."

"Relax. I'm already in the truck. I am on my way. Literally. Not on the couch watching TV and thinking about leaving, but actually driving." Cora honked her horn. A boy in a blue baseball shirt throwing rocks into Falls Creek looked up and scowled at her as she rolled over the bridge. "Did you hear that, Kimmy? That's me in the car."

"Okay good. Now when you get there—"

"Kimmy, have you been drinking?"

"What?" Kimmy's voice tightened to a squeak. "Drinking? Why would you ask that?"

Making the turn onto Union Street, Cora gave the truck more gas, earning a flatulent roar from the engine. She waited for it to level off to answer. "Because if you aren't drinking, you should start right now. You sound like you need an exorcism."

"God, do I need one. The drink, not the exorcism. But I don't dare. It might make things worse. I'm just so *nervous*," Kimmy wailed through the phone.

"Why are *you* nervous? It's not like this is about you."

"I know, I know," Kimmy said. "It's just that Dante's so worked up it's making me crazy. I've never seen him like this. I understand it's a big deal and there's going to be important people there, but he's usually so freaking calm. I wonder if—"

Her sister's voice cut out abruptly. Cora dropped the phone onto the seat, not bothering to look at the screen. It would read zero bars and stay that way until she picked up Route 14 in Granville Summit. Even then, it was going to be spotty off and on until she hit the New York State border. Kimmy was going to have to work out her nerves on her own.

She wasn't the only one with nerves. Cora's stomach was doing sour little flip-flops. Situations involving people she didn't know, crowds, and most especially, cocktail attire, were the kinds she avoided. But Kimmy and Dante were a package deal these days, and with Dante there came the occasional fancy function, things like gallery openings and museum events where his art was on display.

Her stomach had settled by the time she waved to Kimmy from across the four lanes of traffic, mostly because she was too tired to be nervous anymore. Cursing the inventor of high heels, Cora paused between two of the lanes, then darted across, earning a couple of honks in the process. On the sidewalk, she stopped to adjust the strap of her slingback before making her way across the museum parking lot.

"You look like you just ran a marathon." Kimmy stepped out from under the long shadow cast by the museum's facade. "You're red as hell. It didn't hurt your hair, at least. Gave it a little bit of body for once." Kimmy got a stricken look on her face. "You checked things out first, right? Oh my God, did you just get here?"

She had definitely not just gotten there. Cora had pulled into the

Museum of Glass parking lot at four forty-one, only stopping on the way to quickly fill up her gas-guzzling monster's tank. Once there, she'd spent almost an hour stumbling around the sprawling, oddly shaped building, stopping to pick up a Murano paperweight, a baby shoe, a pair of Ray-Ban Wayfarers, a wilted origami crane, and a St. Anthony medal. A maintenance worker emptying trash cans assumed she was drunk and pulled out his cell phone to take pictures. When the place was finally clear and she thought she could reasonably expect to walk inside and not end up on her face, Cora got back into her truck and moved it across the street and parked it behind a YMCA. Her wreck of a ride safely out of sight, Cora had hoofed it across four lanes of traffic back to the museum, the skin on her ankle rubbed into a fat, weeping blister by the strap of her shoe, her long dark hair frizzing up into a Brillo pad.

"Cora, what is it?" Kimmy's face was tight with panic. "If you just got here and you're having one of your—"

Cora stuck her hand out in front of her and cut her sister off. She closed her eyes and took a deep breath. When the volcano of profanity threatening to erupt from her mouth receded, Cora opened her eyes. "No, I did not just get here. No, I'm not having one of my anything. Do you have a damn Band-Aid?"

Kimmy winced. "Sorry. I'm just so—"

"Band-Aid?" Cora said again.

Kimmy shook her head. "I just about managed to get my phone and a lipstick in this thing." She held up her tiny white handbag and shook her head. "No Band-Aids, but there's cocktails in the lobby right now, before the exhibit opens. They're the next best thing, right?" Kimmy cocked her head toward the double doors. "You want?"

"Yes, I want a cocktail. You have no idea." Cora followed her sister toward the door. "I'm surprised you aren't in there already."

Kimmy shook her head. "I came out looking for you. Besides, I told you, Dante's acting weird. I'm going to try to hide until this thing starts. His mom and dad can deal with him until he calms down and everybody sees the installation." She looked at Cora, and her eyes went wide. "I got to see it all put together earlier. Cora, it's incredible. I swear, you are going to be blown away."

She followed Kimmy into a high-ceilinged, echoing space broken up by decorative glass dividers and tiny bar-height tables covered in black cloths. Knots of people were scattered across the floor, and Cora saw waiters circulating with trays.

"I was in the truck forever." Cora pulled her elbow away from her sister. "Let me at least go to the bathroom and maybe comb my hair quick."

"Good idea," Kimmy said, changing direction. "I'll go too. We can kill a little more time and—"

"Kimaya." A handsome man in a slimly cut worsted suit separated himself from a knot of people and headed for them. "There you are. Hi, Cora." Dante gave Cora a quick hug, then took Kimmy's hand. Kimmy was right; he did seem nervous. His free hand was ticking to some unheard beat, and he was jiggling on his heels. He looked happy enough, though, his black eyes sparkling. "Sweetheart, there's a couple people I want you to meet."

"I'll find you in a minute," Cora said, letting her sister be led away, then making her escape to the ladies' room.

Inside, she wasted as much time as possible. When her hands were washed and meticulously dried, Cora combed her hair. She found a Band-Aid in the amenities kit on the counter amongst the sewing kits and tiny packets of Advil and stuck it over the raw place on her heel, then helped herself to a packet of mints. When she couldn't kill any more time, Cora tucked her bag under her elbow and charged back out the door.

Directly into a man with a glass of wine in his hand.

He was quick and managed to scoot backward out of the way. A wave of red arced out of the glass and hit the floor with a splat. He avoided all the spatter but for a few tiny drops that ended up on his shiny dress shoes.

"Shit." Cora slapped her hand across her face. It had just slipped out, and louder than necessary. A couple heads turned their way, and she felt her cheeks start to burn. "I mean, shoot," she whispered. "I'm so sorry. I'll ..."

Cora looked up from the man's shoes, dots of wine across their surface like a constellation, and into a familiar face.

13

"**Y**ou," Cora said. His eyes were a clear, crystalline green she hadn't been able to make out when he'd been standing in the darkness of her front porch.

"Me," he said, lips twitching up at the corners. "Come on. We'd better flee the scene while we can still make a clean getaway." He caught the eye of a server with an empty tray and nodded to the mess on the floor, then took Cora by the elbow and steered her to a small bar set up in the corner. He put down his dripping glass and picked up a napkin, then knelt to wipe the wine from his shoes.

"What are you doing here?" Cora said. It came out sounding like an accusation. She fumbled to soften it. "I mean … it's a surprise, running into you again."

His ox-blood shoes restored to a mirror shine, he stood. "Red or white?"

"What?"

He tipped his head toward the bartender who was waiting silently behind the bar. "Wine. Would you prefer red or white?"

"Er, white please."

"Two," he said to the bartender, then turned back toward Cora. "Good idea. Less likely to show in case of an *accident*."

"Sorry about that." Cora was able to hide the blush by turning to take a glass of pale golden wine from the man behind the bar. "I didn't get it anywhere beside your shoes, did I, Jacob? It is Jacob, right?"

"You remembered." He smiled, revealing teeth that were perfect except for a little turn in one of his canines. Examining the legs of his suit pants, a shade of blue neither somber nor bright but somewhere appropriately in between, he nodded. Cora was no judge of suits, but it fit so perfectly it looked like it had been made for him. "Not a drop that I can find. And anyway, it's only a suit."

Probably a very expensive one, Cora imagined. He looked very expensive altogether: big shiny watch, gold cufflinks with a border of enamel that exactly matched the suit, signet ring on his finger with an A picked out in diamonds on the surface. She realized he was waiting, watching her examine him.

"What *are* you doing here?" she said.

He stepped away from the bar and Cora followed. There were square, metal-block benches scattered around the room, and he gestured for her to sit. When he sat next to her, Cora could smell the cologne he was wearing, prickly but pleasant, like fresh pepper and clove.

"Just a happy coincidence, I think," Jacob said, "running into you again. Avery's family has a financial stake in the materials industry here. Her father used to bring her with him when he came to the city on business and take her to the museum. I'm not surprised she ended up involved with the place as an adult. She had a hand in funding this new exhibit. It's a shame she isn't here to see it. I had planned to head back home after I met with you but decided to delay it a little and see it for the both of us."

"Jesus, I'm so sorry, Jacob. I had no idea. I wonder if my sister knows. I—"

Jacob waved a hand to cut her off. "I hope you won't be enlightening her, if she doesn't. The last thing Avery would have wanted was attention drawn to herself. She was like that; she didn't want her name attached to anything she supported. She hated any kind of recognition."

Cora considered her wineglass, spinning the stem slowly between her fingers. She felt a small guilty twinge in her gut. Jacob had come to her asking for help finding out who killed his fiancée and she'd turned him down. Now it appeared the woman was at least partly responsible for Dante's success. She tipped her head up to find him looking at her.

"It seems more strange to find you here than me," Jacob said. "This is pretty far from, what's it called"—he thought for a second—"Pine Gulch?"

"Pine Gap. I'm surprised you were that close. There's not much to remember. Not even a proper stoplight and more cows than people. If you'd been blinking on your way through you might have missed it altogether."

"I don't know," Jacob said. "Granted I was only there for a little while, but it left an impression." He gave her an indecipherable look. "Still," he said, deftly turning the conversation back to his original question, "it's a pretty good distance from here."

Cora searched the room, looking for Kimmy. She was easy to find, her white outfit standing out in the crowd of dark dresses and suits. Kimmy was standing next to Dante and a pair she guessed were his parents.

"Over there, in the white dress, that's my sister Kimmy." Jacob found her and nodded. "Her boyfriend, Dante, is an artist. I'm supposedly here for moral support, but it doesn't look like Kimmy really needs it." Cora frowned. Kimmy was chattering away, smiling, one of her hands tucked in Dante's elbow. If Cora hadn't run into Jacob, she'd probably be backed up to a wall pretending to be interested in her phone or her wine, an awkward figure in a thrift shop dress.

"Dante Abaya is your sister's boyfriend? He's very talented." Jacob saw Cora purse her lips. "What?"

She laughed, stifling it with her hand. "I'm sorry. It's just every time I hear his last name out loud, I remember that if things work out between them my sister's going to be Kimaya Abaya."

He smiled, eyes crinkling in the corners. Across the room, someone clapped for attention.

"It's starting," Jacob said. "I'm anxious to see it. Avery thought it was going to blow people away."

Cora stood, finding Kimmy again, hoping she'd turn to search her out, but Dante was already towing her toward the large double doors being pulled open. Jacob took the wineglass from Cora's hand

and set it down on the bench, then held out his arm. "Come on. Let me escort you in."

Seeing Kimmy disappear through the doors without a backward glance, Cora slid her hand into the crook of Jacob's proffered arm. At the door, he stepped aside to let her walk through ahead of him.

"Holy shit." Cora stopped walking so abruptly Jacob crashed into her back. He got a hand under her elbow to catch her before she fell and pulled her to the side to let the stream of people behind them pass. It wasn't completely embarrassing, at least. She saw plenty of people stop short and heard more than one 'holy shit' slip past someone else's lips.

When she moved forward again, Cora went more carefully. The floor beneath them felt too deep, like her heel might sink into the mirrored surface that ran from wall to wall without a visible seam or break. It took her a moment to orient herself and look up at the installation suspended from the ceiling and reflected on the floor below.

It started just over the entry door with a single strand of translucent white glass, long and thin as a pool cue. It shot out parallel to the ground, then exploded into other rods in coral and cobalt and emerald and rose, like rainbow sparks from the tip of a magician's wand. Farther on, each of *those* rods exploded outward, bursting into its own firework of glass in new colors: lilac and black, vermilion, silver, tawny yellow.

Some burst on and on, colors growing fiercer as they traveled forward; umber to fiery red, pale yellow to bright shimmering gold. Some stopped, the path dying with the rounded end of a length of amethyst or copper or peridot or jet-black glass. Others doubled back, turning in a sharp vee to rejoin the explosion at another intersection. Each one was mirrored so clearly on the floor they seemed to move in invisible waves as they grew and then shrank in number, flowing in a rainbow toward the other end of the room.

"What do you think, Cora?" Dante had come up beside her while she gaped. He was smiling so hard it looked like it might hurt. She couldn't blame him. It was a triumph of a night for him. This display he'd created was to become a permanent part of the museum, the room they were in an anteroom into the exhibits beyond. Going over as well as this seemed to be, it was sure to lead to other commissions.

"Come on, let me walk you through it." Dante grabbed Kimmy's hand and started to lead them back to the doors they'd entered through, when he noticed Jacob standing behind Cora.

"Hello." Dante held out his hand. "Who's this? Cora, did you sneak in a date?"

She felt Jacob's hand gently touch the back of her arm. When she turned, he gave her a warning look. She understood; he didn't want her to say anything about his connection, or at least his late fiancée's, to the exhibit. She nodded slightly, turning back to Dante. "Dante, this is Jacob. He's a ... an acquaintance of mine. We happened to run into each other outside." Cora snuck a look at Kimmy. Her sister examined Jacob without losing her smile. Cora was pretty sure she didn't have any acquaintances Kimmy didn't know, but it didn't look like she was going to grill Cora for more information, at least not right now.

"Good to meet you," Dante said. He let go of Jacob's hand. "So, this." He pointed above them, at the intricate pick-up stick creation. "You know how you get roped into a group message, on your phone?" Dante's smile looked almost embarrassed, and he shrugged, trying to explain. "I thought of it when Kimmy sent some message to me and like fifteen other people about getting together for drinks. I already knew I was going, and that half the other people on the list were too, but the messages just kept pinging in. Yesses and nos. Then silly stuff like a smiley face or a thumbs-up, but times fifteen, because your phone blows up every time somebody adds something. And those people, all the ones answering, you know they've probably got the same thing going with ten other people. In my mind, this is just what it looked like."

Cora looked up at the very first pearlescent white rod. "Kimmy?"

He broke into a bright, wide smile. "Kimmy."

Cora looked toward her sister, who had ahold of Dante's arm and looked like she might cry. They were so happy it was almost depressing.

Dante led the way through the installation, the mirrored floor making it look close enough to reach up and touch, its twin under their feet so perfectly reflected Cora expected to hear a crunch when she put her feet down on the fragile-looking twins of the pieces above. She marveled at the hundreds of lengths of glass. "Every rod is handmade," Dante explained. "And every line of conversation is its own unique shade. There was no way to move this from my studio in one piece, so most of the assembly had to be done right here with a portable torch and a scaffold. And there had to be multiples of everything, just in case. I broke a lot of glass, let me tell you."

They reached the far end of the room, where the profusion of glass *messages* had tapered back down to one single white rod. It made Cora smile, to think it had all been inspired by her sister.

"Congratulations, Dante," Cora said. "This is really impressive."

He grinned, though she thought it looked suddenly strained. "Thanks. Make sure you stick around. There's a nice reception after this. That will be impressive." He put a hand on Cora's arm. "Don't miss it, okay?"

14

Eventually the last stragglers found their way through the exhibit and into a plush reception room. Dante had been claimed by one knot of people after another, Kimmy staying glued to his side, and Cora found herself left again with Jacob. She was glad now that she'd run into him, even if it had been with a glass of wine. It was much better to look like part of a pair than to wander around trying not to look awkward and alone, twiddling a wineglass around and around.

A long table set against one wall groaned with trays of cheese and fruit, piles of canapes, a mountain of shrimp cocktail in a silver tureen of ice. Making their way down the slow-moving line, she felt a flutter of warmth when Jacob leaned over and whispered in her ear. "Have you noticed that the more food there is, the tinier the plates are? In my experience, your best bet is to get two plates in one hand and one in the other, load them up, and run."

Cora settled for two in one hand, snagging a glass of champagne with the other. She followed Jacob to a table in the corner, out of the way but in sight of Kimmy and Dante.

"Those must be Dante's parents." Cora swallowed a bite of cheese and washed it down with champagne. It was bubblier than she expected, and she had to wipe her eyes with her napkin. "I've never met them, but my sister is totally scared of them. Look at her."

Dante's mother was silver haired and bony, so short the edge of the table was even with her chest. Kimmy was sitting bolt upright beside her, mouth shut, lips set in a stiff, forced smile. On her other side, Dante was talking to his father, as round as his wife was angular, bald head gleaming, champagne glass ticking back and forth while he talked. Cora watched Kimmy's eyes flick back and forth nervously between the tiny woman and her large husband.

"Why's she so scared of them?" Jacob asked. "Wait, let me guess. They're secretly total weirdos, and last time she was at their house looking for a bathroom she found their sex dungeon."

Cora snorted, trying to cover it up with the undersized cocktail napkin. "Kimmy could probably deal with a senior sex dungeon." Her laugh fell away, and she lowered her voice to a whisper. "They don't think Kimmy's good enough for Dante. They don't like the idea of their son running around with a hairdresser from the sticks, at least that's what Kimmy told me." Suddenly the food in front of her didn't look so appetizing and she pushed the small plates away, picking up her glass instead and draining the champagne.

"I don't think that will stop them." Jacob got up swiftly and picked up two more glasses of champagne, bringing them back and setting one down in front of her. "I mean, look at Dante. He's paying attention to his father, but every two seconds he's slipping a glance at your sister."

"They really are great together," Cora said. "Honestly, they have no idea how good Kimmy is for him. They can say what they want about her not being educated enough or good enough for him or whatever, but he's such an … artist."

Jacob cocked an eyebrow, biting back a grin.

"I mean, Dante's a great guy," Cora explained, "but when it comes to practical stuff, he can hardly remember to put socks on. She probably made sure his suit was clean and pressed, got him in it and tied his tie. And got them out of the house on time. And remembered to put gas in the car. And paid the water bill. And made sure the rent was on time. For Christ's sake—" Cora lowered her voice, the Christ having come out louder than she expected, turning a few nearby heads. She had to stop doing that. "For Christ's sake," Cora whispered, "Kimmy works three jobs some days. But none of them is the right kind, I guess. I wonder if they'd be more okay with her if she had a hundred thousand dollars in student loans for some bullshit history degree or something."

"Hey there, killer. Take it easy." Jacob sat back and crossed his arms, though there was a twinkle in his eye.

"The history degree or the student loans?"

Jacob uncrossed his arms and pushed aside his plate, leaning toward her and putting his elbows on the table. He was close enough for her to see the white half-moons of his fingernails, buffed to a soft shine.

"Let me guess. It's the history degree?" she said.

"How'd you know?"

She shrugged like it was just a good guess, but the truth was, his fingernails weren't the only thing about him that was polished. He was perfectly put together, but not forced together, like the items of clothing went together so well because they had the common theme of being expensive. The watch alone probably would have covered a college degree with money left over.

"In my defense," he said, "it was only a history minor."

"How are you doing?" Cora abruptly blurted out. "Sorry. I'm just amazed how great you seem somewhere that must have meant so much to your fiancée, and so soon after—" She looked at Kimmy and Dante. If something happened to Dante, what would Kimmy be like? Shattered, Cora imagined. She turned back to Jacob, who was staring in her sister's direction.

"Don't be sorry. I'm doing fine. And Avery and I, we … we weren't like them." His eyes flicked back to Cora. "God knows I loved Avery, but the truth is, things were on the downhill between us. I just hadn't really accepted it. I wondered all the time, when she didn't answer her phone or didn't call, if there was someone else. She sounded good last time I talked to her, excited to get back to the city, but for all I know she was coming back to break it off and tell me it was over. Now I guess I'll never know."

She wished she hadn't asked. Cora toyed with her champagne flute. Neither of them spoke. The clink of a fork against a champagne glass finally broke the silence.

"Excuse me, everyone." At Dante and Kimmy's table, a man in a crisp black suit and a bow tie pushed his chair out and stood. He tapped the flute again and the last bits of conversation faded away.

"Good evening, everyone. For those of you who don't know me, my name is Forester McClean. I have the privilege of being the chairman of the board here at …"

Cora fought the yawn that sprang up almost instantly when the man started talking. She held her jaw shut forcibly, wondering if anyone really enjoyed speeches besides the people giving them. She looked across at Jacob, who was paying scrupulous attention, head turned toward the speaker, hands tented in front of him, and decided that there was something seriously wrong with her attention span. Then Jacob turned his head the slightest bit toward her and rolled his eyes before returning to rapt attention.

Eventually, Mr. Chairman of the Board started to ramp down like he was getting ready to wrap it up. Cora eyed the end of the refreshment table with its filled glasses of champagne.

"Again, thank you all for coming," McClean said, "and for your continued support of the organization. Now, a few words from the artist whose work I know you all found as forthright and awakening as I did, a tangible representation of the power of a global and interconnected society." There was another subtle eye roll from Jacob that made Cora grin. "A round of applause for our artist, Mr. Dante Abaya. Dante."

"Poor guy is sweating bullets." Jacob edged his chair closer to hers while Dante rebuttoned his suit jacket. "I would have thought the hard part was over."

Cora nodded. Dante looked as nervous as he had before the exhibit doors opened. Maybe he had a fear of public speaking she didn't know about. Maybe he desperately needed to use the bathroom. Whatever it was, he looked ready to jump out of his skin.

"Good evening, everyone," Dante said. "Thank you for coming. I hope you enjoyed the exhibit and maybe even found it thought provoking. If nothing else, I hope you at least thought it was pretty." There was a smattering of polite laughter. "I'd like to thank the people who made it possible. First and foremost, the board and fellows of the Corning Museum of Glass." There was some self-congratulatory nodding and a few pats on the back.

"And of course, none of it would have been possible without the support of my parents." Dante's mother beamed, and his father looked about ready to explode out of his already stressed buttons. "Most especially I would like to thank my girlfriend, Kimaya Gilbert, who was both the inspiration for and driving force behind the installation." Dante paused for a moment, then cleared his throat and adjusted his tie. "In fact, there's not much I could do without her." Kimmy was looking down at the table, flushed but smiling. Maybe this would give Dante's parents a little shove toward being more appreciative of her. "That being the case, I don't want to risk there ever being a time when she isn't there to steer the ship and inspire me." His hand slid into his pocket. "So, I hope that she can make this very important day the *most* important one in my life so far and agree to be my wife."

Cora smiled robotically through the clapping and the congratulations. She hugged her sister, hugged Dante, shook hands with his parents, toasted the beaming couple. She was happy, but the development had thrown her deep into thought. Thankfully Kimmy was too busy glowing, shyly showing off the diamond and pearl engagement ring, to notice. After another glass of celebratory champagne, Cora decided to quietly make her escape.

She slid a sideways look at Jacob, who'd been her silent shadow through it all. Cora picked up her bag from the table and slid it under her arm. "Leaving?" he said. Cora nodded and shot a glance at the people around her sister and Dante. She could slip out now without a fuss, talk about it all with her sister later. "I'll walk you out." Jacob took her arm, and they made their exit.

Coming back out through the exhibit was very different than going in. The lights had been dimmed, and the colors of the hundreds of glass rods were muted and bled into each other, less a bright firework and more a dark spider, hanging by its web over their heads. Cora found herself scurrying under it and through the far door.

Outside, the day's humidity had given way to light rain, the air mercifully cooler. She looked up at the thin fingernail paring of a moon for a moment, watching it grow clear and sharp, then fade away behind a scrim of moving clouds. When she looked down, she saw Jacob staring at her. "Where are you parked?" he asked. "I'll walk you to your car."

That was the last thing she wanted, having him hike her across a four-lane highway to a YMCA parking lot and hoist her into her rust-bucket truck. "Thanks," she said, "but I think I'm just going to hang out here for a bit and get some air."

He looked at her a moment longer, opened his mouth like he was going to say something, then closed it. Jacob nodded and headed down the sidewalk, stepping off the curb into the parking lot, hard-soled shoe touching down with a clap.

"Jacob, wait." He stopped and turned back. "Are you going back home, wherever that is, or are you going to be around here a little longer?"

He shrugged, retracing his steps back over the curb and up the sidewalk toward her. "I don't have any concrete plans. I've been a bit adrift, I admit. Why?"

"Do you still want me to take you up to where …" Cora swallowed. "I mean, do you want me and Rocky to take you up to the cemetery to look around?" She held her breath and waited. Maybe he'd changed his mind since the night on her porch. Maybe the last thing he wanted to do was be reminded of his fiancée lying broken and cold on an old grave in an abandoned cemetery. Maybe her words made it as visceral and ugly to him as it was in her head, a clot on this otherwise peaceful, quiet moment. She started to wish she hadn't spoken, but a moment later, Jacob smiled a grim smile and nodded.

"I would still like that very much."

"Day after tomorrow, if you can. Nine a.m.," Cora said. "You know where to find me."

He nodded, and she watched him walk away across the parking

lot and climb into his car. Only after it left the parking lot and the red taillights blinked out of sight did she step off the sidewalk.

Cora took her heels off and walked barefoot in the rain, aware of the full, unfamiliar darkness and how her handbag had been too small for the can of mace that usually went everywhere with her. She did her best to stay focused and aware until she'd crossed the empty YMCA lot and climbed into her truck. When she was on the road, Cora felt free to think, absently following the yellow lines through the miles and miles of darkness.

She hoped Jacob attributed her change of mind to their better acquaintance. The truth was, Kimmy was going to get married, and if Kimmy wanted a big wedding or money for a honeymoon or toward a house, she should have it. If Cora added the money from the lockbox to what she'd accumulated in the bank, if she got Harold to take a couple more items and put everything she could squeeze out of her budget in, topped off with Jacob's money, she might be able to give Kimmy her half of the house. She'd been creeping closer to the goal, but now, meeting it felt urgent.

Cora smiled grimly to herself in the dark, driving toward the silver sickle of moon that hung over the hills. He might change his mind. Jacob Adler might think about it and decide that he didn't want to be taken on what would probably be a fruitless trip into the woods after all. But she hoped he didn't change his mind. She found that his coming wasn't a distasteful prospect, money or no. His sea-green eyes and the curve of his smile were things Cora wouldn't mind seeing again.

15

"**C**ome on, Rocky," Cora leaned out the front door and yelled across the yard. She waited for the dog to squeeze himself through the gap in the fence between her house and Mr. Debusher's. The old man had been nice enough to keep the dog overnight, promising to let him out this morning to do his business and make his way back home. "Rocky, breakfast." She shook his dish, the kibble rattling like scattershot in the bottom, but he didn't appear. He was probably passed out on the old man's porch, full of dog treats.

Cora set the bowl back inside and stepped out, letting the squalling screen door fall shut behind her. At the edge of the porch, she felt a familiar hum start in her fingertips and her vision blurred. She missed the first step and stumbled the rest of the way down, partly because she couldn't see clearly and partly because it was so unexpected. It wasn't as if she didn't find things close to home now and then, but whatever was tugging at her, it hadn't been there when she'd gotten home last night.

Pulling herself up with the porch railing, Cora dusted off her knees and turned until she found the right direction and took a step forward. The tingling feeling intensified. When she hit her front gate she corrected again, hoping none of the neighbors was near a window to see her lurching around, growing more and more red faced, looking like she was just rolling in from an all-night bender.

She started toward Mr. Debusher's but had to stop and turn around when she lost her vision. When she got back to where her truck was parked at the edge of the street, the tingle became a burn.

Rocky appeared, nosing up the fork latch on Mr. Debusher's gate and pushing it open. He trotted over and sat on his haunches a few feet away from her, eyeing her curiously. Cora took another step, stumbling off the curb and letting fly a stream of profanity. When she got to her feet, the feeling fell away. Cora knelt and felt around under the edge of her front tire. "Where did you come from?" She held up a single wireless headphone earbud.

There was a clatter of glass across the narrow street. A teenage boy was dragging a full trash bag out the front door of a singlewide trailer, bottles clanking against each other as they slid down one uneven step then the next. He hauled the bag to the curb and heaved it into the trash can.

"Tiddles," Cora yelled out. Rocky trotted across the street, then waited patiently on the crumbling sidewalk in front of the blue and white trailer while Eugene Tiddles put the lid back on the trash can. He hitched his low-hanging jeans higher on his narrow hips and looked both ways before coming over to Cora's side of the street, Rocky glued to his side.

"When did you get back from your dad's?" Cora asked. Tiddles pushed the flat brim of his ball cap up so he could see, some of the curly brown hair he was trying to hide under it escaping.

"Last night, real late." He was so soft-spoken Cora could hardly hear him. "I guess it was really this morning."

"How was it?"

"Good." Tiddles shrugged. He bent down to pet Rocky, who knocked the hat off his head trying to lick his face. Tiddles picked it up and dusted off the brim carefully before putting it back on. "I was gonna stay another week, but then he found out he's gotta go to Texas again. That's where the work is right now, I guess."

Tiddles's dad went where the natural gas was. It had brought him here just long enough to meet Marla Tiddles and make Eugene Tiddles Jr., and to discover the former had a serious alcohol problem. Across the street, Cora saw the twitch of the curtain over one of the trailer's small, cloudy windows. "How's your mom?"

Scratching absently at his thin chest through his t-shirt, Tiddles just shrugged and looked over his shoulder. The Hefty bag of empty Nikolai bottles he'd just hauled out to the curb said enough.

"Oh wait." She held out the white earbud in her palm. "This isn't yours, is it?"

Tiddles's face brightened and a smile broke out, showing a surprisingly decent set of teeth behind the thin lips. "Where did you find it? I thought I lost it in the cab last night. My dad bought those for me for an early birthday present."

Cora dropped it into his eager hand. He fished a little case out of his saggy pants and flipped it open, popping the earbud in next to its mate. "I was so mad at myself for losing it. Only had them for two days, and these things are expensive. Where was it at?"

She pointed to where the earbud had been resting against the tire of her truck. If she hadn't gotten the pull to find it, she would have crunched it into white plastic shrapnel when she pulled out.

"Thanks, Cora." Tiddles reached down to scratch Rocky, who was nosing at his hand. "Oh, hey." He looked up at her. "Were you in your backyard last night? Like after midnight?"

"Out back?" Cora shook her head. "No. I got home around eleven and I was dead to the world by eleven thirty. I didn't come out again until just now."

Tiddles's eyes narrowed. "You sure?" She nodded. "When I got home, I thought I saw you go around the back of the house. Somebody did. I just figured it was you taking Rocky out or something. I was gonna yell, but I didn't want to risk waking my mom up." Rocky whined, and Tiddles reached down to rub his nose. "Gotta go, dude. Catch you later, Cora."

She waved and mumbled something in response, turning back around and heading toward her yard. "Rocky, was there somebody in the yard? Go look." She waved her hands, ushering him toward the back. He took one uninterested look at her and went to the corner by the front gate to paw at his burial ground. "Some guard dog you are," Cora muttered.

Between her house and the fence she shared with Mr. Debusher was a six-foot-wide swath of grass. The grass was overdue to be cut; long, and matted down in spots, but she couldn't tell if that was Rocky's doing or someone on two legs. Around the back of the house was a different story. A towering sugar maple cut out most of the sunlight, the ground beneath it bare save for a few pale, spindly blades of grass. In the dirt, soft from the incessant rain, were unmistakable shoe prints.

They were big, a man's shoe, with a heavy tread. They went to the window of the locked bedroom with its cover of cardboard, its old wooden frame nailed shut. From there they traveled up the back steps, clear muddy prints stopping in front of her door and then coming back down. Next, they traveled to the other bedroom, her bedroom. The sheer curtain fluttered out the window she left open to sleep last night.

She hurried around to the front. "Come here, boy. I need your collar." Unclipping it, she went to the back bedroom and gathered up what she needed. Locking it back up tightly, she checked the windows, closing and locking hers, pulling down the old roller shade. "Come on, Rocky. Let's get out of here."

Stopping at the gate to replace his collar, Cora looked back at her little house, and shivered.

16

"**C**ora, I didn't think to see you again so soon." Harold saw her coming and opened the door of the pawnshop, kicking a rubber wedge under the frame to keep it open. Back behind the counter, he ran an old cotton handkerchief over his forehead and tucked it back into the pocket of his pants.

"It's an oven in here, Harold. Did your AC break or something?" The morning had been flat and cool, but as soon as the sun got a grip on the day the temperature had risen to a sticky, swampy level. There weren't any clouds darkening the sky yet, but it was so thick and stifling Cora didn't have to look at the forecast to know it was coming. Tonight, she'd be sleeping to the hammer of rain on the tin roof and the maple outside knocking against the windows to get in.

Harold waved a hand dismissively. "Didn't run it during the summer. I'm sure as hell not gonna start in the fall. Go on, let the heat have one last at it. I consider it training for when I retire to Florida."

"Florida, as in that place where everybody's nice and cool because they're smart enough to stay inside and run the air instead of suffering?"

"Smart ass," Harold said, "but I'm glad you come in."

That was a good sign, if it wasn't just Harold passing the time. "I'm glad you're glad." Cora thumped her bag down on the front case. It was heavier than usual today, and Harold winced at the solid clunk it made against the glass. "Sorry. Listen, Harold, I'm not going to beat around the bush. I need to scrape together as much cash as I can asap. I'm giving you first shot. Anything you don't make me a decent offer on, no hard feelings, but I'm going to take right over to Penny Pawn in Troy and after that, cash for gold in Monroeton."

"That place is a skinning joint, kid. Where's the fire?" Harold watched her begin to pull things out of her bag. He leaned over to examine a shell-inlaid Zippo while Cora dug back into her bag.

"Kimmy's getting married. She still owns half the house, and I want to buy her out. I always planned to, since it's not like I'm going anywhere"—she reached into her bag and pulled out a cloisonne bracelet and set it down next to the ring—"but I'm in a little more of a hurry to get it done now. That way Kimmy can have a big wedding and a nice honeymoon, and some left over to put toward a house or triplets, whatever she wants." Cora looked up at Harold. "It's what my mom would have wanted me to do." She hated to prime the pump with a sob story, but today, Cora would have squeezed out some tears to go with it if she could have. She was determined to move everything she could, get the money in the bank, and hand her sister a check. A check that wasn't postdated and wouldn't bounce. "Here you go." She clinked the last item onto the counter. "Let's make a deal."

She wandered around the store while Harold went over the items, not wanting to hover while he looked. He wouldn't take it all, she knew, but he would give her a fair offer on anything he thought he could turn around. Cora was idly running her fingers over a set of carved-bone chess men when Harold spoke from across the store.

"You want the good news first or the bad news?"

"How bad is the bad news?"

"For you, not very. For me, eh." Harold picked up the Zippo lighter. "I'll give you fifty bucks for this." He slid it over and picked up the heavy silver and onyx man's ring next to it. "Same for this. The silver's real, but the stone's about to come out so I'm gonna have to do some work on it. These are nice, but I got no market for tchotchkes." He passed over the trio of jade figurines. She'd predicted as much, but thought she'd try anyway.

Harold went on down the line, keeping a gold herringbone necklace, a carnival glass lampshade, a gold-plated money clip inlaid with an ebony cross, a World War II purple heart, a switchblade with a mother-of-pearl handle, a ring shaped like a sunflower—the seeds tiny diamond chips—and a brass hair comb set with garnets and seed pearls. She'd thought about giving that one to Kimmy to wear for her wedding, knowing she would have loved the bright white of the pearls against the darker red stones, but she watched Harold push it aside and nodded at the offer of seventy dollars. She'd rather give her sister all the money now than the gift later. And who knew, maybe she'd find something else to give Kimmy between now and the wedding.

"Here's the bad news. For me, I mean." Harold grabbed the calculator from next to the register and began to tot up the numbers. She held her breath. If his bad news was that he couldn't pay her now, she was going to have to load everything up and walk back out to try her luck at Penny Pawn, where the owner was frostier and the likelihood of selling everything even slimmer.

He pointed toward the last item she'd pulled from her bag. It was a round pendant edged with moonstones on an old book chain. "What's under the glass there? My eyes ain't that good anymore."

Cora ran a finger over the milky glass. "I think pressed flowers." They might have been any color when the necklace was new, but over the years the blossoms had faded to a uniform tired-looking brown.

"Too bad. I had this young guy in yesterday, big good-looking fella, looking for a necklace for his wife. Sounded a lot like this, what he was looking for, heavy gold chain, stones around and all that. But he wanted diamonds or rubies, not moonstones. And hair."

"Hair?" Cora looked up from examining the tiny pressed flowers under the glass.

"People used to put all kinds of stuff like that in jewelry. Little braids and whatnot, for funerals and such, I think. But I can't say as I've seen any, and for sure nothing that checked all those boxes." He pointed down through the glass case to the gaudy parrot necklace. "Tried to sell him on that. Told him ladies like something newer and a little more shiny like. But no deal."

"Big surprise there. You're going to have to wait for someone blind to come in to sell that piece of crap."

"You want me to hit subtract here?" Harold paused with a thick finger over the calculator.

"Don't you dare."

"I told him I didn't have anything like that," Harold said. "But maybe I can convince him on this one. They ain't diamonds, but the moonstones is nice, and the chain is good. Might be it'll do. He said he'd stop back in, should anything turn up."

"Hair, huh?" Cora shook her head. "I found a jewelry box with a baby curl in it, but that's about it."

Harold pointed a thick finger out the door, to where Rocky was sitting in the open truck window, tongue lolling out the side of his mouth. "Too bad you can't train him to find what you want. Nosing up stuff like this is impressive, but just imagine."

"I would have pointed him toward a diamond mine a long time ago, Harold." If only it were that easy. If she could pick and choose what hit her, she would have chosen to turn the whole damn process off. There was no rhyme or reason to it she'd ever been able to figure out, except that the things she found had been lost. A lot of what she found was jewelry or coins, but that was probably because they were things people had on them to lose. *Too bad people don't carry around gold bricks*, she thought, *or I'd put in a lot less miles.*

"Shame. Man said he'd pay just about anything for the right piece. And my cut of just about anything would go a long way toward slow roasting to death in Sarasota." Harold spun the calculator around so Cora could see the screen.

The number wasn't what she'd hoped for, but it was more than she expected. She nodded and Harold opened the register. Cora gathered up the items he hadn't been interested in and stuck them back in her bag.

"Thanks, Harold." She waved the fist clenched around the roll of bills as she went out the door. "And turn the AC on. Live a little."

The AC in her truck had died a year ago. Cora had the windows down, but the air inside the cab was still a simmering soup that made her hair cling damply to her neck. But it was worth the discomfort, when they got to Troy. Marcia at Penny Pawn was frigid and unfriendly as always, but she knew coins, and she took a roll of steel wheat pennies, a Roosevelt dime, the silver eagle in its plastic case she'd found at the fairgrounds, and a 2005 Kansas quarter that read "In God We Rust."

The cash for gold place *was* a skinning joint, but desperate times called for desperate measures. She turned a handful of broken chains, mateless earrings, and kinked bracelets into a couple hundred dollars.

When she got back to Pine Gap and parked the truck in front of her house, she was tired, but it was a good tired. She paused rolling up the window to look across the yard. It was a little house, just five rooms counting the tiny bathroom, a front porch that badly needed to be scraped and painted, and a towering sugar maple in the backyard that would soon dump a knee-high pile of leaves on the ground. It wasn't worth much, but it was the only place she'd ever lived, the only place she probably ever would, and after nearly four years of scrimping and selling her finds, she was within spitting distance of being able to buy Kimmy out. If she got lucky and sold a couple of things she had listed online, if Jacob showed up as planned tomorrow and paid her, she could write the check and give it to Kimmy knowing it would clear. Just the thought took a little bit of the tired off the day.

Rocky wandered across the yard, and Cora went inside, filling his food bowl, frowning over the almost-empty bag of kibble. It was going to be tight for a little while, until she recouped some funds. She shook the bowl, but there was no scratching at the front door.

"Dinner, Rocky. Time to come in." She went to the back and listened for him, hearing only the low, throaty growl of thunder, the beginning of the storm the close, heavy weather promised. "Hurry up, dog, before it gets going."

Near the sugar maple, he was standing quietly, staring intently across the shaded backyard. He turned to come in, then stopped midway, looking watchfully at the spatter of raindrops that struck the bare dirt by the back fence like buckshot. When he was inside, she closed the door and locked it, shooting the deadbolt for good measure, remembering what Tiddles had seen and the tracks in the dirt. Cora checked that her bedroom window was still closed and locked as well, knowing that it meant an uncomfortably sticky night in syrupy air pushed around by the fan.

Most nights Cora found the sound of rain on the tin roof soothing, its ting and patter as good as Nyquil at sending her off to sleep. But tonight, mixed with the angry grumble of thunder and her concerns about whoever had been prowling outside, about getting the money together, about the unknown factor that was Jacob Adler, Cora found herself lying rigid in bed, staring at the shaded window. The storm drew over the house, and the rain turned to thick, pummeling fists, then to sharp, icy darts of hail, then back again. The thunder cracked like logs split one by one with a giant's axe, the lightning turning the window shade into a shadow box, where wind-thrown branches were scrabbling fingers and dancing branches were masked men, creeping around the border of the house. At the height of the storm came a great bolt of lightning, so close the flash was in time with the deafening crash of thunder. It painted a thick bright line of light outside the window, hot and incandescent, a long coppery bolt, brilliant and shining as a braid of long red hair.

17

"So how much do you know about this place?" Jacob spoke from the driver's seat without taking his eyes off the road. They had passed the point where Mountain Road was tarred and chipped and were bouncing over the rutted dirt lane that climbed toward Blackwell Cemetery. The surface had been graded in the spring, but heavy rain and runoff had cut washout lines back and forth across the dirt. One of the ruts caught the back tire and the rear end of the vehicle swung out, tossing them from side to side.

If they'd been in her truck with its terminally ill suspension, they would have been bouncing around inside like popcorn. In his big SUV with its large, deep-tread tires, she didn't have to worry about getting stuck or breaking down and having to walk back to civilization, but she hated to think what Rocky's nails were doing to the soft tan leather of the back seat.

"Yes? No? Maybe?"

"What?" Cora said. "Sorry. I was in space. Lightning hit the tree in my backyard last night and the part it took off just missed my roof. I couldn't get to sleep after that. What did you say?"

"I just wondered how much you knew about the place, the lake, the cemetery, any of it. I looked into it a little after Avery died." Jacob paused when Cora stuck her hand out, pointing to the left side of the fork in the road ahead. He nodded and made the turn. "It seemed too crazy to be real. Especially when I started hitting stuff about a town under the water and the graveyard being haunted and stuff like that."

The left front tire dropped into a pothole and Cora was thrown sideways. Her shoulder fell against Jacob's, and she had to grab the panic bar above her window to keep from ending up in his lap. Cora looked down, in case she'd gone red, and saw something glinting on the floor mat. She reached down and picked it up. It was an earring, a heart made of gold. Cora set it in a little groove in the console between them. Jacob looked at it, then at her.

"Avery's. I keep finding things like that."

Cora wished she hadn't picked it up. She sat imagining the dead woman sitting in the same seat, tossing her head or running her fingers through her bright red hair, the earring tumbling down unnoticed.

"Well?" Jacob said. He was looking at her expectantly.

"Sorry. Well what?" It appeared Jacob wasn't imagining what she was. Maybe that was good.

"Well, how much of what I heard about this place is true?"

"Crazy as it sounds, a lot of it's true," she said. "Where the lake is now, there was a town where all the people that worked up in the Blackwell Mine lived. One night the mine collapsed and the slurry dam broke."

"The what?"

"Slurry is all the stuff that's left over when they wash the coal or something like that. Anyway, it was this massive amount of dirty black water, and it all came down off the mountain and filled the valley. It killed most of the people in the town and made the lake. Supposedly, the guy that owned the mine blew it on purpose because he found out one of the miners there was sleeping with his wife."

"Are you kidding? Is that true?"

Cora shrugged. "I said a lot of it's true. Did you catch the 'supposedly' before that last part? But the mine *did* collapse and destroy the town where the lake is now. It was a huge disaster."

"What about the cemetery?" The SUV jounced again. This time, when their shoulders came together, he looked over and smiled.

"What about it? It's just a bunch of crumbly old gravestones and the foundations of a church and a couple other buildings. It was higher up, so it didn't get flattened when the town did. Slow down, we're taking the next right."

"Where? I don't see a sign."

Cora rolled her eyes. "We are way past there being road signs." She pointed to a dent in the tree line. "Right there."

Jacob slowed the SUV to a crawl and put on his blinker. Cora let out a laugh before she could stop herself. "What?" Jacob said.

"Sorry. No, no you're right. Don't forget to signal. With all this traffic, I mean, it's the right thing to do." They hadn't seen another vehicle since turning off Southside Road twenty minutes ago. "The entrance to the old Snowhill Mine is over there." She shifted to look over her shoulder after they made the turn. "There used to be a sign for *that*. They took it down to make it harder to find. Kids were coming up to drink and smoke and whatever. You can imagine the recreational opportunities around here, if getting high in an abandoned coal mine is the best option on a Friday night."

They rolled to a stop in front of a rough gate set up to keep vehicles off the old road to the cemetery. Cora got out and opened the back door for Rocky, then watched him jump the barrier in one clean leap and dart off into the woods. She knelt and pretended to retie her boots, taking a moment to close her eyes and feel for anything that might be out there waiting to skew her vision and send her searching. It would be impossible to hide, up here, alone with Jacob. She was happy to feel nothing more than a faint, distant hum and still, warm ground under her fingertips.

Jacob came around the side of the SUV, buttoning the keys carefully into his pocket. He'd shown up dressed for the woods, in practical canvas pants, a long-sleeved shirt, and hiking boots. They all looked like the L.L. Bean tags had been cut off that morning, but at least he wasn't going to spend the night removing deer ticks. *Looks good on him*, she couldn't help but think. "You okay?" he said, reaching down a hand to help her up.

"Great." Cora let him pull her up and shook her hair down her back, wishing she'd brought something to get it out of her face. She'd left it down because it looked nicer that way, lying against the dark green shirt she'd chosen after trying on and discarding a dozen others. Cora felt herself growing warm with embarrassment. This wasn't a date. It was a paid excursion to show him where his fiancée had been murdered. Realizing she was still holding his hand, Cora pulled it away.

If he found it awkward, he had the good grace not to show it. Jacob turned and headed toward the gate, skirting a giant mud puddle in front of it. "I have a feeling I'm going to wish I'd worn hip waders instead of hikers," he said. "I didn't realize it was going to be so muddy or I would have brought something to change into instead of dragging the whole forest home on my boots later. I can toss them in the back and drive in my socks, I guess. Could be worse."

"At least you went with the all-weather mats," Cora said. "Mine are carpet, so I'm tempted to burn my truck and start over every time Rocky gets carsick."

"The dog gets carsick?"

"You insisted on driving." Cora started after him, pleased to see an amused look on his face. This might not be a pleasure trip, and Jacob had to be hurting, but he was managing to smile, showing his brilliant white teeth with their one charming little imperfection.

It was drier farther up the little road, where it curved around and out of sight into the trees, and wide enough that they could walk side by side, one of them in each of the faint wheel ruts. "There's the cemetery, up there," she said when they rounded the bend, pointing to a pair of waist-high piles of stones, all that was left of pillars that had once flanked the cemetery's entrance. Beyond them, scattered grave markers dotted a hump of land, standing like broken, crooked teeth. "That"—she pointed to a loam-covered square that poked up from the dirt—"is the foundation of a church. The ones on the other side were houses or something. Over there is the lake." Jacob's eyes followed her hand. "You can see a little bit of the water through the trees from the other side."

Rocky came bounding out of the brush and streaked across the clearing, snaking around the headstones in a flash of black. He skidded to a halt in a pile of last year's leaves next to Cora and Jacob. Nosing around a fallen marker, he began to paw at the ground at the base of a leaning slab of white marble.

"Rocky, stop it." Cora nudged him with her toe. "No grave digging." Rocky stopped, gave her a dark look, then started to wander away, sniffing along a deer track that ran between the graves.

"Is this …" Jacob looked down at the place the dog had pawed, then looked over at her. "Is this where you…?"

Cora shook her head. "Not here." She pointed east to where the trees opened and there was a clear view of gray sky and the valley below. The green of the forest was mottled with red and orange, clumps of early turning maples. At the edge of the vista was the tilted headstone, stark black and casting a long, dark shadow over the place Cora had found Avery Benson's body.

Jacob followed her to the grave, but he didn't look down, not right away. He stood staring off into the distance for a moment, scanning the tree line and watching Rocky nose his way around the stones and fallen trees. Above them, a red-tailed hawk circled lazily, drifting in widening circles. She heard it call, sharp and lonely, and receive no reply.

"Hell of a view, I guess," Jacob finally said. "Why were you even up here to find her the way you did?"

"It wasn't me, it was Rocky." The lie she told over and over came quickly and easily to her lips. "We hike the trails below here fairly often. He took off and this is where I ended up chasing him to. Otherwise, I steer clear of this place, for the most part."

Jacob's eyes ticked over toward her, green as jade in the sunlight. "Why?"

"Well, there's the ghost of a young woman in a long white dress that walks around the tombstones at night. And you can hear children laughing, the ones that died when the incline went off the rails and crashed through the schoolhouse. Oh, and when there's a full moon, you can hear the ring of pickaxes from underground, the ghosts of the miners that died in the Penny Lode mine collapse."

"Really?"

She let him stare at her for a moment, until she couldn't keep a straight face anymore, then she laughed. "No, not really. I don't like to come here because it's a graveyard. Normal people don't spend their free time in graveyards. Plus, Rocky likes to dig holes. Letting your dog dig up graves is a no-no. Do you know how much trouble I'd be in if he dragged home a human shin bone?"

Jacob finally looked down at the stone. Unlike most of the other markers, it was black, made from a seamless block of marble. Thankfully the rain had washed it clean. Cora remembered how it looked last time she'd been here, blood running in a dark, treacly stream down the stone. She knelt to swipe away the leaves on the ground. Her brushing only uncovered the top of a few letters carved near the base of the sunken, tilted marker, not enough to read.

When she looked up, Jacob had already moved away. He was looking at the ground, swiping away leaves with his foot. "The police went over the whole place for days." Cora got up and dusted off her hands on her pant legs. "They picked up everything that wasn't a leaf or stick. They even brought in special dogs."

She looked to Rocky, so he knew that didn't include him, and found he'd wandered off. Cora put two fingers between her lips and blasted out a shrill whistle. The dog came bounding back from across the cemetery, quickly, for once. His fur was a mess of leaves and dirt. "Come here, boy," she said when he got close. Then she got a whiff of him. "Never mind, go away. What have you been rolling in?" Cora almost added *a dead body* but caught herself.

"Do a lot of people come here, do you think?" Jacob said. He turned to Cora, the look in his eyes so intense and probing she looked away. When she looked back a moment later, it was gone, and she wondered if she'd imagined it.

"Probably more than you'd think," she said. "It's close to Blackwell Lake and there's a decent path from here to there. The upper trails through the game lands come right past, and then there's the way we came. It's rough but not terrible. Plenty of people will risk a busted axle to come look at the gravestones during the day, or try and hang out with the ghosts at night." She added the last part with a wry smile.

"Yes of course. The ghosts." Jacob looked across the scattered gravestones to the distant hummocks of the old foundations. "I believe this place *does* have ghosts," he said. "Too bad they don't seem to be talking. They might know something. Somebody does. They didn't just disappear, the person that took … that took her away from me. Everything, everyone, is somewhere. Everything can be found, can't it?"

He walked away from her and didn't see her shake her head. Jacob hadn't held a world's worth of lost things in his hands. He hadn't held knives still wearing a rusty coating of dried blood, guns with the serial numbers filed off and a single bullet left in the magazine, photographs of children with naked skin and hurt empty eyes, bodies dead and broken and discarded. Maybe everything could be found. But not everything should.

18

Cora prepared herself for an awkward ride home as they started back to the SUV, Jacob walking silently in front of her. It would be twenty uncomfortable minutes of riding shotgun and wishing the miles away while he wallowed in his disappointment and fumed over the wasted time. And wasted money. That was the part that had Cora most worried. Even if they'd found a bloody knife lying across the gravestone, would the trip have been worth a thousand dollars? She didn't see how.

They were rounding the bend that brought the gate and the SUV into sight when Rocky came barreling out of the woods. She heard the da, da, dum, da, da, dum of his big paws on the dirt in time to turn around and see him skate across a puddle of cocoa-colored water. He missed the frog that had been sitting at its edge but managed to kick up a fusillade of mud into the air. Most of it hit Jacob, covering his brand-new clothes with a wave of brown muck. Jacob looked at Rocky, looked at his pants, then back at the dog.

Then he burst out laughing.

When he finally stopped, Jacob wiped the corner of his eye. Either she'd been reading his mood all wrong, or he really *had* found some sort of closure or peace, because the brooding, thoughtful Jacob of a moment ago had disappeared.

He was still laughing when he opened the rear door for the dog, not even flinching when Rocky clambered in, mud and all. Cora did her best to stomp her boots off as well as she could, not wanting to think about the state of the four furry paws that had scrambled across the tan leather.

Jacob got in and started the car, taking a moment to play with the radio. He found a country music station, then turned it down low enough to talk over. "We spent an evening at the museum and a morning in a cemetery together, and I still don't know anything about you, you know that? What do you do, Cora?" he said. "I mean, when you're not following Rin-Tin-Tin here around the woods." He looked over his shoulder and began to back the SUV deftly out of the narrow lane.

"I mostly buy and resell things online. Right now, at least." Cora shrugged and left off. It was the answer she gave on the rare occasion someone asked her what she did. She thought it sounded especially pitiful coming out of her mouth today. Even the truth seemed sad and insubstantial. She might have some weird extra perception that led her to find things, but looking at what it got her, it didn't feel like it amounted to much.

But Jacob didn't seem as unimpressed as she felt. "That sounds amazing, being in control of your own time, being your own boss." He pulled out onto the dirt road, and they began the rattle and bang crawl back down off the mountain.

"I guess," she said. It was the kind of answer anyone would give, to make nice. But he sounded genuine, and there was an easy smile on his face. Her eyes lingered for a moment on the edge of his jaw, framed by the clean sharp line of his beard. "What about you?" Cora asked.

"Me? I—Hold on." Another vehicle was coming the opposite direction, a dark blue pickup, bright and shiny except for the spatter of mud it had picked up from the back road. Jacob carefully squeezed as far off the single lane as he could, riding the edge precariously. The truck flashed by, and Cora saw a glimpse of yellow hair that was somehow familiar, but it passed too quickly for her to decide who it was.

"Sorry. Damn this is narrow." Jacob pulled back into the center of the road. "What do I do?" he said. "I'm an engineer. Environmental. My firm deals mostly with hydrology issues: freshwater management, stormwater reclamation, shoreline development, stuff like that. Our corporate office is in the same building as Avery's father's. That's how we met."

Cora thought about finding an old souvenir spoon, taping it into an envelope, and shipping it off for a whopping thirty-five dollars and felt like nothing. It must have shown on her face, but Jacob thought the change in expression meant something different.

"I can talk about her, don't worry," he said. "I might not have the answers I want, but I accept that she's gone. I also accept that we were never going to end up together. I am sad because she died, because I did love her, though in the end I guess it was more as a friend than anything else." He paused for a second, looking in the rearview mirror. "So don't worry, I can say her name without the bottom dropping out."

The SUV rocked violently when the left front tire disappeared into a giant pothole. Cora's shoulder smashed into the window painfully and she let out a yelp.

"You okay?" Jacob asked.

"Fine. There are minefields with less holes than this road."

"You're not kidding." There was a silent moment while Jacob eased the SUV back out of the pothole. Cora watched shadow branches roll over the dash and onto her lap before skating away. She looked into the rearview mirror, catching Jacob's eyes briefly. He was looking at her, but she only had a fleeting second to consider what it meant, because in the back seat, Rocky's mirror image was making some unattractive heaving motions.

"Stop. Jacob, pull over. He's gonna blow. Quick, before it's too—"

Jacob started to cut the wheel, but it was too late.

⊰◈⊱

"I am so sorry, Jacob. There's a car wash about a mile and a half from here. I can take it and hose the mats off. I'll get some of those leather wipes they sell for the rest."

Jacob had borne it with good grace, and he'd done way better than she had with the gagging. The smell was incredible. They'd ridden the rest of the way home with all four windows and the sunroof open, but the inside of the SUV still reeked like an overflowed septic tank.

"It's fine," he said. "Don't worry about it. I think I'll just take the whole thing into a back alley somewhere and set it on fire." He got out and opened the back door for the dog. Cora was mortified, probably still bright red around the cheeks, but Rocky jumped out like he hadn't just painted the back seat a pea-green shade of dog barf. He nosed open the front gate and went about happily destroying his favorite corner of the yard.

"Maybe go find a back field or someplace like that," Cora said, sliding down from the SUV. "Somewhere where there's no chance of a witness. After you double-check your insurance is paid up, of course." She managed a smile. He really *didn't* seem that bothered.

"Speaking of paying up." Jacob reached past her into the passenger side of the car and opened the glove box. He pulled out a crisp white bank envelope and held it out. "Here you go. You more than held up your end of the bargain."

Cora willed her hand to stay by her side. "It's okay. I really can't take that. I mean, I didn't do anything." She hoped her words sounded more sincere than they really were. It was everything she could do not to snatch the envelope out of his hand and run.

"No, I insist. We had a deal, and it's not that much, anyway. I would have gone higher if you'd negotiated."

Not that much? Would have gone higher? She hesitated a few seconds longer, then slowly reached out and took the envelope. It was a lot to her. "Um, thanks. I don't feel like I was much help but ..." Cora trailed off and shrugged.

Jacob just nodded and she tucked the envelope into her back pocket. "Well, I guess goodbye, then." Cora turned and started toward the house. When she stopped and looked back halfway up the sidewalk, he was still standing beside the car, hand in his pockets, looking down at his feet. He looked ... lonely. She spoke before she could talk herself out of it.

"Are you headed back today, or"—he looked up at the sound of her voice—"or are you going to be around a little longer?"

"I honestly have no idea when I'm headed back," he said. "I haven't made any definite plans. I've just been wandering."

"If you aren't busy tonight, a bunch of people are getting together at this bar called P.J.'s. It's kind of a dive, but it has good food and …" Cora realized she was rambling and cut to the chase. "We're getting together to celebrate my sister and Dante getting engaged. Kind of an impromptu engagement party, I guess. You should come."

A smile pulled at the corner of his mouth. In the sunlight, his eyes were a light, seawater green. "You don't think that would be weird? I don't really know them."

Cora waved his concern away with her hand. "You *were* there when he asked her. And it's not, like, a formal party. It's just drinks at a bar with a bunch of people. P.J.'s Tavern on Church Street. Seven thirty."

"Okay," he said. "I'd love to. I'll see you soon."

She turned and started up her front steps so he wouldn't see the great big stupid smile on her face.

19

"Rocky, where are you?" Cora flung open the back door and yelled out into the yard. "Come on, dog. We're going to be late." Where was that damn dog?

As soon as Jacob turned at the end of the street, Cora had grabbed her accumulated cash from the box in the back bedroom, stuffed it into her bag with the envelope of crisp new bills, and sped to town, headed for the bank. It had taken half an hour: depositing the cash, juggling her savings into her checking and closing the bone-dry account, cashing in immature savings bonds, but when Cora left the bank, there had been a triumphant smile plastered on her face.

When she got home, she sat down on the couch and laid the check for Kimmy on the coffee table to admire. It had taken a lot of time, and she was officially flat broke, but she'd done it. Then Cora closed her eyes, just for a minute. Somehow that minute had turned into the entire afternoon.

"Next time I find something, it better be a time machine," she grumbled, rushing back through the house and poking her head out the front. She needed one if she was going to wrestle vomity, smelly Rocky into a bath, get herself showered and put together, and make it to the bar without being seriously late. "Where the hell are you, dog?"

Rocky lifted his head up from where he'd been sleeping on the sidewalk. Across the street, the singlewide trailer with its strip of dirty white running across the middle gave her an idea. "Rocky, I'm a genius," she said. "Can you say genius?" His look said something closer to *you're an idiot*, and he put his head back down on his paws and let his tongue loll out.

Cora unclipped his collar and ran back inside. She fumbled the lock open on the back bedroom and pulled open a bin, rifling through until she found what she was looking for. Then she snagged a bottle of shampoo out of the shower and ran back out the door. "Come on, mutt. Let's go get Tiddles."

The teenager pulled open the lopsided screen after the first knock. "Hey, Cora." He was wearing his usual, a baggy t-shirt and jeans so low they were threatening to slide off his nonexistent ass. But Cora didn't have time for a lecture about belts. She held out the sunglasses and the shampoo bottle.

"I'll give you these Ray-Bans if you give Rocky a bath. I've got to get ready to go out."

Tiddles grabbed the sunglasses, turning his hat around backward and putting them on. "Hell yeah. These are sweet. Are they real?" He stuck out his hand for the bottle of shampoo. "I mean, if they are, that's way too much just for giving Rocko a bath. I'd do that for free." The kid was smiling a lopsided smile. The sunglasses looked pretty good on him.

"They're real. And they're yours. Rocky found them, anyway," she felt compelled to add, "so they didn't cost me anything."

"Way to go, Rock. Ready for a bath, huh?" Tiddles said. His eyes slid back toward the trailer. "We don't got an outside hose, though. I don't—"

"Use mine," Cora said. "It's out back. You're a lifesaver."

When she climbed up into the truck half an hour later, Rocky was squeaky clean and smelled faintly of strawberries. She kept an eye on him while she drove, holding her breath that he wouldn't throw up and undo all Tiddles's work on the way to the bar.

"Alright, pup. Behave," she said, when they pulled into P.J.'s parking lot. Cora yanked up the bustline of her shirt—it was a little low cut, but the blue looked good on her—and patted her back pocket to confirm the check for Kimmy hadn't fallen out. She scanned the cars hopefully but didn't see the big two-tone SUV Jacob drove. As much as she wanted him to show, if he didn't, at least Cora wouldn't have to explain his presence to her sister. *Hey, Kimmy, you remember Jacob from the art opening? Well, I spent the day in the graveyard with him—you know, the place where I found his fiancée dead, brains leaking all over a headstone. Why? Well, for money. Yes, I swear that's all he wanted. But we did have a swell time. It was so much fun I decided, hell, why not invite him to celebrate your engagement.*

There was a tap on her truck window. She'd been so involved with the voice in her head that it made her jump, sliding away across the bench seat almost to the passenger door. "Jacob," she said, whispering the name before she looked and saw who was standing there.

"Sorry, I didn't mean to scare you." It wasn't Jacob. Sam Cooper waved a hand, then opened the door and let Rocky out. Cora slid out of the cab and onto the ground, hard boot heels clicking on the pavement. She was as tall as he was in them, his dark eyes dead even with hers. She saw them flick down, then up again, meeting hers. "You look nice."

"Thanks," Cora managed. Sam always seemed so businesslike, and the compliment threw her off. Then again, she was usually out in the woods dressed like a lumberjack and covered in burdocks when she ran into him, so maybe it was just surprise that had made him say anything. "Rocky, wait."

The dog had started across the parking lot, heading for the door. She started after him, when out of nowhere, it hit her.

"Shit," Cora blurted out. Her vision blurred and she stumbled, just managing to catch herself before her knees hit the ground. Gravel crushed into her palms, but she barely felt it over the tingle and burn in her hands.

"Cora, what's wrong?" Sam's voice seemed far away though he was right beside her. She felt hands on her shoulders, trying to pull her up, but she shrugged them off sharply.

"Just … wait …" Cora opened herself up, let the pull guide her hand, to get it over with so it would all go away. She swiped her hands across the blacktop, then swiped again. "Give me a second to …" She had it.

Everything cleared. This time, she allowed herself to be pulled up. Sam held her steady, one warm hand clamped on each of her shoulders until her eyes focused on him.

"Jesus, one second you were there, the next …" He shook his head. "What happened?"

"I suddenly got really dizzy. Need to eat, I guess."

He looked down at her hand. "What's that?"

Cora opened her hand. A heavy dart with a blue barrel and black flight sat in her palm. "Um, nothing. I just stumbled on this when I was down there." She looked it over, then held it out to Sam. "There's a dartboard back by the pool tables, right? Maybe somebody lost it."

He took it and looked at it, then at her. "Maybe." She let out a breath when he nodded and didn't ask any more questions, just headed for the front door, where Rocky was waiting impatiently outside the foggy glass door. "This place looks a little busy tonight."

"Probably mostly Kimmy and Dante's friends," Cora said. "Rocky, heel." He heeled, just not to her. She rolled her eyes when Rocky slid over to Sam's side. "Asshole," she muttered under her breath.

"Sorry, what?"

"Nothing. Kimmy and Dante—have you ever met Kimmy's boyfriend?" Cora asked. "Well, he's her fiancé now. A bunch of their friends are getting together to celebrate."

"Private thing?" Sam paused, hand on the door. Cora shook her head.

"Nope, nothing like that. Come on."

The bar was already full to overflowing, mostly with people she knew by sight at least. Kimmy was standing at the bar with her back to them. Her hair was woven into an intricate flat braid that hung almost to the waist of her little white dress. The braid whipped around when Rocky nosed at the back of her leg.

"Rocky, my sweet little boy." Kimmy leaned down and kissed the dog right on the wet nose. Cora was glad she'd had Tiddles use the good shampoo on him earlier, so he didn't smell like dog vomit, at least not yet. She looked behind the bar, happy to see P.J. was too busy serving drinks to be feeding him jalapeño poppers.

"Cora, did you bring Sam?" Kimmy looked back and forth at the two of them, appearing thrilled with the idea. "That's great."

Sam shook his head. "I ran into her in the parking lot." He held up the dart. "I'm going to go see if this belongs to somebody."

"Sam, you're going to hang around a little bit, right?" Kimmy tugged on his shirt sleeve when he went by. "We have some celebrating to do."

"Yes, ma'am. I'll be here." He smiled and wove through the people and out of sight. Kimmy tugged on Cora's arm not as playfully.

"Damn it, I was so excited when I saw you two walk in together. Thought maybe he'd finally pulled his head out of that cute little rear end and asked you out."

"Sam? He's like, old."

"Old." Kimmy put her hands on her hips indignantly. "He graduated a year ahead of me in high school."

"Right? Like I said, he's old."

Kimmy scowled and hauled her over to their usual table. Someone had stuck a crepe paper wedding bell in the middle.

"*Is* his old rear end cute?" Cora slid into a seat. "I never really noticed, but I promise I'll look next time I see him, just to make you happy." Kimmy's grin returned; the scowl had been entirely fake anyway, and she could never keep one on for long. "Enough about Sam's ass," Cora said. "It's about your ass tonight." She reached out and grabbed her sister's hand so she could get a better look at the ring.

Kimmy giggled. "It's perfect, right?" It *was* perfect, a teardrop-shape diamond with a slightly smaller pearl mounted just shy of the diamond's point.

"Absolutely," Cora said. "Mom would be so happy, Kimmy."

Kimmy held her hand in front of her for a moment, examining the ring, then tucked her hand in her lap. "I never thought she wouldn't be around when I got married," Kimmy said. "I guess nobody thinks that. But you're right"—Kimmy leaned back and crossed her hands resolutely across her chest—"she *would* be happy. And she'd be proud. Of both of us."

"Yeah, of course. So proud." Cora leaned back and crossed her own arms across her chest, then raised one eyebrow. "I mean, look how good we turned out. We don't swear."

"Never fucking ever." Kimmy giggled. "And we don't drink."

"Never." Cora looked up when Dante swung by. He put a bright blue drink with a pick of maraschino cherries in front of Kimmy, kissed her on the cheek, then slid away. "Not even on special occasions. And no drugs." Cora pursed her lips, trying to keep a straight face.

"God no, not even one little teeny tiny joint at the drive-in when you were seventeen," Kimmy said, almost shaking with the repressed laughter.

"Heavens, no. We would never imbibe in the wacko tobacco, not even for experimental medical purposes," Cora said. "God, I was high as a kite. Of course, it didn't fix my little problem, but it did make me think the doll I found while we were high was talking to me. Wait, what else? Oh, and we don't gamble."

"Those scratchers at the gas station don't count, do they?"

"I don't know, do you buy those?"

"Only about once a week. And Powerball on Wednesdays."

"Then no," Cora said, "those definitely don't count."

"And no—" Kimmy burst out laughing, then tried to pull it back together. "And no … no premarital sex." Kimmy had her head down on the table, shaking with laughter, and Cora was using the stupid paper bell to mop up the tears running down her face when Dante came back.

He shook his head and put a beer in front of Cora, a little puff of mist still drifting out of the neck. "I seriously wonder about you two." He went behind Kimmy and draped his arms around her shoulders. "I'd ask what's so funny, but I've made that mistake before. You'll try to explain it, I won't get it, and you'll be peeing yourselves all over again." Cora was about to tell Dante how right he was, when his eyes went to the front of the bar. "Where do I know that guy from?" he said. Kimmy finally raised her head and wiped a hand across her eyes. "Was he at the museum for the opening? That's it, isn't it?"

Kimmy looked, but Cora didn't need to turn her head to know who they were talking about. It looked like Jacob had decided to come after all.

"I wonder what he's doing here?" Kimmy said.

Taking a long drink, Cora slid down off her barstool. "I invited him."

20

She turned her head sideways very slowly, far enough to see Kimmy out of the corner of her eye. Kimmy's head moved just in time to avoid Cora's gaze. It wasn't the first time she'd caught her sister looking. *What was her problem?* Cora thought about going over and giving her braid a yank and asking her.

Then Jacob reached out and touched her hand. It was just a brush of fingers across the ridge of her knuckles, meant to bring her attention back to their conversation, but it sent a thrilling, burning line down the back of her neck.

"You're kidding, right. There's no way that's his actual name." Jacob was grinning, and Kimmy was forgotten. He didn't pull his hand away while he waited for her to answer.

"It is," Cora said. "I swear. It's on the liquor license behind the bar, if you don't believe me. P.J. stands for Percival Johannes. Percival Johannes Buckley." They both looked over to the bar, at the fat man in the beer-spotted t-shirt, and burst out laughing. P.J. turned their way, and for a split second she thought he'd heard them. She felt a stab of guilt, but Jacob brushing across her knuckles again distracted her.

"You're making that up," he said. "I'm going to go check. You know what, actually, I'll just ask him." He started to get up, but she grabbed his hand, pulling him back into his seat.

"Don't you dare."

"Oh, I'd like to see you stop me." He gave her a wicked smile and twitched his hand out of hers, then got up and slipped deftly through the crowd. The bar was wall-to-wall people, though she'd hardly noticed from their dark corner table. Cora watched him go. Jacob looked like a glimmering goldfish gliding through a frog pond, the best dressed, best looking—even Kimmy wouldn't be able to debate that when they eventually hashed the night over—classiest person in here. There were ten tons of denim and camouflage and flannel, and then there was Jacob: crisp gray pants, black shirt tailored perfectly to his broad shoulders, shined black shoes, and the watch and signet ring that had to be worth more than the check in her pocket.

It wasn't just the alcohol talking. She'd been struck by how good he looked the second he walked in, the crowd of familiar faces parting in front of him, the smile on his face as he headed directly for her. Granted the alcohol might be talking now—just a little—but it hadn't been then.

He came back, two beers in one hand, two shot glasses in the other. Ducking neatly around two of Kimmy's coworkers from Mane Event, turning away from the once-over they were giving him in the process, he set the drinks on the table. "Okay, fine. You win."

"You did not." She snorted, then clapped her hand across her face. He burst out laughing.

"No, I didn't. I couldn't. I looked on the license. And anyway, I didn't want to interrupt. I think he's teaching Rocky how to make a Manhattan."

"Rocky's probably teaching P.J. how to make a Manhattan."

Jacob pushed a shot glass across the table with the tip of one long, slender finger. Cora raised an eyebrow. "What's this one?" It was a suspicious dark brown, the color of bad decisions.

"I asked for the best whiskey he had." Jacob shook his head and picked up his glass. "Which is apparently Jim Beam. Here's to the unexpected."

"Was Jim Beam that unexpected?" Cora picked up her glass. It felt cool as an ice cube against her flushed skin.

"Not at all. What's unexpected is sitting across the table from a woman far too beautiful and interesting for this place. And enjoying today at all, let alone this much. To the unexpected." He threw back his shot, then neatly wiped up a drop of spilled liquor from the glass with a napkin. Cora paused for a moment, holding hers between her thumb and index finger. It felt like a strange dream, that someone as attractive and urbane and smooth around the edges as Jacob, someone who probably never imagined a place as small and backwoods as Pine Gap existed, found her beautiful and interesting. Maybe he was just saying it, or maybe he was the one seeing things through beer goggles, but why would he have agreed to come at all, to spend more time with her, if he didn't see something in her? She threw back her shot, making a wish on the burning candle flame that trickled down her throat.

Her eyes were watering when she set the empty glass down. She picked up her beer and took a healthy swallow to wash the fire from her throat. "Are you hungry?" Jacob said. "Do you want me to order something to eat?" Jacob looked over at the greasy menu propped up between the salt and pepper shakers.

Cora shook her head. "I'm okay."

He nodded and picked up his beer. In truth, Cora was hungry enough to eat a horse, but she was on a razor-thin budget and anything not already in her cupboards wasn't on it, at least until she sold a few of the things she had listed online. She'd been too rushed this afternoon to make herself a meal, and now the shots and beer and the god-awful strong vodka and cranberry she'd had earlier were sloshing around in her stomach and slowly but surely going to her head.

"You sure you don't want anything?" Jacob asked. "There's a huge jar of some funny-colored eggs on the counter. Unless those aren't for eating? It is October. I guess it could be part of the Halloween decorations."

Cora laughed and looked at her beer. Somehow it had gotten half empty while she wasn't looking. It wasn't the first. The last couple seemed to have evaporated while they'd been talking. It was just that Jacob was so interested. He wanted to know all about her, and he somehow made the things that sounded silly and small-town when they came out of her mouth seem charming and even enviable. She took another swallow and put the almost-empty bottle down with a click. "They're pickled eggs," she said. "The jar comes with sausages in it. When they're gone you put hardboiled eggs in."

"Why?"

She laughed loudly, not caring if a head or two turned at the sound. "To eat. Maybe you should go try one."

"Maybe I will. You want one?"

Shaking her head, Cora snuck another look at Kimmy, then slipped her hand down and felt for the outline of the check in her pocket. "Nope. That's a hard pass." The check was a reminder that even a couple pickled eggs weren't in the budget. Writing it had brought the balance in her checking down to nineteen dollars and twenty-two cents. Dinner tonight was going to have to be of the liquid variety. Even that was going to be too much, if she went and got the next round like she should.

"Your sister keeps looking over. I probably shouldn't have kept you to myself all this time." Jacob's eyes, bottle green in the low light, crinkled at the corners when he smiled, and he ran a finger idly across the back of her hand where it curved around her bottle. Her fingers tingled and buzzed, though for once not in response to something lost. "I didn't mean to steal you away, but I couldn't help it. Will she be mad?"

It took Cora a minute to answer. Her fingers uncurled from the bottle, brushed his. "She'll be fine."

The band started with a clatter of drums and the scream of an out-of-tune guitar. When Jacob turned toward the noise, Cora made herself not look at Kimmy, focusing on the clean line of his hair instead, where it ended in a precise dark line against the skin of his neck. When Jacob had walked in, Kimmy had been polite, but Cora knew her sister well enough to feel the chilliness in her tone.

Cora fumed silently, feeling the bottle in her hand vibrate with the music. After everything she'd done, scrimping and saving, selling things low to get a quicker return, draining her accounts dry, going without to scrape together every penny for her sister's sake, to have Kimmy instantly decide to dislike Jacob irritated Cora. What reason could her sister possibly have for not liking him? Was she jealous? Had she really thought Cora was going to show up with Sam? Was she bothered it might take some of the attention away from her on her big night? The check was starting to feel like a stone in her pocket. To think Cora had been chomping at the bit to give it to her. *I think I'll hold on to it until tomorrow and give her a chance to explain why she's being so snotty.*

"What is it?" Jacob had turned back toward her and caught the collapse of her smile.

"Nothing." She shook her head. He might have asked again, and she might have told him, he looked so genuinely worried, but there came a sudden shrill yip, followed by cheering. She saw a jalapeño popper sail into the air, followed by the tip of Rocky's snout as he leapt up to grab it, eliciting another round of cheering. Jacob shook his head, picking up his beer.

"He's the life of the party. Must be entertaining, having him around."

"Oh yes, it's a thrilling life." Cora rolled her eyes and finished her beer, setting the empty aside with a clink. She put the check, Kimmy, everything aside with it. There'd be time to hash it out later.

"Seriously, though, I read some of the news stories after he found Avery." Jacob said the name without pause, not a hint of sadness, the corners of his mouth staying in their mischievous grin. "Finding missing kids, finding bodies, that I actually kind of get. There's plenty of dogs that can find people. But there were articles where he found other stuff too. Like that lady's wedding ring she lost like fifteen years ago. I mean, how is that even possible?"

Shrugging, Cora started to speak, when Jacob slipped out of his chair and disappeared. "Sorry," he said, when he reappeared a moment later, hands full again. "Hope you held that thought. I figured I'd better get refills before P.J. got out another round of dog treats."

Groaning, Cora reached for the shot glass and threw it back without asking what it was. When it was down, she still didn't know, but it didn't burn as much as the last one. Her empty stomach had settled into a pleasant sloshy numbness. "Ugh, he'd better not be feeding him any more crap. One round of cleaning up dog barf a day is more than enough."

"Amen to that." Jacob tossed back his shot and cleaned up his glass. Then he leaned back and unbuttoned the top button of his black shirt. She realized she was leaning forward, thinking about reaching up and running a hand across the incredibly smooth-looking skin, and caught herself, dropping her eyes. Cora felt a fiery flush creeping up her neck.

"What's the most interesting thing he's found?" Jacob asked nonchalantly. Thankfully he didn't seem to have noticed the ogling.

Leaning back, Cora twirled the neck of a new, full bottle of beer between her fingers. She thought about it and tried to focus enough to not slip and say *I* instead of *Rocky*. "Let me think." She took a drink and set the bottle back down. This beer was different from the last one, darker and more bitter, but delicious in a thick, heavy sort of way. It burned her tongue and slid down into her stomach like molasses. "The car, probably." Cora winced. She'd slurred over the second B.

"A car?" Jacob raised an eyebrow. "That's not interesting." He smiled. "I mean, I could find a car."

"It was a 1954 Datsun convertible. And it was completely buried under the ground. The only thing sticking out was the tip of the ratty fox tail that was wired to the antenna. Maybe that's what Rocky smelled, to find it. Anyway, it was next to the little league fields, a foot from the home dugout. The keys were still in the ignition."

"Buried under the ground. You're kidding."

"I'm not. Swear to God." Cora paused to shake her hair back from her shoulders, knowing she was doing it to see if his eyes followed the toss of her head, feeling shallowly gratified when they did. "I guess there was a bad flood here in nineteen seventy-two. The fields are next to Falls Creek, and it turns out the owner had to leave it there after his son's game because it wouldn't start. He couldn't get a mechanic for a couple days, and by that time the creek had turned into a river and the water was over the dugout. When the water dropped back down it was gone. He thought the car washed away with the dugouts and the bleachers and half the houses along the creek, but it must have just gotten swallowed by the mud."

"That's crazy. The whole car, just sucked into the ground." Jacob shook his head, leaning closer to be heard over the band. His breath was warm and sweet with beer.

"Yep. Anyway, after Rocky found it, they dug it up, took it apart and put it back together, and when they were done, it started right up."

"That's insane." He grinned, not leaning away at the end of the story. "What else? Was that the most valuable thing he ever found?"

Shrugging, Cora looked down at her hands, trying not to stare directly into his eyes, the only things she was having any luck focusing on. "That was it, probably. I mean, he finds jewelry and things like that lady's ring sometimes, but nothing like that for a while."

"How long is a while?" he pressed. His eyes looked hungrily over at her.

She tried to think back. "I don't know. He found a sapphire bracelet a while back." Why did it matter? Jacob stared a moment longer. Then his face softened. "Come on. Let's dance."

"God, no. No way."

"Come on." Jacob grabbed her by the hand, dragging her out to the small dance floor.

21

The ray of sunshine that fell across her face was warm and so bright it felt like a hot poker to the eyeballs. Cora rolled away with a groan, reaching for the pillow on the other side of the bed and cramming it over her head. Did it smell like pepper and clove, the heady cologne she'd inhaled so deeply when she'd been pressed against Jacob on the dance floor, or was it the ghost of the scent lingering on her own skin?

She remembered that part, the deafening music, the heat of him against her, but through dark, amber-colored glass. After that, the night disintegrated into shreds of sound and memory; being pulled laughing across the parking lot, the ping of rain like steel drums on the cars around them. Flying down the road behind the flip-flip of the windshield wipers, the air steamy and close inside his car. On her front porch, his hand against her neck, against her face, the sound of thunder and the sound of breathing. Then nothing. After that, there was nothing at all.

Cora hazarded a peek out from under the pillow. It felt like there was a finger rammed into her eye socket, deep enough to tap the back of her skull in a jagged tump-tump-tump perfectly in time with her heart. Closing her eye again dampened the beat but did nothing for the seasick heaving in her stomach.

Rolling onto her side, Cora stretched her legs out under the rumpled sheet. She was sore, muscles complaining loudly about last night's dancing. And what else? She didn't know. She didn't remember. Her stomach climbed up into her throat, part hangover, part regret and embarrassment. She'd had too much to drink before, but she'd never lost time like this. Cora held still, willing the nausea away with deep, slow breaths, grimacing as she exhaled sour morning breath.

When her stomach was settled enough, Cora squinted blearily out from under the pillow and eyed the other side of the bed. It was rumpled, the bedding pushed back, the second pillow on the floor. He'd been here, hadn't he, in the bed beside her? He must have been. But he wasn't here now.

"Jacob," she called out. Her throat felt like sandpaper, and his name came out a croak. She shouldn't have bothered. After a lifetime, Cora was familiar enough with the sighs and creaks in the little house to know there was no one here but her. Not even the dog.

Where was the dog? Where was Jacob?

She remembered the whispered words on the dance floor—most of them, at least—and the feel of his arm across the small of her back, the touch of his lips, deliciously hot as he whispered in her ear. *I couldn't wait to blow this town. God, Cora, now I don't think I could go if I tried. You're just ...* Those eyes and that wicked, wicked smile. *Let's get out of here.*

"He'll be back," she rasped aloud, like saying it would make him appear. But the only thing her words brought about was a buzzing from the kitchen, her phone, plugged in on the counter, chittering across the Formica. It was faint, but it still managed to set off the bass drum inside her head.

"Jacob." She stood, then regretted it, weaving unsteadily. Then she sat back down. She'd never given him her number. He hadn't asked. It couldn't be him.

She let the phone keep vibrating. Cora didn't remember putting it on the charger or setting it to silent, but she didn't remember hanging her bag on the knob of the bedroom door instead of in its usual place by the door, either. Yet there it was, hanging open like a mouth with a dislocated jaw.

The phone stopped buzzing and stillness descended. For a moment. When it started again, Cora thought about letting it go and lying back down to see if she could sleep away her hangover and some of the remorse that was creeping in. She went as far as pulling the covers back over her legs when the phone stopped and then immediately started vibrating again. Cora heaved herself back to her feet and shuffled out of the bedroom.

In the kitchen she could hear the leftover dribble from last night's storm running off the edge of the tin roof and spattering on the porch steps. The sound juggled another shred of last night into place, and she remembered how cool the fallen drops had made his hands when he cupped her face and caressed her neck on the front porch. Running a finger across her bottom lip, Cora searched for the memory of kissing him.

There were watermarks across the floor, the prints of her boot heels lit up in the painfully bright sunlight coming through the hall window. There were tracks past her bedroom as well, though not hers. They were bigger and fainter, impressions left in the film of dust on top of the old oak planks. These tracks led past her bedroom, to the locked second bedroom and back again. She eyed them for a moment, until the sun disappeared behind a cloud and erased them. The phone stopped vibrating. After a heartbeat, it began again.

Flipping it over, Cora's hand hovered over the phone. It was Kimmy. The last memory she had of Kimmy was through the crowd on the dance floor. She'd been trying to get Cora's attention. Jacob had pressed himself against her, drawing her away as quickly as it took his lips to find her neck. When she'd turned back, Kimmy had been gone.

Before it could start vibrating again, Cora answered. "Hello." She tucked the phone between her shoulder and her ear and got a glass down from the cabinet and filled it from the tap.

"He's gone, right?" Kimmy said. Cora didn't say anything, but her silence answered Kimmy's question well enough. "Big surprise. Well?"

"Well, what?" Cora downed the glass of water and refilled it, then opened the cabinet and got out the ibuprofen. She tried to open it noiselessly, but the pills rattled when she palmed off the cap.

"Yeah, I bet you need some Tylenol this morning. You probably need about half a damn bottle."

"Like you've never had a hangover, Kimmy."

"Oh, I've had a hangover. But not the kind you get from about fifteen shots of tequila. And I never went home wrecked with a complete stranger. And I sure as shit never left my dog at a bar."

"You don't have a dog."

"Do *you*? Do you even know where Rocky is, Cora?"

Cora put the phone on speaker and looked through the cabinet for some Pepto. The closest she could find was Tums, and she tossed a handful in her mouth, chewed and swallowed with a grimace. "He's outside." She went to the door and opened it, hoping that was true.

"If he is, it's because Sam Cooper brought him over."

"Bullshit," Cora said. Rocky was asleep on the mat. She wished *she* was asleep. "He's right here. Say hi to mean old Aunt Kimmy, Rocky." The dog opened one eye to glare at her, then went back to sleep.

"Don't pretend like you remembered him. I know for a fact you didn't. I can't believe you forgot all about him and went home with that guy."

"Are you kidding me?" Raising her voice set the bell in Cora's skull ringing for Sunday morning services. She let the door fall shut and closed her eyes. "Why are you giving me such a hard time about this, Kimmy? You tell me how bad I need to get out and meet somebody about ten times a week. I finally do, and now you're lecturing me?"

"That was not meeting somebody." Kimmy's voice had taken on a tone so close to their mother's that Cora had to stop and lean against the counter. "That was you getting out of control drunk. Honestly, I'm amazed you were even standing, seeing the tab. The tab you two ran out on, by the way. I had to pay that, Cora. It was more than I made in tips this weekend. I can't believe you'd do that to me. Or to P.J. What the hell were you thinking?"

Most of the space in Cora's head had been taken up with jabs of pain and creeping guilt. Now anger was starting to compete for some of the room. Had she had a little too much and suspended all adult judgment? Yep. Was she proud of it? Nope. Was she paying for it? Sure as shit. But nobody was hurt, or at least nobody would be when she felt like a human being again. How was it her sister's business who she brought home? If it was the money Kimmy was so upset about, Cora would figure out how to pay her back. It was just an accident, skipping out on the tab. They'd been in a hurry.

"He probably just forgot about the bill, Kimmy. You said it yourself, we had a lot to drink. What do you have against Jacob, anyway? You wouldn't care if this was somebody else. If it was Sam, you probably would have bought the drinks all night and shoved me in his truck with him."

"What do I have against Jacob?" Kimmy said. "That man's fiancée's only been dead like what, two weeks or something. If I was dead and that was Dante—"

"He isn't Dante. And I'm not you. Sorry I don't have everything all lined up like you do, perfect hair, perfect man, perfect life. Everything but a perfect sister. I know how hard you've tried to make me like you, but I don't fit, do I. Never have, never will. Why don't you give it a rest, Kimmy."

"Don't turn this around on me because you feel all sorry for yourself."

"Sorry for myself?" Cora barked. "You have no idea what it's like to be me, Kimmy. You weren't dumped in the middle of the road two seconds after you were born. You aren't a walking metal detector, stumbling around town like you're disabled. Do you know how hard it is to—"

"No, Cora, I don't." Kimmy cut her off. "I don't know what it's like to be you, to have that in your life. But I know you sure as hell like the excuse. That way you don't have to do anything. You want life to be different? Then do something about it. What would Mom say? If—"

"No." Her anger was so quick and so severe Cora almost threw the phone. She clenched it in her hands so hard the knuckles went white. "No, don't you dare, Kimmy. Don't you bring Mom into this. You don't know what she would think. You're not her—"

"Cora, I—"

Cora hung up the phone, cutting off whatever it was her sister started to say.

22

At first Cora thought she couldn't find her keys because she was so angry she couldn't focus. The contents of her bag were spread out across the kitchen table, the bag itself inside out on the chair. The keys weren't in the pockets of the pants she found halfway through the bedroom door, or under the bed, or in the cushions of the couch with the dust bunnies and the ghosts of old potato chips. But when her temper had simmered down to a more reasonable level, the keys were still missing.

Giving up indoors, Cora went outside to look. Mr. Debusher was checking his mail, gathering damp wadded flyers from the box with his gnarled hands. He gave her a knowing look. "Got a bottle of scotch 'bove the icebox, if you need a little hair of the dog."

Just the thought tugged her roiling stomach up into her throat. "No, thank you. Did Rocky wander over here at all this morning? Maybe with my car keys," she managed. Maybe he'd dragged her keys over out of spite. Please God, he hadn't buried them in the corner of the yard with the rest of his treasures.

"Don't think so," the old man said. "He come over for a treat after that nice feller dropped him off and brung up my paper like usual, but no keys that I saw."

She walked up the street then back down to her house. Cora circled her yard, looking for freshly dug holes, but the ground was featureless. The rain had washed it clean of dog prints and the footprints around the border of the fence.

"Whatcha looking for?" There was a clink of glass bottles. Tiddles dropped the black bag of trash he was carrying into the can and snapped down the lid before crossing over to her side of the street.

"Keys," Cora mumbled.

"To what? Your truck's not even here." Tiddles eyed Cora. Her hair was wadded up into a knot on top of her head, and she was dressed in saggy sweats and old flip-flops. Where Mr. Debusher had looked amused, Tiddles looked disappointed. Probably when you had to watch your mother drink herself into oblivion day after day, seeing someone hungover like Cora wasn't very amusing.

"I left it at P.J.'s last night." She couldn't quite meet his eyes, looking away and pretending to scan the ground. "Kimmy got engaged, so they had a little party. But the keys have to be around here somewhere. If I didn't have them when I got home, I wouldn't have been able to get into the house."

He sighed. It made her feel like she was the teenager and he was the adult. Tiddles hitched up his low-slung jeans and pushed up the brim of his hat. "I'll help you look."

Fifteen minutes later, the yard and street had been checked and rechecked, and her house gone over again. There was still no sign of them.

"If they're here, they're slid down somewhere they ain't ever coming back from," Tiddles said. "Whatcha gonna do?"

She shrugged. "Hell if I know. I've got a spare for the truck. I hope Kimmy still has a key to the house. I should probably change the locks, though, just in case." At least she kept the key to the back bedroom separate. If she'd lost that one, with the double lock, she would have had to go to the Feed and Seed and buy a sledgehammer. Maybe she should start keeping all the keys on Rocky's collar.

"Thanks anyway, Tiddles." Cora gave him a half-hearted wave and headed back inside. When she went to the pantry for dog food, Cora wondered if she'd tried to find the keys last night and didn't remember. She was tidy, at least enough to know when things were out of place. This morning every drawer she opened seemed the slightest bit off, like she'd rifled through the contents. She was putting the mostly empty bag of dog food back in the cupboard when she heard the squall of the rusty screen door spring followed by an efficient double knock.

She caught a glimpse of herself in the little mirror by the door. She looked like hell, but there wasn't anything she could do about it. Maybe it was Tiddles, with her keys. That would be a relief. Maybe it was Jacob.

It wasn't either. She opened the door and saw Sam Cooper retreating to a dark blue pickup truck parked on the curb.

Cora watched him flip open the cover of the silver toolbox behind the cab. He rummaged around for a moment, then shut it and started back up the walk with a blue and yellow can in his hand.

"That thing sounds like somebody's torturing a bag full of baby cats. Hold on." Sam pulled the cap off the can of WD-40 and wiggled the little red straw into the opening on the nozzle. He shot a burst of liquid across the spring and worked it back and forth. By the third time, the blood-curdling squawk had receded to a defeated squeak. "There," he said, setting the can down on the porch railing.

"Um, thanks. For that, and for the dog. I hear you brought Rocky home last night." Cora leaned against the frame of the open front door. Sam gave her a once-over. There was a politely blank expression on his face, the kind that covered something else. Irritation? Disgust? Pity? She couldn't quite read him, but whatever he was thinking, it probably wasn't going to make her feel any better.

"No problem, about Rocky. As for that spring, I'd probably have ended up coming by later and doing it if I didn't now. I have a problem with leaving things not figured out and finished. It saves time in the long run just to do them and move on."

"How's that go in your line of work?" she said. He was in his Game Commission uniform this morning, less the hat; head-to-toe forest green broken only by the patches on the sleeves and the badge over his heart. "I wouldn't think it's one of those jobs where you can just finish everything in a day. Or do the poachers and trashcan bandit bears only work during your shift?"

He smiled, eyes crinkling in the corners. "I wish," he said. "But it does make me very good at paperwork. Mine is always done on time. Speaking of time"—he looked at his watch—"I went by P.J.'s a couple hours ago, after I dropped the dog off. You know you left your truck there last night, right?"

Cora looked away, embarrassed, stumbling to the side when Rocky squeezed himself in beside her legs and stared up at Sam. "I wasn't in any shape to drive," she mumbled.

"That was a smart move. But the doors were hanging wide open, and I can't imagine you left them that way. It looked like it had been rifled through pretty good. Hope you didn't have anything valuable in there."

Cora shook her head. "Maybe some duct tape and an ice scraper. I'm pretty sure I locked it, but honestly, it's so old the locks don't always catch. Anyway, if they'd had any decency, whoever went through it would have set it on fire so I could collect some insurance money. I should start leaving matches and a gas can in the back."

"Well, better luck next time. But seriously, you did know there's been a couple break-ins around town, right? Harold's Pawn got hit, Curious Curio, Steele's Secondhand, one of the places up to Blackwell Lake."

"Harold's?" She hadn't known. "Anybody get hurt?"

Sam shook his head. "Not that I heard. Sounds like it was all at night when the stores were closed. Stuff stolen, door or window forced, things like that."

Cora thought about the tracks around the back of her house. Sam must have noticed the change in her expression. "What?"

"Nothing, probably." She shook her head. "Tiddles … Eugene Tiddles, the kid that lives in the trailer across the street, he said he saw somebody sneaking around the house a couple nights ago. There were shoe prints out back."

Sam started down the stairs, but she called him back. "They're long gone, Sam. The rain washed them out." He didn't stop, disappearing around the corner of the yard. When he reappeared, he just nodded to confirm what she already knew.

"You want a ride to P.J.'s? To get your truck?"

Cora shook her head. "Thanks, I think I'll just take Rocky and walk."

He nodded, then stepped down onto the sidewalk. "Definitely take him with you if you're out roaming around. Just in case."

When he was gone, Cora looked at Rocky, who'd flopped down onto the porch, long pink tongue hanging out the side of his mouth. "Yeah, right," Cora said. "I think I'll take the mace. Like you'd raise a paw to protect me."

Rocky snorted and closed his eyes.

23

Cora pulled Kimmy's check out of last night's jeans and stuffed them into the hamper. The check somehow felt heavier this morning, like some of her guilt had soaked into the silver-edged paper. Last night she should have given it to Kimmy and made her happy. Instead, she'd had too much to drink and made an ass of herself, and now they weren't talking.

And for what? She stripped the bed angrily, wishing she could wash away her disgust along with the smell of her alcohol-tinged sweat. *To wake up alone and sick with no memory of what happened with a man I'll probably never hear from again?* She tore the pillowcase off her pillow and flung the pillow back on the bed. What did she think, that he was some city Prince Charming so bowled over by her he couldn't resist? She felt foolish for taking the things he'd said at face value because she was lonely and naive enough to want them to be true.

In the kitchen, she turned her bag right side out and swept the scattered contents back inside, then dug the spare truck key from the junk drawer.

"Come on, Rocky. Let's go." She opened the front door and Rocky pushed past her legs and into the kitchen. "Other way. Go. As in go for a walk."

He ignored her and spent a moment pacing the short hallway at the back of the house. Rocky stopped at her bedroom door, sniffed around the jamb, then went to the locked room next. "Rocky, please. If I have to drag you out of here, I'll throw up." Giving the door one last sniff,

117

he came, but slowly, eyeing her bedroom door as he padded silently toward her. Maybe it was the smell of someone else in the house, the lingering aroma of a ghost still in the air. "Yeah, me too, dog. You have no damn idea."

Once she coaxed Rocky outside, Cora turned the door lock and the deadbolt from inside, then squeezed herself out the front window, pulling it not quite shut behind her so she could get back in. It made her nervous, leaving the house unsecured when someone was prowling the town, breaking into stores, sneaking around people's houses. She'd get her truck, come back home, and lock the place up tight behind her. Then she'd have to call Kimmy and eat crow so she could ask her sister for the spare key.

When Cora turned onto Church Street, she found it quiet and closed up the way only a very small town can be on Sunday morning. Maybe it was the emptiness, but the walk from one end of Church to the other seemed endless. It was an age until she passed Harold's, where a square of plywood covered the bottom half of the door where the glass had been broken. Just beyond the pawnshop, Cora's vision turned to static and there was a tingle in her fingertips. It had never been so unwelcome, and she followed it angrily. Wasn't this what was responsible for her problems, really? This crippling strangeness she'd been born with that had kept her from living like a normal person, from having a job or friends or leaving this dead, disintegrating little town? When the feeling fell away and she found the blue glass perfume bottle at the edge of the sidewalk, Cora ground it under her boot heel, back and forth until it was glittering dust.

Her rusty truck sat like an island in the middle of P.J.'s parking lot. Cora picked her registration and insurance papers up off the floor mat and stuffed them back into the glove compartment. Closing it, she let Rocky in and started the engine. It fired up with its usual burp and grumble, but she sat there for a moment without putting it in drive. She wasn't ready to call her sister, and she certainly wasn't ready to go back home and try to piece the night back together, either.

"Rocky, I hope you've got some more walk in you today." Rocky's ears perked up. For once they were on the same page. She reached over and rolled down his window so he could hang his head out while they drove. She did the same on her side, letting the fresh air wash over her.

When she made the turn into the trailhead for the game lands, Rocky woofed out the window. The small gravel lot was full, vehicles parked tightly one after another. A man in camouflage and blaze orange was putting a compound bow into the bed of a pickup truck. She watched him turn sideways to fit between his cab and the vehicle beside it, then shifted into reverse. "Change of plans," she said, as much to herself as to Rocky. She had no desire to run into anyone right now, and even less to get skewered by someone looking for a trophy buck.

Back on the road, Cora drove aimlessly. The pull of things was fleeting when she moved, tingling and receding, fading away then returning, the way radio stations came in and out along the highway. The farther she got from houses and people, the fainter it got, so she stuck to the back roads. When the feeling faded away entirely, Cora found herself at the pull off by Blackwell Cemetery. She pulled the truck to a stop in front of the wooden gate.

Cora sat staring through the windshield, looking down the dark tunnel the trees made over the old road. It was quiet here, and calm. Her vision was clear, and there wasn't even the faintest tingling in her fingers or toes. When she came here the day Avery Benson was killed, it had been unbearable, the tear and burn. When she'd been here with Jacob, and again today, it held nothing more worth finding. Maybe she'd just sit here forever.

Then Rocky jumped out the open window.

"Rocky, what the hell." She called after him, but he was a black streak disappearing down the road. "Rocky, get back here!" Cora called again. Rocky was as big as a deer, and here, on the upper edge of the game lands, there might be hunters, ready to let fly at the first flash of fur.

"Shit. Where is it?" Cora tipped the truck seat forward and rummaged around in the space behind it until she came up with an orange vest. A little more ferreting around and she found Rocky's, a contraption of blaze fabric and Velcro that fastened around his neck and under his flanks. Shoving her arms through hers, she stuffed Rocky's into her pocket and ran after him.

He hadn't gone far. She found him standing stock still, rigid as a statue where the old overgrown road ended and the forest opened up to make space for the little cemetery. She wondered what he saw. Kimmy had told her once that dogs saw more than people, that their noses were so sensitive they painted a picture of what was around them just from the odors. Cora wondered if they could see what had happened in the same way, from what was left behind. Did he see the ghosts of people who had been here yesterday or the day before, roaming between the headstones, stepping over the windfalls strewn like pickup sticks among the graves? Did he see Cora and Jacob? Did he see the ghost of Avery Benson, her head striking stone again and again?

Cora shivered. She'd seen too many episodes of *Graveyard Tales*. There were no such things as ghosts, and even if there were, why would they walk the cemetery when there was an entire lake of misery for them to haunt, just through the trees.

"Come here, boy." Cora pulled Rocky's orange vest out of her pocket. He didn't move. She went to him instead, and he didn't try to wriggle away when she slid the orange vest over his head and buckled it under his stomach. "Rock, what are we doing here?"

He didn't answer, of course.

She left him standing and wandered amongst the stones, reading the names on the ones that still stood. Falsey, O'Rourke, Bevridge, Dobbins, O'Herron, Walsh, McTigue, Sullivan, Fitzpatrick, Holland, Mannix. Cora walked and read names until she found herself at the tipsy marker of black marble. Cora knelt and dug her hand into the ground, scraped away the thick layer of decaying leaves, sinking her fingernails into the soft black dirt and scooping out a space in front of the stone. She uncovered the curlicued letters that ran along the face of the marker.

"Fiona Clennan Blackwell, eighteen ninety to nineteen oh nine." Cora ran a finger across the carved letters as she read. Nineteen years old. Younger than she was. Avery Benson hadn't been much older and was just as dead. And here was Cora, wallowing in self-pity and regret.

"Rocky, come on. Damn it, I hate when Kimmy's right." She said it in a kinder voice than she usually reserved for the dog. He must have noticed the change, because he came and snuffled his nose into her hand, leaning against her side. "Let's go find some cell service." Kimmy was her sister. She would forgive Cora. She would forgive her and then she'd commiserate with her, and they'd find something to laugh about in the terrible mess that was the night before. Then Cora would give her sister the check in her pocket and that would erase any last bits of remaining ugliness.

She stopped before the turn onto Southside Road to message her sister. *I'm sorry, sis. Is it okay if I stop by? BTW, do you still have a house key?* Cora pressed send and pulled out onto the road.

24

There was still no response from Kimmy when Cora hit the edge of town. She wondered if Kimmy was making her sweat and decided she might have to just call and grovel, when three little dots appeared on the screen. They came and went, started again, then disappeared. Good, she was answering. But what was Kimmy doing, writing a novel?

It turned out to be a short message when it finally came through. *I'm at your house. I'll wait for you inside.* Very short. It sounded like Kimmy was still mad. But if she was in the house, then she had the spare house key, which was good news. Cora would patch things up when she got there.

K. Be there soon.

There was no answer, no more little dots telling her Kimmy was typing. Cora shoved the phone into her bag and headed for the house.

The day was already beginning to darken, the ancient flickery streetlamps starting to come on by the time she pulled up behind Kimmy's little white Camry. "Kimmy." Cora pushed open the door. Behind her, Rocky gave a low guttural snarl, an angry, vicious sound she'd never heard him make before.

"Jesus, Rocky. What the—"

Rocky's growl sank into something even deeper and more threatening.

"Jacob!" Her face broke into a smile. She'd tried not to kid herself, but Cora had been holding on to just a little hope that he'd show up and fill in the gaps in her memory, reassure her that his words hadn't been just a come-on and she hadn't meant nothing. And here he was. A flush rose in her cheeks. He was standing in the curved opening between the kitchen and the living room, looking giant under her low ceiling. The familiar green eyes that turned toward her nearly glowed in the light from the open doorway.

"Get inside and shut the door."

"Jacob, what are you—"

"I said get inside and shut the door. Slowly." The set of his jaw was hard, as rigid as the line of his body. "Do it and keep your hands where I can see them." When she didn't immediately move, he lifted his hand from his side. Jacob used the gun in his hand to wave her forward.

She moved robotically, going from surprised to confused to scared in a few dizzying seconds. Cora reached behind her blindly, afraid to turn her head, and pushed the front door shut.

"Lock it. I don't want any unexpected company." Another wave of the handgun. She felt for the latch and turned it, the bolt falling shut with a dreadful final click.

"Good. Now put down your bag. On the table." Cora dropped her shoulder and let the bag slide off, the mace canister making a heavy, useless clunk against the scarred wood of the tabletop. He saw her eyes flick toward it and laughed, not the light, entertained laugh she remembered, but a bitter, cruel one. "Don't even think about it. I saw that mace when I took your keys. Make sure it stays in there."

"You took my—"

"Shut up," he snapped, all laughter gone. "Walk in here, nice and slow."

He backed up into the living room as she approached. Jacob didn't take his eyes off her, and she didn't take hers off the ugly black gun in his hand. It had a too-long slender barrel ending in a black, staring eye that was trained on her chest. She couldn't bring herself to even blink, until she was through the doorway. Then a flash of white on the other side of the room made her turn her head. Bound hand and foot to one of the chairs from Cora's kitchen, eyes showing wild and white above the length of silver duct tape over her mouth, was Kimmy.

"Shut the dog up." Jacob's voice was unrecognizable, no longer cultured and honeyed but icy and sharp, each word clipped into its own sentence. "Shut. Him. Up. Now."

Rocky stood in front of her, hackles raised, hair standing on end and making him look half again his usual size. The agitated tick of his tail back and forth, back and forth, whipped across her shins. His growl was so low and fierce she could feel it rumbling in the floor under her feet.

"Cora." Jacob lowered the muzzle of the handgun and pointed it toward the dog. "Now."

"Jacob, I—"

"Shut it," he said. "Take care of the dog or I will. Put him in the bedroom and lock him in. Keep your hands where I can see them. Wait." Cora froze, bending to take Rocky's collar. "Stand back up." She stood, trying to control the shake that had crept into her hands. "Take off your shirt."

When she froze, Jacob rolled his eyes. "I need to know you aren't hiding anything. What's the problem? You weren't very shy last night. You had your shirt off before we got through the front door." A leering smile crept onto his lips and quickly faded. "Off. Drop it and empty your pockets."

Her fingers were shaking so badly she couldn't get the top button out of its hole. Jacob sighed and took a step toward Kimmy. He lowered the gun and pressed the barrel against her head. A garbled squeal came from behind the duct tape across Kimmy's mouth. Cora got hold of her shirt and yanked, sending the buttons skittering across the floor. Shrugging the shirt off, she shuffled around in a circle, heart jumping into her throat for the seconds when her back was to Jacob.

"Turn out your pockets. One hand at a time." There was nothing in her front pockets. Cora pulled them out and let them hang like white flags of surrender on either side of her pants. She turned around and pulled out the only thing that was in the back pockets. The check for Kimmy.

"Drop the paper and turn back around." The folded rectangle

fluttered to the floor, landing in a little tent beside her shoes. In front of her, Rocky gave another threatening snarl.

"Now put the God damned dog in your bedroom. Don't try anything. You understand me?"

"Come on, Rocky," Cora whispered, tensing when she spoke, afraid to make a single sound or motion that might set Jacob off. "Rocky, please."

"Right now." Jacob swung the gun back in her direction. Cora felt Rocky tense and grabbed him before he could lunge. He didn't fight her when she began to drag him toward the bedroom, but he didn't come willingly, either. The growl in his throat stuttered when she pulled the collar against his windpipe, choking him, but he remained stiff legged, nails drawing lines across the floor as she dragged him. Cora set her feet and leaned in, manhandling him through the door.

Turning back to the living room, Cora caught sight of the second bedroom. The door hung wide open, the jamb splintered, the hinges twisted apart. She could see one of the shelving units tipped over onto the desk, contents scattered and broken across its surface.

"It's not in there," Jacob called out. She flinched at the sound of Rocky throwing himself against the other side of her bedroom door. His nails scrabbled against the wood. "I thought it had to be. God knows I looked everywhere else in this dump while you were passed out. Where *do* you keep that key, Cora?" Her eyes flicked toward the bedroom, where Rocky was attacking the door. Jacob shook his head. "Of course. On the fucking dog. If I had been able to get in and find it and get out before you came home, it would have been so much better. Then of course, your sister had to turn up."

Cora's eyes slid to the side, toward the bathroom at the other end of the hall, trying to think of anything she could use as a weapon, any way to get to the small window and scream for help.

"If you try anything …" He tapped the muzzle of the gun against the top of Kimmy's head, tap, tap, tap. "Now get out here." Cora came slowly back into the living room. Her sister's eyes were wet, tears running in little shining rivers down her cheeks and over the tape covering her mouth. Jacob dabbed idly at the wetness with the cuff of his shirt. Kimmy flinched away from his touch.

"Where is it, Cora? It's not in there. It's not in this house. It's not in your piece of shit truck. It would have been better if I'd found it, Cora. I'd be gone, and Kimmy here …" Jacob moved the gun, grinding the barrel into her temple.

Kimmy jerked away from it, whipping her head back and forth, her braids skating out in a fan around her. Jacob struck her in the back of the head with the butt of the handgun. "Stop it." Kimmy stopped thrashing. A dark stain spread out from the crotch of her white denim pants.

"Stop," Cora begged. "Please stop. Don't hurt her."

"I'll hurt her, the dog, you, and anyone else who walks through the door until you tell me where it is. I know you have it. It wasn't in Avery's house. The police didn't recover it at the scene or it would have showed up with the evidence. Somebody found it between when I killed her and when the police got there. I know that, and I know who that leaves. You. Where is it, Cora?"

Cora shook her head wildly. "I don't know what you're talking about. Jacob, I—"

"Liar," he spat. "I see all your stuff in here, your online auctions, the crap you take to the pawnshop. If you thought you were going to be able to sell it like the rest of your garbage, you're crazy. I looked through your computer. You haven't sold it yet, which means you still have it." Jacob's voice rose to a roar, a thin snake of vein appearing across the smooth surface of his forehead. "Where is it?" he screamed. "Where the fuck is it!"

"I don't know what you're talking about." Cora's voice was thick with tears as she watched a line of blood trickle from her sister's scalp down to her shoulder, a thin red ribbon against the dark skin. When it reached her shirt, the red bloomed like a flower across the stark white. "Please, let her go, Jacob. We don't have anything of yours."

"Oh, I know *she* doesn't. We had a conversation when she stumbled in, didn't we?" He looked down at Kimmy, whose head had dropped forward. Her chest was heaving in quick spasms. "Not nice of you, keeping things from your sister. You were going to keep it for yourself, weren't you, you selfish bitch?" He grabbed Kimmy's braids and pulled her head up, exposing her throat, pushing the barrel of the gun up into the soft skin under her neck. "Give it to me, Cora, or I swear to God, I will kill her. I will kill her like I did Avery. Give me the fucking necklace. The one you picked up in the cemetery. It's mine. Hand it over, or I swear to God, your sister is going to die."

25

"I don't know what you're talking about." Cora's words were nearly unintelligible, jammed up by the fear squeezing her throat. She had to force them out in tight bursts, gagging between syllables.

"You don't, do you? You sure about that?" He took the gun from where it was pressed against Kimmy's neck. Her sister seemed to wilt from relief, then pull tight again when the barrel pressed against one of the hands taped to the arm of Cora's old kitchen chair. "Well, I don't believe you. So, what I'm going to do is take off one part at a time until your story changes." He ground the muzzle into the delicate bones in Kimmy's hand. Cora could hear them crunching like twigs under a heavy boot. "We'll see how much hair she can style without hands."

Kimmy thrashed and rocked in the chair, trying futilely to get her hand out from under the muzzle of the gun. "Last chance, Cora. And if you think I won't pull this trigger, you're dead wrong." His lips—lips she'd thought perfect, lips she'd felt pressed against her throat—were pressed into a thin, malignant line. "I'll do it and sleep like a baby tonight. This is kiddie shit compared to what I did to Avery. Her head cracked like an egg on that tombstone." To make his point, he rammed the gun barrel into the bones of Kimmy's hands again, forcing a muffled scream from under the duct tape.

All this interminable time, which afterward, Cora knew could not have been more than a few short minutes, Rocky had been on the other side of the bedroom door, throwing himself against it, claws stripping away the paint on top of the old pine veneer. In his fury, he tore off the old crackle-finished knob. With the knob gone, the lock disengaged.

When Kimmy screamed, Rocky threw himself against the door. It rebounded from the impact and opened a crack. Rocky clawed his way out and shot across the narrow hallway and into the living room, a terrible vision of wide-open jaws and bared white teeth, launching himself toward Jacob. If he hadn't skidded on the wood floor, scrabbling for purchase before he leapt, he might have made it. But that short second gave Jacob time to react. He swung the gun up and pulled the trigger.

The sound was a mute whip crack. Momentum carried the dog past Jacob, and Rocky slid in a boneless pile across the living room floor. The blood on his fur painted a wide brush stroke behind him across the wood.

"I hate that fucking dog." Jacob stared at the black figure splayed in front of him. "This is all his fault in the first place, you know that? If he hadn't dragged you into the cemetery when he did, you wouldn't be in this mess. You should thank me."

One of Rocky's back legs twitched feebly, the way it did when he ran in his dreams. It stopped when it fetched up against the rag rug. Cora couldn't move. She was frozen, smelling the hot, burnt smell of the spent bullet. A glistening red snake slithered away from the dog's side.

The sight of the dog lying beside her, close enough for her to touch if she'd been able to move her white tennis shoe away from the leg of the chair, set Kimmy on fire. She thrashed so desperately the chair arms groaned and flexed.

"Stop that." Jacob hit Kimmy again, cracking her across the face this time with an open hand. Her head ricocheted backward with a snap, then fell forward, her chin on her chest. "Shit," he said, shaking his head. "I need her to be awake, to help convince you to tell the truth." Then he shrugged. "Have to wake her back up, I guess."

Jacob reached behind his back and pulled out a knife, the blade flatly black, the handle small enough to disappear into his hand. "Better switch to old school. These silencers, they're bullshit." He waved the gun clenched in his other hand. "It's not like on TV, you know. They're impossible to get, and then you really only get a couple good shots before they're worthless. And anyway"—his lips pulled wide into an evil smile—"this is way more fun. Now." He pushed the point of the knife against Kimmy's throat. It was so sharp it bit with only the slightest pressure. A bulb of red collected then burst. A new red ribbon trailed down the other side of Kimmy's neck, meeting the line of blood from Jacob's first blow and joining it, painting a ruby chain around her collar. "Now, I want you to tell me where it is, Cora. Until you do, I'm going to start removing skin. I'm going to peel her like a grape, and it's going to be your fault."

He drew the knife downward, drawing a thin red line down Kimmy's neck from ear to collarbone. Cora lunged forward, but Jacob whipped the gun toward her. "I get it, Cora. I really do. Being dirt poor's a son of a bitch. If you weren't screwing me over, I might even admire your commitment to digging yourself out of this white trash shithole a dollar at a time. But the necklace, it belongs to me. It should have been mine from the beginning. Now that Avery's dead, it's going to be."

"Jacob, stop," Cora pleaded. Jacob pulled the knife away from Kimmy's neck and laid it across her throat, pressing down. The pain brought Kimmy back to consciousness. Her eyes fluttered for a moment, then focused on Cora.

Jacob's hand tensed, tendons shifting and pulling taut. "Last chance."

"Wait." Cora threw her hands up in front of her. "Wait, wait. I'll tell you. Put the knife down. I'll tell you where it is."

26

Jacob's hand relaxed, the blade making a small sucking sound when he pulled it away from Kimmy's throat. "That's better." He wiped the blade slowly and deliberately back and forth across the sleeve of Kimmy's shirt. The blood left a feathery pattern with each pass, painting a pair of red wings on the white cotton.

"Let her go, and then I'll tell you." Cora looked Kimmy in the eyes, seeing the fear and now the confusion.

"Tell me, then she can go," Jacob said.

Taking a deep breath, Cora's mind raced through his words, through all the things she'd found, the places things were kept, searching for something believable, something that might give them a chance. "It's at Harold's, at the pawnshop," she spit out. It was Sunday. Harold's was closed; he wouldn't be there. If Jacob left to try to go there, she could get help, call the police.

Jacob's eyes narrowed. "I was there. I was there right after Avery died. I was there again yesterday. You didn't sell it to him."

She scrambled for an explanation. "I did. I swear. It's there. It's in the safe. In the back room. He doesn't leave anything that valuable in the case over the weekend, in case the place gets robbed." Cora forced herself to look at him. His eyes narrowed and her heart hammered in her chest.

"There was no safe."

"It's in the floor. Under the carpet." Cora didn't dare look at her sister, or the lies would crumble in her mouth.

Jacob examined her for a minute. Then he nodded. She let the breath she'd been holding escape. "I got the impression you were a selfish bitch, but I had no idea. I can't believe you let me hurt your sister just to keep it for yourself." He took a step and used his toe to prod Rocky's leg where it was splayed across the rag rug. His sides were still rising and falling shallowly, and he let out a whimper. When Jacob's eyes left Kimmy, Cora made a move toward her sister. Kimmy's head was rocking back and forth in small erratic movements as she fought to stay conscious.

"Stop." Jacob's hand came up, and Cora stepped back, away from the gun. "We're not quite finished yet. You'd better be able to get into that safe, or I'm going to be paying that guy Harold a call after I leave here. Tell me exactly where it is and how to get it."

Cora stuttered for a moment, trying to think of a convincing lie. *All I have to do is get him out of here,* she thought, *tell him anything, just so long as he goes.* "It's in the floor, under a flap of carpet in the back left corner." She'd never been in the back room at Harold's and hoped to God what she was telling him was even possible. For all she knew there was a refrigerator in the back left corner. "I don't know the combination." *Sorry, Harold, but I'll get help before he can get to you, if he buys this.* "But it's there, I swear it."

Kimmy lifted her head. She opened her eyes and found Cora's. There were tears in the long feathery eyelashes, fear in the large dark eyes, and a thick ring of red soaked her shirt from the collar to the shoulders. It broke Cora's heart.

"Good," Jacob said. He smiled and Cora wanted to throw herself at him, claw his eyes out with her fingernails. "Very good. I'm disappointed in you, Cora. I knew you weren't a genius, but I never imagined you were absolutely heartless. I doubt she'll ever forgive you." He ticked the knife in his hand back and forth like a scolding finger.

"You know where it is. Let her go," Cora said, the words tumbling out in a breathless flood. They must have come out too quickly, or something in her tone was unconvincing, because Jacob's lips tightened, his hands clenching the knife in his right hand and the gun in his left. He leaned menacingly over Kimmy. She tried to lean away from, rocking in the chair. He lowered the knife to rest against her throat once more, and she went still, eyes closing in terror.

"Just for the sake of conservation, tell me, what did it look like?"

What did it look like? She didn't know. How could she know? A few words from what seemed like another lifetime worked their way from the back of her mind. A conversation at Harold's. Jacob said he'd been to the pawnshop more than once, now, trying to find this mysterious necklace he was so sure Cora had found. She closed her eyes and tried to remember Harold's words.

"I had this young guy in yesterday, big good-looking fella, looking for a necklace for his wife. Sounded a lot like this, what he was looking for; heavy gold chain, stones around and all that. But he wanted diamonds or rubies, not moonstones. And hair."

"A necklace on a long gold chain. With diamonds and rubies. A lock of hair."

His smile was immediate and brilliant. For a second it was the smile of the man she'd been so taken with and taken in by. Cora sagged with relief.

"I knew it," he said. "Harold's, in the back, under the rug. Too bad you don't know the combination. Guess I'm going to need Harold." Jacob shook his head. "Who I don't need anymore is her."

Jacob's wrist tensed briefly, tendons shifting and pulling taut. Then, in one brief, fluid motion, he cut Kimmy's throat.

Cora opened her mouth to scream. She didn't get a chance.

"And I definitely don't need you." Jacob leveled the gun at Cora and pulled the trigger.

She fell like a broken doll to the floor, but Cora felt no pain, just the softness of the braided rug against her cheek. She lay still, while the cool dry rug became warm and wet by degrees as the pool of blood grew beneath her.

That's my blood, she realized. *It's going to ruin the rug. This was Mom's rug.* Cora wished she believed she was going to see her mom again now. And Kimmy. She was glad she couldn't move, couldn't turn her head and see her sister. There was no hurt in her body, not yet. But inside her head, the pain was extraordinary. Her sister was dead, and the last image of her Cora had was with her head fallen forward, the clean lines of the parts between her braids, vulnerable and exposed above the bib of blood that poured from her open throat.

There was a sound of splashing, and a sharp tang in her nostrils. *Gasoline*, Cora thought. She heard a labored breath that wasn't her own, and a pained, canine grunt. But a whoosh drowned it out.

"Goodbye, Cora."

Jacob's shoes showed briefly in her limited vision. Behind them, a ring of flames licked upward. When his feet moved away, she watched the fire inch toward her in orange and yellow tongues, licking hungrily at the rug, snapping at the fabric covering the couch.

In front of her, the flames crawled closer. They reached the fold of paper on the floor, the little teepee of the check intended for Kimmy. The fire caught, crawled up from the corner of the paper, then devoured it. The last thing she saw was the check, crumbling to ashes.

PART 2

LOSERS WEEPERS

27

She heard a car pull up behind her and the squeal and chunk of the door as it opened and closed, but Cora didn't turn around. The fire had reduced the little house to an outline of jagged charred teeth around an ugly black mouth, piles of white ash like dirty snow circling it like a funeral wreath. The sugar maple in the backyard had burned to a charcoal spire, pointing skyward like an accusatory finger.

A slow patter of paws finally caused her to turn toward the street.

"I thought you might be here." Sam Cooper pulled off his uniform hat and turned it restlessly around and around in his hands. "I was going to wait until you got back to town, but he wouldn't settle down. I thought I'd better come find you."

Rocky limped up the sidewalk, his paws making an uneven trail over the fall of ashes. His right front leg only kissed the ground briefly, leaving a feathery brush mark instead of a print like his other paws. "Dr. Lister said he'll always limp a little, but not this bad. I left his medicine with Harold. He said he'd put it in the apartment for you before he hit the road."

Cora nodded numbly. Sam eyed her for a moment, but when she didn't speak, he turned around to look across the street. "I don't know how he made it." He eyed the faded burgundy smear that ran off the edge of the sidewalk and across the pavement to the blue and white trailer. Somehow Rocky had dragged himself out of the house and across the street, baying like a wolf until Tiddles opened the door and saw Cora's house, flames flickering behind the windows like the eyes of a jack-o'-lantern.

"The kid should get a medal," Sam said, turning back toward Cora, "running inside like that and pulling you out." Eugene Tiddles had burns down both arms from dragging an unconscious Cora out of the house. "He's healing fast, but he's beating himself up for not going back inside to get Kimmy, even though …" *Even though she was beyond anyone's help by then.* That was what Sam didn't finish saying. "He's a good kid. Said he'd take care of Rocky until you're back on your feet if you needed him to. Probably be happier here with him than with me."

Cora shook her head. "No. I can do it."

"You sure? You just got out of the hospital. Should you even be on your feet?"

Her hand went unconsciously to her head, pulling at the knit hat that covered the clipped-off hair. The place where the bullet had creased her skull felt dull and numb under the thick pad of bandages. "I'm fine."

"Are you?"

"I said I'm fine." Her voice was husky and cracked from all the smoke and tears. Sam looked like he was going to say something but changed his mind. Nodding, he put his hat back on, straightening it with a practiced hand, then got back into his truck and pulled away.

Rocky padded forward, three-legged and unsteady, nosing the patch of ground where the porch steps had been, his breath stirring up a flurry of gray ashes. "She's gone," Cora said dully. "Kimmy isn't here." Rocky whined. "She isn't here, stupid." Her voice was louder, angry. "She isn't anywhere. She's nowhere. She'd dead. Kimmy is dead, you stupid, stupid dog."

He nosed another patch of ground, then picked his head up and yipped. Cora watched him through red-rimmed eyes. "She's not there. She's dead, God damn it. She's never coming back."

Rocky looked up. He padded over, head bobbing up and down as he limped, staring her down with liquid black eyes. "You heard me, dog. She's dead. She's dead, and it's my fault. She's dead and I wish you were dead, and I wish I was dead too. It's my fault." Her voice had risen to a shout. "She's dead." Cora screamed into the emptiness that had been the house, falling to her knees. Her head felt like it was being torn open again, a pain as jagged and unendurable as the pain inside her heart, wringing burning tears from her eyes.

Coming a step closer, Rocky laid his head on Cora's knees. She shoved him away. "Go away. I hate you." She pushed him away again. He didn't flinch at the halfhearted blows, just steadied himself and came again.

"God damn it, Rocky, she's dead." Her voice shrank back to a whisper.

Rocky pointed his snout toward the sky. She saw his chest expand, his shoulders hitch, and then he let out a long, broken-hearted howl. She had not thought a dog could cry. There was indescribable pain in that terrible wail. Cora knew exactly how he felt. Slumping forward, she pulled a still-howling Rocky to her and wrapped her arms around his neck, feeling herself shaking under the torrent of tears. They howled together.

28

Cora was staring out the window of the apartment over the pawn-shop, watching the cars roll slowly down Church Street. One by one they paused at the blinking light, then faded into the distance. She heard a knock on the door. It could have been the first or the fiftieth. Whoever was out there might have been knocking for an hour; Cora didn't know. The last few weeks had been a slowly swirling black hole, a semiconscious stream of waking, sleeping, waking, sleeping, days at a time blowing by in a haze. To make it worse, what awareness she did have slipped and slid here in town, where so many people and so many lost things meant there was always snow at the edge of her vision and a low vibration under everything.

"Cora?" The brisk knock came again. "You in there?" Cora went to the door, sliding the chain out of its little slot and turning the deadbolt. Sam was heading back down the narrow stairwell but stopped and looked back when he heard the door open. "Sorry, I wouldn't have pounded like that, but I thought maybe you couldn't hear me over the racket downstairs."

"Downstairs?" That had slid away too. Cora paused to listen. There it was, the sound of a saw, the shrill whine as a board was pushed against the spinning blade. "That must be it. I guess I didn't hear you." The saw cut off and it was suddenly silent, the workmen below stopping to cross the street to the diner for lunch. Or maybe they had finally finished repairing the damage Jacob had caused searching where Cora sent him with her bluff.

Shutting the door behind Sam, Cora crossed back to the table and sat down. He looked around the small apartment for a moment, then came and took the chair across from her. "Harold decided to stay down there for good, then?"

She nodded. "Sunny Sarasota. He's listing the building as soon as it's put back together." When it sold, Cora would have to find somewhere else to stay. She hadn't wanted to take Harold up on his offer to use the apartment above it in the first place, but she didn't have anywhere else to go.

"How are you doing?" Sam asked. "You look thin as hell," he added. Cora just shrugged. Sam was right. When she bothered to look in the mirror, she saw a hollow-eyed, washed-out version of herself. She *was* thin, even more on the inside than out. Grief and anger had rubbed away at her, sanding her down bit by bit until she felt like little more than a paper shell. "How are you set up for food?" he said. "I can run across the street for something."

Something like a laugh came out of her throat, though it was jagged and out of practice. Sam looked at her with concern, but she shook her head. "I have plenty of food."

Tuna casserole, chicken casserole, baked meatballs, baked ziti, scalloped potatoes and au gratin potatoes and funeral potatoes; all these and more were crammed into the freezer. Pine Gap was a small town, and in small towns, casseroles followed funerals, as if enough covered dishes could fill up the hole left by death. They all tasted like ashes to Cora, so she was thawing them out and feeding them to Rocky little by little. The dog was going to be fat as a prize pig by the time the snow started to fly.

Sam sat for a silent moment, examining her. "Is there anything new?" he finally asked.

"Still nothing. They got his car going through a traffic camera." Cora corrected herself. "Her car, I mean." The big shiny SUV Jacob drove had belonged to Avery Benson, stolen after her murder. Cora felt sick at the memory of riding in it beside him, of the earring she found on the floor. "It was only the once and it hasn't shown up again. The investigator, Diaz, she said he's probably dumped it by now. But that was three weeks ago. There hasn't been anything since, and I don't dare keep calling all the time …" Cora trailed off and her eyes drifted back toward the window.

"Why not?" Sam reached out and touched her hand to get her attention. She jerked it away.

"Sorry." Cora turned to meet his eyes. "It's just, I'm starting to get the impression the police don't believe things happened the way they did." Cora looked down at her hands, at the gnawed nails and the dry, burn-scarred knuckles. "Then again, why *would* they believe me? It's not like any of it makes sense. I can hardly believe it happened, and I was there." Cora leaned her head against the window, so the cool glass pressed against the thick surgical scar that ran up the side of her head.

"The police will figure out what you told them was the truth. They'll find him."

Would they? It hadn't occurred to Cora that Jacob Adler wouldn't be found, not in the beginning. But after nearly a month, doubt was seeping in. The only thing anyone knew for sure was that his name wasn't really Jacob Adler. He'd been careful, hadn't left a single fingerprint that could be found. Cora remembered him casually wiping away a stray drop of liquor from his shot glass, removing any trace of himself, and felt like a fool for the thousandth time. Security cameras and traffic cameras were few and far between in Pine Gap, and he'd never turned his face to the ones he did pass. The only image of him anyone had managed to turn up was in the background of a picture taken the night of Kimmy's party, a useless sliver of his face between Dante and a beaming, bright, alive Kimmy. Jacob Adler, whoever he really was, was a ghost.

Cora turned to watch Rocky, sprawled out on his side. His legs kicked fitfully while he chased a dream rabbit through a dream field, paws brushing the fringe of the rug that lay over the faded linoleum. He opened one black marble eye to look at her, then closed it again.

She rubbed her eyes, ground her knuckles into them. When she looked back up, red eyed and blinking, Sam was the one staring out the window, watching a car as it approached, then passed by. Was he looking for Jacob Adler in every car, the way Cora did?

"They're probably trying a lot harder to find him for killing Avery Benson," Cora spat out, suddenly angry. "Rich white girl from the city. Kimmy was poor and Black, so nobody gives a shit." The sharp, frustrated edge in her voice made Rocky get up and pad over to her chair. Cora leaned over and gently smoothed the place on his shoulder where the hair had been shaved and was growing back soft and downy around the quickly healing scar. "Avery Benson. She's where this all started. He was after what she had. When I find out about that, then maybe I can find out who he is."

"What do you mean *you*?" Sam stood, head nearly touching the low ceiling. He wasn't a big man, but he seemed to fill the small space. "Tell me you aren't doing anything—"

"Anything what? Stupid? Dangerous?" Cora said. "I would, if it would help. But right now, I'm just trying to find some answers. I'm going to go to Blackwell Lake and ask some questions. Or I'm going to try to. They're tight up there," she admitted. "I called and I didn't get beyond the front office. They aren't going to just let me walk in and start grilling people. I'm thinking if I hike up the back way, maybe I can slip in."

"Don't do that."

"Sam, you can't stop me, I—"

"Don't sneak in the back," he interrupted her. "Somebody who got shot in the head last month probably shouldn't be going on five-mile hikes through the woods." She started to protest, but he threw his hands up. "I don't care what you say, you shouldn't. And besides, if they catch you, they'll throw you out on your ass."

"Let them. I'm still going to try. It's the best I can come up with, unless you have a better idea." She crossed her arms over her chest and turned away from him, toward the window. Cora heard the creak of the floor as he stepped up behind her and put a hand on her shoulder. She twitched at the touch but didn't jerk away.

"Maybe I do have a better plan," Sam said. "What if I could get you in up at Blackwell Lake through the front door?"

29

"He's fine. Did you see the way he jumped down out of the truck? Didn't even hesitate." Sam slowed ahead of the turn onto Mountain Road. "And your neighbor, I thought the old guy was going to cry when he saw Rocky."

"I know. You're right," Cora said. It was silly to worry about Rocky. He was getting around fine, and he'd spent plenty of time with Mr. Debusher before. But now, Cora felt anxious when the dog was out of her sight for more than a minute.

The truck bucked over a rut in the road, and Cora reached for the panic bar over her head. "Sorry," Sam said. "These roads are twice as bad as usual this year, with all the rain."

"So, you still haven't told me your master plan." Cora let go of the bar and settled her hand into her lap, fiddling with the buttons on her sweater. The clothes felt foreign, donations from the Red Cross that felt stiff and unfamiliar, and too big on her shrunken frame. "I hope you aren't thinking we can lie our way in. I already tried posing as a travel blogger and as a journalist doing a story on the town under the lake. I got hung up on both times."

The few turns off Mountain Road were either marked with tin signs fighting to be seen through the heavy overgrowth or weren't marked at all. The way to Blackwell Lake, on the other hand, was impossible to miss. A bronze plaque in a stacked stone surround read *The Blackwell Lake Resort*, and underneath in letters nearly as big, *Registered Guests Only*.

"I tried that route too." Cora nodded at the sign as they made the turn. "Booking a stay. But they're about to close for the season. And even if they were taking reservations, I would have had to sell a kidney to be able to afford it."

"I guess you have to charge a lot to keep the bills paid when you're only open for the good weather. This place just sits for half the year. Couple months of that, the roads up here aren't even passable."

It might be a different story in January, but at present, the approach to Blackwell Lake was in better shape than any of the other roads on the mountain, the neatly paved drive like a slick black snake winding away in front of them. The trees and bushes had been trimmed back in a precise strip on each side of the road to make room for a border of manicured grass.

"Sam, stop." Cora threw her hands up over her face, suddenly unable to see. She turned her head back and forth, trying to clear her vision, but in a moving vehicle it was like trying to look through a jar of Vaseline. "Damn it, please not now."

The tires ground to a halt. She heard his door open, then felt an inrush of cool air when he opened hers. "Cora, what's wrong? Is it your head?"

She felt his hand grasp her arm, but Cora shrugged it off, sliding out of the truck. Her knees buckled when she hit the ground, but she dragged herself back up by the door frame. On her feet, Cora spun blindly in a circle, feeling the tingle in her fingers crawl inward like fire ants marching up her arms.

"Cora." Sam took her by both shoulders and gave her a gentle shake. "Cora, look at me. What is it?" She turned her head and the center of her vision cleared to a perfect round tunnel beyond his shoulder. "Jesus, you're white as a damn sheet. What's wrong?"

"Nothing," Cora said. "Just give me a minute." She shook him off again. "Let me go, Sam. Just let me—" Free of his grasp, she took a slow step forward. It never left her alone, not for long. It never would. Because of it, she'd found Avery Benson. Because of it, Jacob Adler came into her life. Because of it, because of her, Kimmy was dead. It just kept going, and there wasn't anything she could do to stop it.

Cora let herself be dragged along, fumble footed, off the road and into the closely grown pine trees, tears leaking from her eyes. A branch raked her hand, drawing thin raised lines across the pale skin like fingernail scratches, but she barely noticed.

Sam caught her by the shoulder again, pulling her to a stop and spinning her around, steadying her when she lurched sideways, losing her sight again. "Just stop, Cora. Where are you going?" He let go of her shoulder, putting the back of his hand to her cheek. "You're burning up. You're not okay. Get back in the truck. I'll take you to the—"

"No. Not yet." Cora turned her head to find the path again. "Let me go. I need to …" She took one step forward, and just like that, it stopped. The fire burned away and there was nothing in front of her eyes but clear air, dust motes dancing through the light coming through the pine branches. It happened so quickly Cora went from being about to burst to feeling empty and cold.

The leather band blended perfectly into the bed of fallen pine needles, but a glint of gold from the buckle gave it away. Cora picked it up and turned it over, brushing off the back of the watch to read the spidery engraving. "Can't have been here very long," Cora said, murmuring absently to herself. "The band isn't even damp."

"Cora, what is it?"

She held it out to him. "It's a watch."

He took it from her, turning it over and letting it rest flat in his large, callused palm. Sam looked up at her. "I see that. But how … Cora, what just happened?"

Opening her mouth, she started to give him one of the usual excuses. But something in his eyes stopped her. "I …" She swallowed hard. Cora didn't want to lie to him, but she didn't want to tell him the truth, either, not now. "It was nothing." She reached out and took the watch from Sam's hand and slipped it into her pocket.

"Cora, bullshit. That was not nothing." His eyes bored into hers. There was no malice in them, not even curiosity. He looked what? Concerned? Sam reached out and pulled her hand toward him, examining the dots of blood welling up from the cat-claw scratches the branch had made. He dabbed the blood away with his shirt sleeve. "You can tell me, you know," he said softly.

"Sam, I …" she said. "Sam, please, let's just go."

He looked at her for a moment longer. When he realized he would get nothing more from her on the matter, he didn't press, but she thought he sagged a little. Finally, he shook his head.

"Fine. But I should probably take you back to get checked out, don't you think?" Sam handed her back into the truck and paused in the open door. "That wasn't normal."

"No, that definitely wasn't normal." Cora reached for the door handle. "But I'm okay now. And I need to do this. Let's go."

30

It was a silent ride, up the last stretch of blacktop to the tall metal gates that marked the entrance to the resort. Sam rolled down his window and pushed the intercom button.

"Welcome to the Blackwell Lake Resort," a chipper woman's voice sounded from the speaker. It was familiar; the woman who had hung up on Cora when she'd called before, she realized. "Name, please."

"Sadie, it's Sam."

There was a pause, long enough for Sam's brow to dip into a worried crinkle. Then they heard a metallic clink and the gates parted and started to slowly swing inward. "When the road splits, take the branch to the left, down the access road." The voice from the intercom had dropped to just above a whisper. "Follow it around to the employee lot behind the big house. I'll meet you there. Whatever you do, don't park in the main lot or go past the chalets." The intercom clicked off.

"Who's Sadie?" Cora asked. They drove through the gates, and she watched them roll closed in the rearview mirror.

"Sadie Bickerman. I called earlier and convinced her to let us in to take a look at where Avery Benson was staying. I'm hoping everybody hasn't cleared out for the season, and we can maybe talk to somebody who knew something about her."

The pavement had been replaced with a bed of white crushed shell, and the tires crunched and ground as they drove slowly toward the staff entrance. Before the road wove its way back under the cover of the trees, Cora saw a swath of velvety lawn without a single fallen leaf interrupting the smooth green, and a ring of neat, identical houses strung around the black bowl of the lake.

"Nice this Sadie doesn't mind sneaking you in."

Sam grimaced. "Wasn't maybe the most fun phone call I ever made, asking her. Sadie's my ex-girlfriend."

Cora raised an eyebrow. Sam didn't say anything more as the lake slid out of sight.

The front of the resort's main house was all show, exposed beams hewn from old growth oaks, the stucco between the timber framing pristine white. The back side, facing only forest, was flat and unadorned, painted a faded, peeling white. Battered compacts, minivans, and rusty pickups were packed tightly into a small lot. They were clearly not meant to be seen by the guests any more than the employees who entered through the inobtrusive door tucked under a battered aluminum awning.

A woman was standing in the shade of the awning. She was short and plump, with light brown hair pulled back into a tidy bun and a sprinkle of freckles across her nose and cheeks. Her outfit was something between a stewardess's uniform and a girl scout kit, the narrow hem of the khaki skirt forcing her to walk in short, clipped steps as she hurried toward them. She pulled at the forest-green scarf knotted around her neck and patted her hair.

"There you are," she said. "You didn't run into anybody on your way in, did you?"

Sam bent over and gave her a kiss on the cheek, and her pretty, pale face went pink. "Nobody noticed us."

The woman had been smiling brightly, until Sam said *us*. She watched Cora climb down out of the passenger side. "You didn't tell me you were bringing anybody, Sam." Sadie eyed Cora coolly. "I'm risking my job just letting you through the gate, you know. Maybe this wasn't a great idea."

"Sadie, this is Cora Gilbert. I swear, we won't get you in trouble. Anyway, we're already here. Just give us a little bit of time."

She didn't look entirely convinced. Sadie stared at Cora for a moment, before shaking her head briefly and turning back to Sam. "I have to go tell Helen I'm taking my break early and get her to cover the gate. Go over there." Sadie pointed toward a space beside the employee entrance, where the busy shape of the building made a dark recess. "Stay out of sight until I get back." She turned to go but did manage a small smile for Sam. "I'll only be a couple minutes."

Cora and Sam slid into the shadowy alcove. There was a large planter set in the nook, big as a bathtub, the soil around the spindly yew growing inside dotted with cigarette butts. Cora perched carefully on the edge. "That's your ex-girlfriend?" Cora said. "Does she know that?"

"Well, it wasn't necessarily mutual, the breakup," Sam admitted. He leaned beside her and crossed his arms, looking down at the sharp line the sun drew across the ground at the edge of the alcove. "Do you know my brother?" he asked.

"Which one?" Cora said. "Don't you have like ten?"

Sam laughed, his arm shaking gently against hers. "It felt like it, sometimes, while I was growing up. There's six of us, including me. There was a Cooper on the football team for like fourteen straight years. This year, my oldest brother Carder's boy is playing, so it's starting all over again."

"What does your brother have to do with you and Miss Sadie Smiles-A-Lot?"

"When I met Sadie, she was a teller at the credit union. I'm not going to say she struck me dead or anything like that"—he shrugged—"but she's pretty, you know, in that quiet way. Not flashy, but pretty. You don't remember her from school, do you?" Cora shook her head. "No? She would have been ahead of you, I guess." Cora didn't remember Sadie, but she didn't remember many people. High school had not been the high point in Cora's life.

"I think she asked me out the first time. I don't really remember. After that, we just kind of fell into dating." They both froze at the sound of a door opening and closing. A car started and they heard the crunch of tires on shells as it pulled away. "I didn't think about it till it was over, but she was probably the one towing the boat along. It didn't hurt that my mom really liked Sadie, since she was so interested in the family, always wanted to be doing things with the whole big bunch. As it turned out, my family was what she was interested in."

Raising an eyebrow, Cora turned so she could see him better. "She was after you for your family?"

"Not the whole thing," Sam said. "One night we were, uh, you know, and things were at, um, a certain point, and Sadie yelled out a name. It wasn't the good Lord's. And it wasn't Sam Cooper, either. Close, though. She was only off a couple years on her Coopers."

"No way." Cora slapped a hand across her mouth. Her words had come out loud enough to echo around their dark little nook.

"Yes way. I guess she had a real thing for my brother Clay, like since they were in middle school. Totally unrequited. Clay didn't even remember her. He went away to college and met Virginia, got married. Sadie never got over him, but since he went off the market and there wasn't any chance she'd ever have him, I guess she figured she could at least get close, if she settled for the only Cooper still available."

"That's horrible, Sam."

"It's honestly not." He shrugged. "In fact, it was almost a relief."

"What did you do? I mean, she yelled out your brother's name in bed."

He laughed and his eyes crinkled, making her smile without meaning to. It felt foreign, smiling, like using a muscle that had begun to atrophy. "I knew *she* realized it, when it happened, but I think she was hoping I hadn't, in the heat of the moment. I waited until she was asleep and snuck out."

"That's it?"

"Well, almost. I left a note." Sam grimaced. "Seems childish now."

"What did it say?"

"*Sorry, bed was too crowded.* Then I signed it Cooper and let her decide which one."

"You did not."

"I did. And that was the end of that."

"Was it? She seems pretty smiled up to see you."

Sam shrugged. "Maybe she figured she'd better stay on good terms with the family, in case Clay and his wife ever split up." He grinned but lowered his voice to continue. The door had opened again, and there was the crunch of approaching feet. "She's going to be waiting a long time, if that's the case. Clay told me a couple days ago he and Virginia have one on the way. I think they're in it for the long haul."

Around the corner, they heard Sadie's voice. "Okay, follow me."

31

Cora blinked at the glare when she stepped back out into the sunshine. They followed Sadie's stiff back around the rear of the building and down a narrow, shady path, yet more crushed shell crackling underfoot. Sadie relaxed a little out in the open, the shoulders of the trim uniform slumping slightly.

"I guess it can't really hurt," she said, "letting you look around the chalet quick. The police have been done with it for a while, and they're going to start packing it up tomorrow so the family can come get her stuff. What's left of it, at least. The person that broke in, he cleaned it out pretty good. Probably loaded everything up in her SUV and drove out the front gate." Sadie shivered. "Scary, really. I mean, these people don't even lock the doors, and then to find out a murderer just waltzed in and out."

"Everything else is still in it?" Sam asked. "I was hoping, but after this long ..."

Sadie looked over her shoulder, her blue eyes big and childlike. "I know, right? The resort director was going crazy. First there's a murder and a robbery, which weren't exactly good for business. Bookings are not going to be so hot next year, let me tell you. Now he's got to worry about the family suing the place into bankruptcy. That's why the stuff's all still in there. He didn't dare touch anything or push them to get it all packed up and out. But the season's over, and the place needs to be made over for next year. It was a relief when they finally called."

She managed to bat her eyes and roll them at the same time, ignoring

Cora and addressing Sam. "I thought maybe her family was just going to leave it all. Not like they'd probably miss any of it. And all the really expensive stuff was taken, anyway. These rich people"—she lowered her voice to a whisper, though there wasn't another soul in sight—"they rent a chalet for the whole summer and bring like, everything they own. We have to move out the furniture and move theirs in, even though the places are full of really, really nice stuff. They change the pictures on the walls, the rugs, everything, and then they leave for weeks at a time and don't even enjoy it."

Cora double-stepped to walk beside Sadie. "Did you know her?" Sadie stopped short and looked Cora up and down before she answered. She must not have found much to be threatened by because she answered with a sniff.

"Know her? I'm staff. We're not supposed to *know* anybody. But when I did have to deal with her, she was nice enough. She didn't pretend I didn't exist, like most of the guests. Which is a big deal, if you knew how demanding some of them are. They want everything yesterday, and they want it organic and locally sourced and delivered by invisible fairies. But the Benson woman was polite, at least. She even tipped me when I picked up some stuff for her from that crappy little museum in town. Here we are."

They'd crossed behind the main house that sat on the farthest point of Blackwell Lake and, following Sadie, made their way down the west side, snaking discreetly behind the individual chalets. Cora wondered if that discretion had been as convenient for Jacob when he'd murdered Avery Benson and pillaged the chalet. Although the entrance was gated and there was a fence that ran along the eastern border, the resort was too big to make enclosing the entire thing practical. The privacy and protection of the west side had been left to Mother Nature, with a thick ring of old-growth pines and miles and miles of nothing but the old cemetery.

"It's unlocked." Sadie turned to look nervously back up the path. Sam was already up the large, slab stone steps and heading inside before she could change her mind. Cora quickly followed.

"Holy crap." Cora stopped halfway through the doorway, taken aback. The outside of the chalet was a tinier version of the main house, with dark beams bordering bright, white stucco. The inside was far more opulent. Most of the interior was one large room with a high cathedral ceiling, a loft with scrolled ironwork railings jutting out over their heads. Even though the place was in disarray, drawers hanging open like gaping mouths, contents spilling out over the lips, it was clear everything was high quality and expensive, from the Navajo rug under the tipped-up easy chair to the abstract gold figures lying broken on the marble fireplace mantel.

"Man, look at this place," Sam said. "It's like someone shoved a mansion inside a Bavarian restaurant. So, what are we looking for?"

"Anything," Cora said, picking up a picture frame. Behind the shattered glass, Avery Benson looked up at her, long red hair falling over her shoulders, smiling for the camera. An older man had his arm around her shoulder. Cora set the frame back down sadly. "A name that might be Jacob's real name, a picture, maybe, one to give to the police. Someone has to know him. Maybe she knew him. She must have, don't you think?"

Cora headed up the stairs. Sam followed. The downstairs had been turned out, rummaged through. The loft had been destroyed. Every piece of clothing in the large walk-in closet had been pulled from its hanger, every item taken from its drawer, the drawers pulled from their tracks and tumbled on top. The bedding had been thrown from the bed, then the mattress and pillows ripped open, stuffing scattered like fluffy clouds on the wooden floor. Through an open door they could see a bathroom, the mirror over the sink a disco-ball of gleaming cracks.

"Are you guys upstairs?" Sadie's voice came from below. "Make it quick. I need to get back. My break isn't that long."

On the floor, upside down, was a rectangle of stiff paper. Cora picked it up and read it, then held it out to Sam.

"What's this?" he asked.

"Invitation to Dante's art opening. I can't believe I was stupid enough to believe it was a coincidence."

"It was, though, don't you think? Probably the only real coincidence in all this." Sam examined the embossed card in his hand. "I mean, he was clearly following you, looking for a way into your life to see if you had whatever necklace he was looking for. But it was sheer luck on his part that you were going to be here." He held up the invitation before setting it on the nightstand. "That you were connected to Avery by this."

"But how was he connected?" Cora asked. "That's the only way anyone is ever going to find him." Cora picked up a sheaf of papers and flipped through them, finding nothing but photocopies of old documents stamped Pine Gap Historical Society. She picked up a book and fanned through it. Sam gave a last look around, then shook his head. "You seeing anything?" she said.

"Nothing. Maybe we could talk to some people in the other houses, if there's anybody still here." He paused on the steps and waited for her to follow. "They might know something. Might have even seen him casing the place ahead of time."

"No way, Sam." Sadie came toward the stairs to meet them, sensible heels clip-clopping on the polished wood. "Everybody's gone. And you need to get out of here. I was nice enough to let you look around, but I could lose my job." Sadie put her hands on her hips; her lips had compressed to a thin, hard line.

"Sadie, I won't get you in trouble. And the person who did this, the one that killed Avery Benson, he killed Kimaya Gilbert too. We need to figure out how—"

"You're Kimmy Gilbert's sister." Sadie's head swiveled toward Cora. "I didn't realize. I went to high school with her. I'm so sorry." Her voice had gone soft and sympathetic, and she took a step toward Cora, like she was going to pat her on the shoulder or, God forbid, hug her. Cora slipped past Sadie and out the front door as quickly as she could, stumbling down the steps. She started walking blindly across the grinding, crunching shell path and onto the soft grass at the edge of the lake, putting what distance she could between herself and other people. Cora sank to her knees.

It was always there, always in her mind, that Kimmy was gone. It wasn't like Cora would ever forget. But sometimes she was distracted for a minute or even an hour, long enough to go numb to the fact. Then with a thought or a single word, it returned like a punch in the stomach. All the time Cora had spent finding things, suffering with the feelings that came with it, she hadn't known how close they were to the feelings of loss. Not until Kimmy. The blindness from the tears that wouldn't stop, the burn inside from guilt and anger. But this she couldn't follow to its source and extinguish. She couldn't find her sister and make it all fall away. Kimmy was beyond finding.

Cora got to her feet and stepped onto the dock across from the chalet's front door. She squatted down on the painted wood, staring out across the dark water, hauling in deep breaths and trying to pull herself back together.

"You there, who are you? What are you doing here?"

Raising her head, Cora saw a man with a mane of gray hair charging around the border of the lake. Two figures in burly pantsuit versions of Sadie's uniform flanked him. They were coming straight for her.

32

By the time the trio of men reached the dock, Sam was coming down the front steps of the chalet after Cora. Sadie hung back. Cora thought the woman looked about to make a break for it, but she didn't get the chance.

"Miss Bickerman, who are these people?"

The look in Sadie's eyes was just short of terror. "Director Clivens, I—"

"Miss Bickerman." Clivens stepped toward her, neck puffed up tight against the collar of his crisp button-up shirt. His left hand clenched and unclenched angrily. "Miss Bickerman, answer me. Who are these—"

"Sir," Sam broke in, "we're here because we're interested in possibly—"

"In what?" the man interrupted. "In arranging a stay?" He looked them over with derision. His fingers twitched at his sleeve, pulling it up slightly, then he let it go, crossing his arms in front of his chest instead.

"Excuse me, sir," Sam started again. Cora crept up beside the resort director, examining him. He saw her approach and glowered down at her.

"It's Director. Director Robert Clivens. And these gentlemen, they are Mr. Welsh and Mr. Timmins. They're the men who are going to escort you people off the property immediately. You clearly don't belong here." He eyed Cora while he spoke. She had taken a step closer to him, near enough to touch. "Do it now, gentlemen. And you, Miss

Bickerman, I expect you in my office with a good explanation or a letter of resignation by the end of your shift. Get them out of here."

They went for Sam first. While everyone's attention was away from her, Cora took another step toward Clivens and reached out to stop him, grabbing him by the wrist.

"Young lady, I don't know what you think you're—"

"We came to return your watch."

The man froze. Cora let go of his wrist and he turned back toward her. She reached into her pocket. "I found it out near the road. Sadie"—she turned to the other woman, who was white as a sheet—"I mean, Miss Bickerman answered the intercom at the gate. We told her what we found, and she thought it might be yours. She was helping us find you."

She wasn't sure it was working. Maybe Cora had read it all wrong: the aborted attempts to check the time, the empty wrist she had grabbed. But the engraving on the back of the watch, R.M.C. in fussy, curlicue script, seemed unlikely to be a coincidence. And even more, some part of her thought she could feel something, some connection between the man and the watch, though she couldn't say why. But she wasn't sure. Even as Cora pulled the watch out of her pocket and held it out, she wondered if she was way off.

Director Clivens's whole body relaxed. He reached out and took it from her gently, rubbing his thumb tenderly across the glass face before strapping the watch back on his wrist.

"It was a gift from my late wife." He wasn't quite smiling when he finished adjusting the band and looked up at Cora, but he didn't look ready to bite any more, either. "I had started to give up hope of seeing it again. Where exactly did you say you found it?"

"A few hundred yards up from the sign at the entrance. Just past the edge of the grass, in the pines."

Clivens thought for a moment, then nodded. "I stopped last evening to take a picture of a tree I wanted removed before it fell and blocked the drive." He turned to one of the men behind him. "Mr. Welsh, let the grounds crew know. I want it taken care of before they leave for the day."

"Yes, sir." The two men turned and headed back toward the main house. Sadie looked after them longingly, like she would have run after them if she dared.

"Thank you, Miss ..."

"Gilbert. Cora Gilbert."

"Thank you, Miss Gilbert. I appreciate your returning it. It's quite valuable, even beyond the sentimental. A lot of people would have kept it. Or sold it."

She kept a straight face. "I wouldn't have dreamed of it."

Giving her a nod, Clivens turned to Sadie. "Please be early tomorrow, Miss Bickerman, to supervise housekeeping while they pack up the Benson chalet. It needs to be complete before the family arrives on Friday."

"Yes, sir." Sadie flushed with relief, now that she knew she would still have a job the next day. She gave Sam one last longing look and scurried away.

"Miss Gilbert, again, thank you. Now, I trust you and your friend can see your way out?"

⸻⬥⬦⬥⸻

"Well, that didn't exactly go how I expected." Sam pulled the truck out of the resort's smooth drive and onto the deeply rutted dirt of Mountain Road.

"Really?" Cora was less surprised. It fell well within the boundaries of what she'd come to expect. She didn't elaborate, though she could almost feel how badly Sam wanted to ask. "But at least we got a little bit to work with."

"Did we?" Sam slowed to let the front tire ease into a pothole and back out. "All I got was that there are no cameras around that place. I was sure there would be, maybe even one that caught a glimpse of Jacob Adler coming or going when he robbed the Benson lady's place. Then again, if that was the case the police would have thought of it, and they probably would have found him by now. I should have guessed they're into their privacy, based on the Gates of Mordor back there and Clivens's hairy bodyguards."

"That never crossed my mind," Cora admitted, "to look for cameras. But what about the museum? Sadie said Avery Benson had her running stuff up here from the historical society. There were photocopies from there in her bedroom. It's probably nothing but …"

"But it's worth a look," Sam said, stopping before the turn onto Southside Road. "And I know somebody who works at the museum."

"Not another ex-girlfriend, I hope."

"Thank God, no. My sister-in-law." On paved road once more, Sam sped up, passing a slow-moving SUV painted a motley combination of colors almost as bad as her truck's before speaking again. "How did you do it?"

"Do what?" Cora answered a second too slowly.

He looked away from the road and shot her a raised eyebrow. "Find the watch. You didn't just stumble on it. I was there. And how did you know it was his?"

"That was just a lucky guess, knowing it was his," Cora admitted. "He kept touching his arm and looking like he wanted to check the time, but when I grabbed his wrist, it was bare. And he was all agitated and pissed off, so I thought it might be because he lost something. Though he might be the kind of person who's always pissed off."

"And the other part?"

She didn't answer. The silence held until they made the gentle turn around Potter's Bend and onto what had been her street.

"Cora, you can tell me, you know."

"It was nothing. Just luck, I guess. I—"

"Bullshit." Sam pulled the truck up to the curb across from Mr. Debusher's house. "I don't believe that, Cora."

"Sam, I don't have time for this. I need to get Rocky."

He put the truck in park and turned toward her. "After you tell me what's going on, Cora." Sam looked at her, staring until she turned away toward the window. "The watch, my compass, those missing kids, Avery Benson. And those are just the times that made a stir, aren't they? I'm the one that processes all the lost and found listings on the game lands. Did you know that? I'm the office paper pusher, so every single one comes across my desk. I've always thought there were a lot of them, way more than there should be. After you found my compass, it made me curious. I looked back. Ninety-nine percent of listings over the last few years came from the same email address. I wonder whose that might be."

"So what if Rocky does find—"

"But it's not Rocky, is it, Cora?"

She opened her mouth to protest, but she didn't know what to say. Now that Kimmy was gone, no one knew about the strange ability that blinded her and burned her and set her chasing after anything and everything that was lost. Cora was alone with it. It was a secret, and secrets were sharp and heavy. They wore on you. They wore you down.

"Okay, listen …" She took a deep breath, blowing a patch of fog onto the glass. How big a deal was it, to let him in? Turning to see him waiting patiently for her to answer, Cora thought he might even believe her, as crazy as the whole thing sounded. It had taken a while to put it all together, but her mom had believed it. And Kimmy had.

Kimmy, who was dead because of Cora's ability to find things. Cora should have been dead too, taking her strange and dangerous ability with her. It was safer to keep it to herself. Cora opened the door and got out.

"Cora, come on. I—"

"Goodbye, Sam. I have to go." She walked away and didn't look back, only turning after she heard the truck roll away.

Mr. Debusher was waiting on his front stoop. "He was pinin' for ya. Once it started ta get dark, he wouldn't be still for a second, would ya?" Mr. Debusher reached into his sagging sweater pocket and pulled out a bone-shape treat, brushing off a bit of brown fuzz before holding it out to Rocky. "Yer better now, though, aren't ya." The old man looked up at Cora. "He sure was missin' you."

Rocky took the treat gently, barely brushing the thin-skinned fingers holding it out. Once he had it in his teeth, he crunched it and swallowed. Then he turned to nose Cora. She ruffled his fur, then smoothed it neatly back over his broad forehead. "I missed you too, buddy."

"Young Eugene was by a bit ago, to say his farewells. He was pleased to see our boy before he went."

"I'm sorry I missed him." Cora turned to look at the trailer, Tiddles's small bedroom window dark. "He called to tell me he was going to his dad's for good." She was happy for him. But she would miss him. Looking up and down the street, Cora thought the street would miss him too. She could feel the difference in it. It had always been a quiet place, but with Tiddles gone and the gap where her house had been now an empty space like a missing tooth, it felt desolate.

"You ain't walking ta town by yourself, are ya?" Mr. Debusher asked, watching her peering down the street.

"I'm only going to Church Street," Cora said. "And even with only three good legs, I think Rocky would scare away a black bear. He's bigger than the last one I saw."

"That he be. Still, after what happened ..." Mr. Debusher cast a rheumy eye toward the fence. It was bowed from the heat, the boards shrunken so the spaces between were even wider than before. Beyond it was a black void. What little part of her house that stood after the fire had collapsed into the cellar, all of it waiting to be bulldozed in and leveled out. "Best not to be out running around alone. Don't feel the same anymore. Been giving me the heebies lately, c'aint explain it. Feels like ghosts in the graveyard."

"I'll be okay, Mr. Debusher."

"You gonna try to build back, after they fill it?" He nodded his head toward where Cora's house had been. "Maybe you could bring in one of those already built places, the kind they haul in split right down the middle then pop back together. Probably could get one in before the snow falls. Get you right back here where you belong quick as spit."

"I'm not sure what I'm doing yet," Cora said. "Harold's letting me use his apartment for a while, so it's not a big hurry." She realized when she said it that she *was* sure. Cora had no intention of coming back. She didn't know where she'd go, after Jacob was caught and made to pay for what he'd done, but it wouldn't be here. There were too many memories, the good ones before and the final ones that were worse than anything. Rocky leaned against her leg, like he could feel where her thoughts were going. She reached down and patted his head.

"I'd better go," Cora said, retreating down the steps. "Thanks for taking care of Rocky." She started down the sidewalk, past where her house had stood, and thought maybe Mr. Debusher was right, about something feeling wrong on the street. Maybe it was ghosts; the charred ground was surely a graveyard. Whatever it was, she could feel it, something full and watchful in the day that would grow menacing in the dark. Rocky stayed glued to her knee until they reached Church Street. She locked and bolted the apartment door behind them, but the feeling of being watched didn't quite fade away.

33

Museum at nine. I'll pick you up quarter of.

The message from Sam had woken her, the vibration dragging her up from a fitful sleep. Cora was relieved to hear from him. Last night, she wondered if she would see him again. He had no real reason to be helping her, and she'd been less than forthcoming and a little bit short with him, shutting down and walking away the minute things got uncomfortable.

Pulling on jeans and a heavy sweater, making a pointless pass across her shorn hair with a brush, Cora listened for Sam's knock on the door. She wasn't holding out a great deal of hope of finding anything useful in the little local museum, but it was the only thing she had to go on.

"Come on, Rocky, let's get ready. Sam's coming." Rocky was standing with his paws on the windowsill that overlooked the street. Coming up beside him with his collar, she saw the dark blue pickup truck pull up alongside the curb. Rocky dropped his front paws to the floor and padded across to stand in front of the door. He dropped down onto his haunches obediently when she let Sam in.

Sam juggled the cardboard carrier of coffee cups and the brown bag into one hand so he could reach down and pet him. "I don't know about you, but I think Rocky might actually look happy to see me. He used to give me the hairy eyeball all the time."

"Maybe because you never brought donuts before."

"Probably. Did you know they have doggie donuts?" He handed

Cora the coffee cups and rifled through the carryout bag. "Shaped like a bone and everything. Here you go, boy."

He fed Rocky the donut, breaking it into pieces. When he was done, he stood up and brushed his hands off on his jeans. Cora handed him a coffee.

"I got them both black. Hope that's okay," he said. "They look at you like you've got three eyes when you don't want anything in it, but if I wanted something with four cups of sugar and covered in whipped cream, I'd order a milkshake. Donut?"

Cora shook her head, deciding to stick with coffee. If she was going to go somewhere new, better not to have too much rolling around in her stomach, in case she found herself stumbling around trying to find something.

"Listen, Cora. I'm sorry about yesterday. Your business is your business. I was just ..." He fiddled with the plastic tab on the coffee cup lid, then looked back up. His eyes were brown, like Kimmy's, Cora thought. Darker, but warm like her sister's had been. "I was worried is all. When you jumped out of the truck and headed for the woods after that watch, you didn't look good. I mean you didn't look well. You looked good." He took a too-large sip from the hot coffee, then sputtered into his elbow. "Shit. That's hot. What I mean is I was concerned. But I also don't know how to leave well enough alone, because when I can't fit things in a box the way I think they should go, I tend to kind of fixate on them. Drives me nuts, the way I can't settle until I figure things out."

She remembered him taking the time to fix the spring on her screen door. And at P.J.'s the night after she'd found Avery Benson's body, crawling under the table to wedge a cardboard coaster under the leg so it didn't wobble. It was kind of reassuring that he had his own quirk, even if it had made him a little too aware of hers.

He was still looking intently at her. "It's fine," Cora said. It wasn't much of an answer, but she managed a small smile with it. He looked relieved, pulling a cruller out of the bag and putting half of it away in one bite. Sam swallowed, then looked at the clock. "We'd better go.

Jessica said she'd come in an hour early and meet us. She's not the kind of person you want to make wait."

<hr>

They pulled into the small gravel lot of the museum five minutes later, though museum seemed a very grand word for the old two-story building, sided in an unfortunate shade of green. "What do you think this paint color is called? Baby barf?" Cora asked as they made their way up the steppingstone walk.

"Don't repeat that where Jessica can hear you," Sam said, looking around in case they were overheard. "Not unless you want the whole lecture about how it's a historically accurate shade of Benjamin Moore. It's called Patina on Brass, by the way. I've heard all about it."

"It's not as vomity-looking up close, I guess," Cora said, running a finger across the painted wood beneath a plaque that read *Pine Gap Museum and Historical Society*. "Probably just looks this way in the right light. Maybe it's the sun."

"It's not the sun." The voice spoke from behind them. Cora jerked her hand back down by her side. "It's that God damned yellow house across the street. It clashes and makes the museum look like a bucket of puke. That old cow did it on purpose, two days after this was finished. Nobody paints their house mustard fucking yellow like that unless they have an ulterior motive."

"Lord, Jessica. Tell us how you really feel." Sam grunted when the woman threw her arms around him and squeezed. She was small, shorter than Cora by a foot, compact and trim, and obviously strong enough to make Sam wince. She let go and turned to Cora.

"Jess," Sam said, "this is Cora Gilbert. Have you two ever met?"

Jessica shook her head, light brown curls bouncing like springs. "Nope. I'd remember. I like your hair. Ballsy shave job." She stuck out a hand, short nails painted bright pink to match her sweater.

"Jessica, come on. It looks like that because she got shot in the head."

Jessica pulled her hand away and reached past Cora to insert an old brass key in the door. "So? I still like it. You've got to have good bone structure for short hair. I'm sorry about your sister, by the way." Jiggling the key until it turned, Jessica pushed open the door. Sam looked a little abashed, but Cora found it was a nice change, when someone didn't waste time offering up generic comfort out of politeness. She was starting to like this Jessica already.

"Rocky, sit. We won't be long." The dog sank down onto the steps. "Be good," Cora said.

"Unless some lady with a nasty beehive and support hose comes over." Jessica addressed the dog directly, pointing a finger at him while she talked. His head came up nearly to her chest when he was sitting. He followed her finger up and down. "If you see any cranky old bitches, you bite, you hear me? Bite. Sic 'em."

"Jessica," Sam moaned.

"What? Oh yeah, Carder Jr.'s starting Friday. You're coming to the game, right?"

"Wouldn't miss it." Sam turned to Cora while Jessica locked the door behind them. "Jessica's my oldest brother Carder's wife. Their son—"

"Don't make me come over there," Jessica growled under her breath. She was glaring out the glass side panel of the front door. Across the street in the yellow house—it *was* an awful shade, like some unholy combination of egg yolks and Heinz mustard—the front door was open a sliver, a shadowy figure visible in the opening. They heard Rocky bark. The door to the yellow house clapped shut. "See, the dog gets it. They can sense evil, you know," she said. "That Beecher woman is seriously insane. I had nothing to do with the board giving her wrinkly old ass the boot, but she stares me down every day like I stole this job from her. I am about this close to going over there and shitting on her sidewalk."

"Jessica Cooper, you are all class."

"You know it." Jessica pulled aside the lace curtain and stuck her middle finger up, raising it toward the house across the street.

"Beecher?" Cora said. "Like Marilyn Beecher?"

"Oh shit. Please tell me she isn't like your aunt or something." Jessica turned a porcelain key switch, and the glass-globed fixture overhead came on. It lit a small, dim foyer, all but a few slivers of the cabbage rose wallpaper covered with framed sketches and black and white portraits.

Shaking her head, Cora stood still for a moment, feeling for anything that might be a problem. Thankfully, there wasn't much more than the usual under-the-skin hum and only the slightest blur in her vision, like she'd rubbed her eyes too hard. She turned to Jessica, who had paused with her hand on the switch.

"No," Cora said, "the Beecher lady isn't a relative or anything like that. I don't actually know her. But she's the one who used to arrange the whole Old Home Days stuff, right?" Jessica nodded. "She's the only person in my entire life I ever saw my mom lose her temper with. One year all the schoolkids had to dress up in period costumes and ride on a float in the parade. When the lady handed out all the clothes, she gave Kimmy a field hand costume, because she said it was historically accurate. I thought my mom was going to kill her."

"That woman is a racist bitch. That's half the reason she got fired. That and they're pretty sure she was stealing antiques and selling them on eBay. She's lucky she only got canned and not shipped down to Allenwood for some one-on-one time with a big butch cellmate. I hope she fucking—"

"Jessica," Sam said. She'd drifted back toward the door, peering through a yellowed lace curtain.

"Sorry." She came back and stepped past them. "I mean, I guess I do owe her the job opening. It was a good thing too. What else was I going to do with a history major and no teaching degree? If that piece of crap hadn't gotten herself canned, I'd be listening to my mom say I told you so and defaulting on my student loans for the rest of my life. Okay." Jessica paused to take a breath. "Sam said you wanted the information I gave Avery Benson, the stuff about Blackwell Lake and her family."

"Her family? What do they have to do with the lake?"

"You didn't know?" Jessica beamed at Cora. "Holy fucking shit."

"Jessica," Sam moaned. "Seriously, you have a mouth like a trucker."

"Seriously this, Sam Cooper. I didn't spend all those hours digging up information for that woman and sending it up to the resort so she could make a fucking art project out of it. She was interested in the history because Atticus Blackwell, the man that owned the mountain and the mines, the one who supposedly flooded the town, he was Avery Benson's great-grandfather."

34

They followed Jessica into a room with waist-high glass cases in a ring around the border. Above them hung more photos and sketches and several maps, objects wired to the walls in the spaces between the frames: wooden-handled tools, pieces of crockery, tin signs, each one carefully labeled. In the center of the room was a large oak dining table, an old kerosene lamp with a painted glass globe sitting in the center.

"How would you like to have a guy like Atticus Blackwell in the family tree?" Jessica said. "That guy was a motherfucking mass murderer."

"The grave where Avery Benson was killed, it belonged to a Fiona Blackwell," Cora said. "They've got to be related, right?"

"Fiona Clennan Blackwell," Jessica said. "She was Atticus Blackwell's wife."

Cora stopped short. "Avery Benson was murdered on her great-grandmother's grave?"

"Nope. Same guy, different wife. We really should start from the beginning," Jessica said, waving for them to sit down.

"I have to get to work before eleven, Jessica. Why don't you just tell us what Avery Benson—"

"Why don't you shut the hell up, Sam. I'm in charge, and I don't get to host an episode of *History's Mysteries* every day, you know."

"I want to hear it, if there's time." Cora pulled out one of the heavy carved chairs and sat.

"See." Jessica stabbed a finger at Sam, then pointed it at the chair next to Cora. "Sit your ass down." Sam sighed, but he pulled out a chair and sat, crossing his arms over his chest. "Okay, so where Blackwell Lake is now, there used to be a town called—wait for it—Blackwell. The population was mostly Irish and Scottish, some Chinese, Black, all the people who worked in the mine. It was a company town, like most of the ones up in the mountains around here were."

Going to the wall, Jessica carefully removed a frame. She brought it over and laid it on the table in front of them, tapping a finger on the glass. "This was Blackwell. At the height of coal production, it had more than a thousand residents. They had a company store, a school, two churches, a boarding house, even a theater."

The brown and white image was surprisingly clear, showing a wide dirt street with two-story buildings running along the right-hand side, neat clapboard houses on the left. Beyond them, the street rose and curved out of sight. A church steeple with a cross on top was visible in the distance.

"The land the town was on, the mine above it, pretty much the whole mountain, was owned by Atticus Blackwell. Which makes you wonder how the hell he and Fiona Clennan ended up together." Jessica put the picture back on the wall and straightened it precisely.

"Why?" Cora asked.

"Because they were so far apart on the social ladder they were practically from different planets. His family was rich as shit. Her parents were fresh off the boat from Ireland. Fiona Clennan's father worked in the Blackwell Mine. I wish somebody would write a romance novel about those two and make up a good backstory about how they met, because I would love to know. I don't even care if it's not true."

Jessica pulled a pair of white cotton gloves out of her pocket and put them on. She slid a stack of long, narrow books off the case behind her and put them on the table. "I dug these out when I was looking for stuff for Avery Benson." She pulled the top volume off the pile and opened it carefully. Inside, the pages were brittle and yellowed, bound copies of an old newspaper. A slip of pink paper marked one of the pages. "Half of what's in these newspapers is about how coal production was down again, who ate dinner with who and what color suspenders they had on, shit like that." She flipped carefully to the marked page. "Boring as fuck. But that's what makes it such a good record of what went on around here. There was so little happening that if someone so much as farted in church, it made the paper."

Jessica spun the book around toward Sam and Cora. Sam reached out a finger to run it along the words while he read. *"May the first, nineteen oh seven—"*

Jessica smacked his hand way. "These are old. Get your greasy fingers off."

"They aren't greasy."

"I will snap them off like little twigs," Jessica threatened.

Cora leaned forward, coming close to touching the page herself while she tried to make out the small, smudgy print.

"May the first, nineteen oh seven, Atticus Carmody Blackwell was joined in blessed union to Fiona Eileen Clennan." There was a paragraph under the bolded headline, about who attended, what the bridal party wore. Cora started to skim it, but Jessica pulled the book away and pushed another into its place.

"Here's the next thing about them that shows up." Jessica pointed to a short block of text, squeezed in near the bottom of a water-stained page. *"Mr. and Mrs. Atticus Blackwell are the parents of a beloved baby girl, born to them February the ninth, nineteen oh eight,"* she read. "So, the year after they got married, they had a kid—"

"This is all very interesting," Sam broke in, "but not very useful."

"You have no appreciation for history that didn't happen on a football field, Sam. You're just like your brother." Jessica huffed and thumped the book shut, bumping the glass lamp in the middle of the table in the process. Sam reached out to catch it before it tipped over. "Damn it, Sam, why'd you catch that? Beecher had it labeled as an eighteen-ninety Bradley and Hubbard. More like a nineteen-eighties fake, hand-painted by some kid in a Malaysian sweatshop." She shook her head. "Cora, I'll give you ten bucks to tip it over and break it when you leave."

"Jessica, you're a menace," Sam said.

"Only to that old hag's ass. Seriously, who did she think she was fooling?" Jessica reached for the last book of bound newsprint, paper crumbling away from the edges as she turned to the slip of pink paper between the leaves. "Here, this is where it gets ugly."

Sam and Cora both leaned forward over the page, shoulders touching as they read. "*Blackwell Catastrophe one of Worst in Mining History,*" a thick black headline read. The text underneath was closely set and fuzzy, and Cora had to squint to make it out. "*The unexpected collapse of the Blackwell Mine just before midnight on October the 30, 1909 and the resulting failure of the slurry impoundment below it caused innumerable gallons of foul black water to descend into the sleeping town of Blackwell. Only a very few residents of the town lived to tell the tale, escaping with their lives and the clothing on their backs. The missing and presumed dead include …*"

There was a long list beneath the paragraph. Cora reached out a finger to trace her way through the names, but a look from Jessica made her snatch it away. "All these people." She leaned back in her chair. "It's horrible. I don't see Fiona Clennan Blackwell on here. She must have been one of them, though, right? On her gravestone, it says she died in nineteen oh nine."

"She did die in nineteen oh nine. On the day of the flood, even. Just not *in* the flood." Jessica reached for a sheaf of photocopied pages. "At least according to Fiona's mother, Margaret Clennan. Margaret missed dying when the town went because when the mine blew, she was in church. The Catholic church and the cemetery were slightly above the town."

"She was in church? Didn't it happen at midnight?" Sam said.

"It did," Jessica said. "She'd been there all day, holding vigil over her daughter's dead body."

"Fiona Clennan was already dead?" Cora said, trying to ferret the information out of the pages in front of her. They were a jumble of big headlines and little articles, followed by what looked like pages and pages of legal documents.

"Yep. Here's where it gets crazy. She was already dead because she was murdered earlier that day," Jessica said, "by her husband. According to Fiona's mother, Atticus Blackwell found his wife with another man. It seems Atticus Blackwell was a real bastard, and Fiona was planning to run away and make a new life with a new husband, one of the men who worked in the mine with her father. Fiona's lover made a run for it when they were discovered, but Fiona wasn't as lucky. Atticus caught her by her necklace on the way out the door. And strangled her with the chain."

"Holy shit," Sam whispered.

"Language," Jessica snapped. "Atticus Blackwell killed his wife, and then he went after her lover. Nobody in town would give him up or help Atticus find him, so Atticus got crazier and crazier with rage, and eventually snapped. He blew up his mine and took out the whole town to kill one man."

"This can't be true, can it?" Cora asked.

"Sounds like *Days of our Lives* nineteen hundred edition, doesn't it?" Jessica said. "I mean, Fiona Clennan's mother certainly believed that was what went down. Those pages, the ones in the front, they're where she went to newspapers and magazines and got them to print her version of the story, trying to bring attention to what Atticus Blackwell did. There were a few other survivors, but all they could say for sure is that Blackwell raged through the town before the mine went, looking for his wife's lover. Still, enough people believe that's what happened for it to be the ready explanation today. I mean, everybody who lives here has heard some version of it. It didn't come from nowhere."

"What happened to him?" Sam said. "To Atticus Blackwell."

Jessica picked up the books from the table and stacked them neatly. She turned and put them back on the shelf behind her before she answered. "Nothing."

"What do you mean nothing?" Cora's head was spinning.

"I mean nothing, nothing. Fiona Clennan's mother was a penniless Irish widow with nothing and no one left to back up her story about Atticus killing her daughter. There were a few witnesses that he'd been in town looking for her lover, but no one saw him actually blow up the mine. Atticus Blackwell walked away. He sold the land, moved to New York, got remarried years later, had another kid when he was like, sixty or something gross like that, and lived to the ripe old age of eighty-two. That second family, by the way, that's where Avery Benson came from."

"Was this everything you gave her?" Cora asked. "Did Avery Benson say anything about why she was looking for all this?"

Jessica shrugged. "Nope. I never even actually spoke to her. She emailed the historical society requesting any information I could find on the Blackwell family and the people who died in the mine disaster. I copied what I came across, googled the rest, and Sam's ex-girlfriend came and picked it up." Jessica turned to Sam. "That was awkward, by the way. But better than having to watch her lick her chops over Clay at every family function."

Sam looked red.

"And you didn't find anything about a necklace, did you?" Cora flipped through the photocopied pages.

"I mean, Fiona Clennan was strangled with one," Jessica said. "I wonder if it was the one in the wedding announcement."

Cora froze. "What?"

"Didn't you read it?" Jessica turned and pulled one of the books back down from the shelf and turned to the marked page. "In all the stuff about what everyone was wearing. I remembered it because it seemed a little gross. Here."

She spun the book around toward Cora, who leaned close to read the small print. "*The bride wore ivory satin trimmed with Battenberg lace in a flower and scroll motif, edged in watered green silk that complemented the bride's dark curls and mirrored the color of her groom's eyes. Orange blossoms and myrtle made up the bridal bouquet and the coronet. The wedding jewelry was a gift from the groom; bracelets of heirloom emeralds and a rich pendant with a double border of ruby and diamond, set with a finely woven band of the groom's hair suspended from a double length chain of intricate gold book link.*"

"Gross, right? I mean, people were into that stuff then, but still. Hair? And if Atticus killed her with it," Jessica said, "it was officially the world's shittiest wedding gift."

Cora looked at Sam. "It's what he was looking for."

"What?" Jessica said.

"Jacob Adler was looking for this necklace. This exact same one," Cora said. "He killed Avery Benson for it." She sat back in her chair. "He killed my sister because he thought I found it when I found Avery's body." This was all just too strange to believe. And so far in the past it was hard to imagine what it had to do with the here and now.

Rocky began barking. Jessica got up and looked out the window, to where the door of the yellow house was open again. She looked over at Cora. "Can I borrow your dog?"

"Jessica, no," Sam said.

"What?" Jessica said, heading for the foyer. "I thought I'd take him for a walk for you, see if he needed to use the bathroom. On Beecher's sidewalk."

Standing outside the front door, Rocky's hackles were raised, and he was tense and stiff legged. "See," Jessica said, "he knows there's a psychotic witch over there."

Cora thought the dog was looking down the street, rather than across. She patted his head. "Relax, buddy." He seemed to listen, circling around to push himself between her legs and Sam's. Too bad Cora couldn't relax. Her vision was suddenly foggy and there were telltale prickles building in her fingertips.

"Okay?" Sam asked, examining her. She shook her head. To her relief, the feelings had receded as quickly as they'd come. "Cora, I'll run you home quick so I can make it to work. Jess, I'll see you at the game, okay?"

"Bring the coffee. I'll bring the bourbon." She looked at Cora and shrugged. "High school sports. Nice to meet you."

Cora nodded absently, too much information floating around in her head. She was quiet while they loaded Rocky back into the truck and headed for the pawnshop.

"I'm sorry if I made you late," Cora said when they pulled up in front. She opened the door for Rocky. The dog got out more carefully than he used to, but without too much apparent pain, she was glad to see. He was tense again, though, intent on something she couldn't see.

"I'll be right on time." Sam spoke through the open truck window. "Make sure you lock up behind you, alright? Rocky seems a little edgy. You never know." She nodded. Sam looked at her a moment longer, then started to pull away.

"Sam, wait." He stopped, backed up the few feet he'd gained.

"What are you doing tomorrow?" she asked. "Other than going to a football game?"

He shook his head. "Nothing that I know of. I'm off tomorrow."

"There's someone I think I should talk to, if I can arrange it. Will you go with me?"

35

"I didn't expect to be coming up here again so soon," Sam said. "Or ever."

Sam had picked Cora up, right on time. She had an inkling he was always on time. He'd been surprised when she told him where they were headed, but it hadn't kept him from buckling his seatbelt and heading out of town.

"Maybe they won't let us in," he said, a little hopefully. "Unless you're betting on Sadie coming through again. I wouldn't."

"They're expecting us." Cora looked over her shoulder at Rocky, to make sure he wasn't making any of those lurching movements that were a sure sign of a vomit volcano about to erupt, though it would have been Sam's fault, for bringing another doggie donut. "I spoke to Robert for almost half an hour yesterday."

Sam raised an eyebrow. "Robert?"

"Robert Clivens, the resort guy. He's really not that bad. Little uptight, but I can see why, I guess. He's terrified Avery Benson's father is going to drag them through court and the whole place is going to go under and he and whole lot of other people are going to be out of a job. I don't know that it would be any help, but I told him I'd put in a good word."

Sam put on the blinker and slowed the truck before the turn onto Mountain Road, taking a moment to look at her and shake his head.

"What?" she said.

"Nothing. You're just such a surprise sometimes."

"Ugh. Sam, stop."

Sam pulled off into the gravel and put the truck in park. Cora flung open the door and slid out. It was happening, at the worst possible time and in the quick-hitting, full-bore sort of way it sometimes did, one that had gone from the usual fuzziness and ground-level tingling to blindness and scorched veins in an instant. If Sam thought she was a surprise a moment ago, she couldn't imagine what he thought now.

"Cora, wait. What's wrong?"

But she couldn't wait. Cora stumbled away from the truck. She heard the angry blare of a horn as she crossed Southside Road blindly, a passing car coming so close she felt the air as it sped by. She lost her footing in the opposite ditch, skidding down into the muddy bottom. When she got back up, she suddenly found her vision. Everything fell away, leaving her cold and breathless. Parting the drooping stalks of goldenrod, Cora reached down and picked up a pink plastic wallet with a rainbow on the side, the kind a little girl would carry.

"Are you okay? You missed being run over by a whisker." Sam crossed the road toward her. "What is that?" She handed him the wallet mutely and sat down on the edge of the ditch, feet in the soft brown earth, and put her head on her knees.

"No name on it. But there's a picture in here," Sam's voice sounded out softly. She felt him sit beside her and heard the squish of his boots on the wet ground. "Someone's lost wallet. Lost so there's no way you saw it from the truck. Cora, you can trust me, I swear it. How did you find this?"

The problem with lies and dissembling was that they took a lot of energy. Cora didn't have any left. She prayed that it wouldn't come back on him, knowing, but she was so tired of being alone with the weight of it all. Cora raised her head. "You've pretty much figured out Rocky's really not that great at finding things, right?"

He nodded, slight smile pulling at the corner of his lips. "Yeah, I'd guessed that. I dropped half his donut this morning and it rolled under the couch. I had to go get it for him."

Cora nodded. "I mean, it turns out he is actually amazing. And super smart. He did save my life, after all." She looked across the road. Rocky's head was visible through the back window, watching her intently. "I've screwed up plenty in my life, Sam. You can't even imagine. But adopting that dog, it was the best thing I ever did. Kimmy knew how great he is. I—" She shook her head. "Anyway, when it comes to finding things, Rocky can hardly locate his food dish without a road map. But me?"

She paused. Her mother had known, though Cora had tried to hide it from her as much as she could, to keep her from worrying any more than she already did. But Kimmy, she'd been the only one who ever *really* knew. Sam waited patiently, to his credit. He listened to her draw in a long breath before she finally spoke again. Then Cora told him everything.

He didn't interrupt, and she didn't look at him, speaking to the space between her shoes, one toe idly grinding the mud. When she finished, Cora crossed her arms and turned to see if he was laughing or getting ready to run away and call the straitjacket brigade.

"No shit?" Sam said.

"No shit."

"Cora, that's amazing. You can find, what, anything? It's like a superpower. Where did it come from?"

"It's not amazing, Sam. It's not a gift. It feels more like a damn curse. I don't know where it came from. I just know that some things *want* me to find them."

"How is that a curse? Those two kids would have died out in the woods if you hadn't found them. And those bones you found by Falls Creek, that man's family would have never known what happened to him. They might have searched forever. And you give people important things back, right?" The little pink wallet looked absurd in Sam's large hands. He unzipped it and took out the only thing inside, a single photograph. "Do you know who this is?" he asked, holding it out to Cora. She took the picture and stared at the figures. A little girl sat on the lap of a white-haired lady who was looking down at the tow-headed child like she was holding a fortune in her arms. Cora shook her head.

"No? I do. That"—he pointed to the old woman—"is Peggy Latimer. Works at the Feed and Seed. Or at least she used to. I'm pretty sure she died a couple months ago. So that little girl is probably her grand-daughter. And she's probably heartbroken, missing this. But now, you can find her and return it."

"Sounds perfect, doesn't it? But Sam, multiply this by a hundred, a thousand, all day every single day. And the process is the same, no matter what I find. Did you already forget the part where I walked in front of a moving vehicle? Did you miss the part where I told you about not being able to function because I spend half my time blind and feeling like my hands and feet are about to explode? Where I live now, I can't concentrate, I can barely sleep, because it's there all the time."

"Is it really as bad as all that?"

"It is, Sam, and it's been like this my whole life. Do you know why you don't remember me from school? It's not because I was a couple years younger than you. It's because three days a week I got shipped to the learning support program in North Branch. The other two I spent in the special education building. Calling it a building was a stretch. Don't tell me you don't remember that trailer with the handicapped ramp on the far side of the football stadium. Did you and your friends call it the retard trailer or the sped shed? Everybody else did."

"Cora, come on now, I—"

"Maybe you didn't. I mean, you don't seem like the type that would have called me terrible things to my face, but even if you had"—she shrugged angrily—"I was so gorked out on ADHD medication or pills for whatever they thought was wrong with me that week, I probably wouldn't have even noticed."

Her voice had gotten louder, quieting the chittering birds. She heard Rocky whine through the window, staring at her, worried.

"School was the worst place in the world for me, Sam. With so many people, so many things. I couldn't function. I just sat there day after day, not able to see clearly enough to read, feeling like my body was going to catch fire, or fumbling around like a damn zombie while people laughed at me. I'm not stupid, Sam. Once I could get away and go home or somewhere without everything dragging at me, I could do the work. But then they assumed I was cheating, or that Kimmy was doing my work at night. I dropped out when I was seventeen and got my GED from home. And even that was pointless. What kind of life is this ever going to let me have?"

Cora handed the photo back to Sam. He stared at it for a moment, then zipped it back in the plastic wallet and slipped it into his pocket. Cora swiped away a tear with her sleeve, but just one. That was enough. Self-pity was like quicksand. If she let herself get in too deep, she'd never get out.

Getting up, Cora dusted off the back of her pants. "Come on, we'd better go. He's waiting for us."

36

When they parked behind the moving truck, she could see the resort director standing at a distance. He nodded to Cora then turned, walking away from Avery Benson's chalet, back toward the big house. Cora motioned for Sam to stay with Rocky and turned her attention to a figure sitting in an Adirondack chair at the end of the dock. His broad back was to her, in front of him a lake as flat as glass, a ring of trees and tidy white buildings shown in perfect reverse on its mirror surface.

"Is this place really haunted?" His gravelly voice came when she stepped onto the edge of the dock. He continued without turning. "Are there really such things as ghosts?"

She looked up as a heron passed over, its reflection skating over the dark surface of the water. It dipped low to land. When its feet touched the surface, its mirror twin shattered, rippling outward in rings that shivered the trees and houses painted on the lake. "I don't believe in ghosts," Cora said, "but I do think this place is haunted."

Mr. Benson rose then, turning to Cora. "Yes, I think you're right. I think you're exactly right."

His face was unremarkable: wide, lantern-jawed, with thick dark brows threaded with gray and deep-set eyes. His most striking feature was maybe striking only to Cora, because she recognized it so readily. It was grief. The furrows carved into his forehead, the dark shadows in the hollows of the cheeks, and the emptiness in the eyes. She'd seen the look many times in the mirror.

"I'm very sorry for your loss, Mr. Benson," Cora said quietly.

"And I'm sorry for yours. Call me Reggie," he said. "Pull up a seat, young lady. Now what can I—" His voice closed off, and he swallowed loudly before he continued. "You reminded me of her there, for just a second. Not that you look anything alike, but you move like she does … did. Avery didn't so much sit down as she melted into a chair." Reggie looked back over the lake. It had gone still again, clouds like a herd of silent sheep drifting across its surface. "I see Avery everywhere, seems like. Whenever there's a woman with red in her hair, or a gangly little girl that's all scabs and elbows."

"Every time I see a woman dressed in white," Cora said, "for a second, I know it's going to be my sister. Or I hear just the right laugh. She had this giggle …"

"Then you know." Reggie looked over his shoulder, to where men in blue coveralls were carrying crates from the chalet to the moving truck. "They could have done all this without me, but I told myself I needed to see it, the last place she was. I walked over to the cemetery through the woods, to where you found her. Now that I've been, I find I don't want to be here any longer. So, no disrespect, dear, but you have until they put the last box in that truck to ask your questions."

Cora nodded. "You saw it then, the cemetery?" She waved a hand toward the east side of the lake, in the direction of the old plot. "Where she was found, there was a grave, someone named—"

"Fiona Clennan Blackwell. I knew of it even before—" He shook his head quickly, a little shake. "It was part of the reason Avery was here to begin with."

"She was looking into your family history, right? A genealogy."

Scrubbing a hand through his hair, Reggie let out a tired breath. "Well, not quite. She was pretty square on that part before she came. It was more about …" He looked off into the distance, past the lake and into the deep green of the pines. "My late wife's side of the family, the Blackwell side, they grew money like bread grows mold. Between their money and mine, well, Avery certainly didn't want for anything growing up." Reggie looked over at Cora. "She wasn't spoiled, I promise you. Not at all. She was kindhearted, and generous. If I gave her a twenty-dollar bill when she was a kid, she'd give it away to the first person who needed it more than she did. Of course, as she got older, the twenties turned into fifties, then hundreds, and then into charitable organizations and boards and funds for anything and everything."

His face dimmed, and a drift of clouds crossed the sun at the same moment, painting the lake black, turning the reflections in the water into dirty-handed smears. "She felt guilty about having so much, just by luck of the draw. Entitled. That was her word, not mine, mind you, but if you asked my daughter to describe herself, that's what she would have said."

Reggie sat back in his chair, the wood creaking softly. Somewhere across the lake a junco called to its mate, the eerie trill floating across the water. "My wife died when Avery was sixteen," he said. "Avery and I had gone to a movie. Noreen didn't want to see it. Too much violence, she claimed." Reggie looked skyward. "While we were gone, a man—barely a man. A kid—broke into the house. She tried to fight him off, but …" Reggie ran a hand through his mane of salt and pepper hair. "Noreen's father was still alive then. I wonder if he felt like this, losing a daughter. I don't think it's different when they're two or ten or fifty. But my wife's father, Sylvan Blackwell, he outlived her. It wasn't until last year that he died. Sylvan died and everything belonging to the Blackwells came to Avery. My daughter inherited money, property, jewelry, and a closet full of skeletons."

Cora heard Rocky snuffle and looked to where he sat in front of Sam, who was leaning patiently against the door of his truck. "Do you mind if my friend hears this?"

"Don't see why not. None of it's a state secret."

Cora waved Sam over. Sam carried an Adirondack chair onto the dock and placed it across from Cora and Reggie. He completed the little triangle, but his back was to the lake. *I couldn't sit that way*, Cora thought, looking over his shoulder at the water. With everything that must be beneath the lake, with the low, constant drone of lost things calling to her, whispering like restless spirits, it felt a little too much like a horror movie, where the killer would rise from the lake one last

186

time to drag the screaming victim into the water. The thought made her shiver, and she pulled her sweater more tightly across her chest.

"When the estate was settled," Reggie said, "and the final distributions were made, some of her grandfather's personal effects—heirlooms, old documents, things like that—they were sent to Avery. When she got around to looking at them, she was horrified."

Cora snuck a look at Sam. She had a good idea what Avery Benson had found.

"Her great-grandfather murdered his wife in cold blood and killed an entire town, almost to a person, and then walked away. He spent the next fifty years or so growing the family fortune and grinding anyone who came after him into the dirt. There were records going back as far as nineteen-ten of lawsuits brought by family members of the people drowned in this lake, people he'd wronged or abandoned or cheated, things like that. When he died, his son, Sylvan, my wife's father, picked up right where he left off. Avery absolutely adored Sylvan. For her to find out the grandfather she thought was so great used all his money and power to avoid paying out a single penny to any of Atticus's victims ..." Reggie shook his head sadly.

There was a clatter behind them, a heavy box being dragged over the sill of the chalet's front door. Reggie leaned back in his chair and watched two men carry it down the steps and up the metal ramp into the moving truck. The face that had been animated a moment ago turned to stone while he watched the last days of his daughter's life being packed into cardboard cartons.

Cora was on the verge of saying something to urge him to continue, when he shook his head, shaking off the memories like a dog shaking off water. "When Avery found out what she'd inherited, where it all came from, she was sick over it. I'll never forget it, that phone call. I thought someone had died. I rushed over to her place to find her sitting in the middle of all the papers that had been brought over after the estate settled, just absolutely broken. Scared the wits out of me."

"That's why she came here?" Cora asked.

Reggie nodded. "She wanted to know everything: who her great-grandfather had killed, who they'd left behind, how she could fix any of it. She wanted to see it firsthand, where it had all happened. I tried to talk her out of it, at first, convince her it wasn't her responsibility to make up for the past. Children aren't responsible for the sins of their fathers, and even if they were, she wasn't related to the Blackwells really, not technically. Noreen and I couldn't have a kid of our own." Reggie shook his head sadly. "As bullheaded as my daughter was, you never would have known she wasn't my blood. She was bent on it, so I gave up arguing and got everything set up for her, rented the place, shipped her things to this godforsaken backwater to make it feel like home for her. Now here I am ..." His voice grew thick. "Here I am, watching it go back out in boxes. I feel like I sent her here to die."

Cora looked away. She knew that agonizing feeling of grief mixed with guilt, stoked by anger. It was hot and painful, like a burning cinder in the stomach.

"I'm sorry," Reggie said a moment later, eyes red-rimmed but clear. "I don't think I can stand to be here any longer. I didn't know a place could hold so much God damned death."

He stood, Cora and Sam rising when he did. She didn't want to ask any more of the man, but now was the last chance she had. "Reggie, in the things Avery inherited, was there any jewelry?"

Reggie had taken a step forward, but he stopped. "There was a Rolex of her grandfather's that came down, some ruby bracelets, her great-grandfather's signet ring—hefty gold thing with an A for Atticus set in diamonds—and the necklace. That's what you really want to know about, right? The necklace Atticus Blackwell strangled his wife with."

He turned toward Cora, the look on his face sharp and angry. "I've held that cursed thing in my hand. Gold and diamonds, and a chain heavy as a hangman's noose. I wonder what kind of man kills his wife with something like that and then takes it off and puts it in his pocket to give to his next wife. The kind that kills a whole town for one man, I guess. I told Avery to throw the damn thing away. But she said it would be better to do what she could with it to right some of her family's wrongs. I don't know what she meant by that. I guess I never will."

He walked away, toward the moving truck, where a man was stretching tall to reach the handle of the overhead door to pull it shut. Reggie paused long enough to speak over his shoulder. "I don't know who would want it badly enough to kill for it, or why, and I don't know where it is. Maybe he has it, the man who murdered my daughter and your sister. Maybe it's lost forever. I hope it is. I hope it stays that way. But if it does turn up, do me a favor." Reggie turned to take one last look at Cora, standing on the dock. "If you find it, grind it to dust. Break it so small no one could ever put the pieces back together. Throw it in this godforsaken pit of a lake and let it sink back to where it belongs. That necklace has brought nothing but death."

37

"I guess that could have been worse." Sam looked in the rearview mirror, watching the gates to Blackwell recede behind them. "I mean, we know a little bit we didn't know before. The question about what necklace Jacob Adler was so hot to get his hands on was pretty much answered before, but now it's locked down. I still don't get why, though. I mean, it sounds like it might be worth something, diamonds and rubies and whatnot, but enough to kill for? Some of the other stuff he took was worth way more."

Cora leaned her head back and closed her eyes. She was trying to filter the new information, figure out what might be useful, but the blur and the buzz were distracting. She felt like there were things she should be connecting, things Jacob had said and things she'd seen and heard, but she wasn't quite able to bring the ends together, not here.

When she opened her eyes, Sam was looking at her. "You look a little fuzzed. You ... ah ... doing your thing?"

"Not really," she said. "Well, maybe just a little. It's not horrible, to where I'm going to jump out the window and go play in traffic, but it's annoying, like someone's running a chainsaw in the background. Makes it impossible to finish a thought." Cora lapsed back into silence. When they reached the turnoff onto the hard road, Sam signaled and turned right instead of left.

"Sam, wrong way. I really want to go back to the apartment and think about this."

"I'll take you home but give me a couple minutes first. I want to try something."

Shrugging, Cora looked over her shoulder to where Rocky sat, snout out the partially opened window. "Fine, but it's your upholstery."

A few minutes later, Sam pulled onto the side of the road. A cornfield cut close to the pavement on either side, trapping them between two high walls of green. He put the truck in park and got out.

"Come on." He opened Cora's door and motioned for her to slide down. "Humor me."

With a sigh, she got out. "Rocky, come on. I guess we're humoring people today."

She followed Sam down the narrow space between two rows. The corn was over their heads, the narrow rays of sun that fell between the leaves painting the ground in tiger stripes. A cold breeze blew the stalks against each other, filling the air with a papery whisper like the beating of insect wings.

A hundred yards in, Sam stopped abruptly and turned around.

"Okay, Sam," Cora said, speaking loudly to be heard above the rustle of the stalks. "What's this about?"

His eyes were serious, fixed on hers. He was so close she could see the grains of pollen that had settled like gold dust on his eyelashes. Sam reached out and took her hand. The sudden contact made her shiver. "Can you feel anything around," he said, "like when you found the watch or that little wallet?"

She tried to tug her hand away, but he held on, not painfully but firmly enough she could see the muscles like knotted cords in his forearm. Sam looked slight, but there was a subtle, wiry strength about him that wasn't obvious the way it had been with Jacob. Jacob. She twitched at the memory of her stupidity, and the last man who'd laid a hand on her. Cora tried again to pull away and turn back toward the road.

"Cora, no. Wait. Just give me a minute." Sam held on. "Please."

He pulled her toward him with a quick, hard tug, reaching out and ensnaring her other hand at the same time. Holding them both, he gave them a small, brisk shake. "What's here? What is there to find, Cora? There isn't much, is there?"

She froze, stopped struggling. "How would you know that?"

Sam shrugged, lessening the strength of his grip on her hands, though not releasing them. "Both times I saw it happen, it was like someone had plugged you into an outlet, like there was a current running under your skin. I swear I could smell it, coming off you like ozone."

"You think I smell? What the—"

"Cora." He shook her hands again, focusing her.

"What?"

"Close your eyes."

"What? No."

"I swear, I'm not going to club you over the head and run or anything. Close your eyes."

"Fine." Cora closed her eyes. She swayed slightly, when his hands let go of hers. *What's he doing? Is he going to kiss me? Wait, why would I think that? Do I want him to? What the—*

Then there was a whisper of warm fingers against her wrist. "Okay, open them."

She didn't open them immediately, because she didn't want him to somehow read her thoughts. Clearly, they'd been way off. Cora wasn't sure if she was glad or disappointed.

"You lost everything in the fire, didn't you, all but the clothes on your back, right?" Cora nodded, finally looking up. "Everything but this?" He was holding her silver bracelet, the one with the pendant she'd found in the river as a child. He'd unhooked it and stolen it from her wrist while her eyes had been closed. "I don't think I've ever seen you not wearing it. Must be important to you. Family heirloom?"

She reached out and tried to take it, but he held it out of her reach. "Sam, what the hell are you doing?"

"You find everyone else's things, Cora. Why is that, do you think?" Sam swung her bracelet back and forth in front of her like a hypnotist's pocket watch.

"Because I have really rotten luck, Sam. Give it back."

"You want to know why I think you find the things you do?"

"Because they're lost. Now give me back my bracelet."

"I don't think it's because they're lost." He stopped swinging the bracelet and clamped it tightly in his fist. "Or not just because of that. Plenty of stuff gets lost. There's a whole town under that lake up there. Shouldn't all that stuff have had you going haywire? What about the museum? Plenty of stuff in there belonged to somebody else. At least some of it has to have been lost to end up there. Shouldn't you have been losing your mind? But you weren't."

"It's not predictable, Sam. That's the problem. It's just random."

"Is it? I don't think so. I saw how hard it hit before you found the resort guy's watch. When I saw him again today, I thought to myself, it was almost like you could feel how bad he wanted it. Like in the very moment you were finding it, you could feel how bad he missed it."

Cora opened her mouth to protest but paused. She thought about the moments before she'd handed it back to the man. It was almost as if she'd felt it, his connection to the watch. His want. And was it the first time? What about when she'd returned Sam's compass? And before, when other things had found their way back to their original owners? What had she felt?

"I think it's because someone wants it." Sam spoke the words she couldn't quite pull together in her head. "I don't think it's about being lost. It's about being missed. Would you miss this?" He opened his hand to show her the bracelet that lay like a silver puddle in his palm.

"Stop it, Sam. Don't you dare. Don't you—"

His arm swung over his head, and she lurched forward, her hand reaching out ineffectively after the bracelet. Her vision clouded, her hands and feet exploding into an electric buzz, the hum filling her, surging through her veins. It pulled her … nowhere.

Sam was standing right in front of her, holding the bracelet he had pretended to throw. When she saw it still in his hand, everything fell away.

"That was a shitty thing to do, Sam Cooper." Cora reached to take her bracelet, but he held it out of reach. "What was that supposed to prove, anyway?" She glared at him. He at least had the decency to look sheepish.

"Listen, I'm sorry. That wasn't nice. But I never would have thrown it for real, not unless, well ..."

"Well, what?"

"Nothing, but you felt it, didn't you, for that moment you thought it was lost. I could see it. That means it's not so random after all. You can find your own stuff. And if you can learn to find your own stuff, who knows, maybe you can get a feel for it, learn to control it. Like building up a muscle or something."

"I don't know, Sam."

"You won't until you try. I really think there's a solution to this, but it might take some practice." He started to swing the bracelet on its chain.

"Sam, don't you dare. You said you wouldn't throw it for real."

"I said I wouldn't throw it for real unless."

The bracelet disappeared in a silver arc, swallowed by the cornfield. She didn't have time to give Sam a piece of her mind before her body forced her to follow.

38

"How long are you going to give me the cold shoulder for?" Sam let Rocky out in front of the pawnshop, then came around to open the door for Cora.

"You chucked what is literally the only thing I have left from my life into a cornfield. So forever, probably."

"Aw, come on, Cora. You found it." He grabbed her wrist and shook it, making the bracelet jingle. "I was testing a theory."

"And if you'd been wrong?"

"I would be out there all night with a metal detector. But I'm not, because it worked, didn't it?" He gave her a hopeful grin, one eyebrow raised. He looked like a little boy trying his best to talk himself out of trouble.

"I guess," Cora conceded. "Not that it does anybody any good." *That wasn't necessarily true*, she thought, as soon as the words came out of her mouth. In fact, it was *something*, wasn't it, after all these years, to find even a little rhyme or reason in what she could do. The first time Sam had really thrown her bracelet, sending it soaring into the field, she'd gone to it immediately. She could feel it there, over her shoulder, pulling her like it was attached to a string. And for the first time, Cora knew what she was going to find.

But that wasn't all, though she hadn't said as much to Sam. She couldn't be sure it was enough of a difference to mean anything, but when Sam tossed the bracelet for real before she could protest, she'd been ready to murder him, but she'd also been able to see him. She could feel it, down the long row of corn, and although her vision was still fuzzy, it wasn't entirely obscured the way it had been the first time. Her fingers and feet buzzed and crackled, but they hadn't burst into flames.

"I hope you realize how lucky you are that worked." Cora slid down out of the truck seat. "Because if it hadn't, you'd be buried out in that cornfield right now, and I certainly wouldn't help anybody find *you*." She gave him a scathing look. Or tried to. It didn't have much threat behind it. And anyway, all this, it was beside the point. "None of that got us any closer to finding out who Jacob Adler really is. Or where he is."

"I thought maybe if you could get used to finding your own stuff, or stuff you want to find, then maybe you could—"

"I can't find *him*," Cora said, "if that's what you're thinking. Not unless he's hiding across the street in the diner. One thing I do know is when I find things, they're never that far away from where I start feeling them. I'm strictly short range, I guess. The farthest I think it's ever really worked was when I found Avery Benson. And Jacob is on the other side of the country, if he has half a brain."

"That's not what I was thinking, that you should find him."

She looked up in surprise. "No?"

Sam walked to the door, waited while she dug the key to the outside door from her pocket and let Rocky in. Cora was happy to see him pad across the foyer and up the stairs with barely a limp. She leaned back against the brick wall, cold now that the sun had gone below the horizon. Sam came to stand in front of her.

He leaned closer, and for a moment, a part of her thought once again, *He's going to kiss me*. His lips parted, his head tilted forward, and his arms came to rest on the brick on either side of her. "The necklace," he said.

Cora closed her eyes briefly and felt like an idiot. Not wanting to look as stupid as she felt, Cora ducked out from under his arm and stepped inside the doorway.

"What about the necklace?" she said. Sam looked up the stairwell to where the dog was waiting, pacing the small landing in front of the apartment door. Sam ran his hand through his hair, took a deep breath before looking back at Cora.

"I wasn't thinking that you might be able to find Jacob. That's the last thing you should want. He's dangerous. But what if you could find the necklace?"

Cora felt a flare of heat rise in her chest. "I would have found it already, if I could, don't you think? I would have found it and handed it over to him to save my sister's life. All the places it supposedly was, at the graveyard, in Avery's house, I was there, and it wasn't, or at least it wasn't calling to me. Reggie assumed his daughter brought it with her, but that might not even be true. For all we know she put it in a safe deposit box or sold it or lost it between her car seats. Maybe it hasn't been here since Atticus Blackwell used it to strangle his wife. God, I wish they'd buried it with her."

She stopped to take a breath, shake away some of the bitterness that had risen in her throat. "Besides," she said more quietly. "What good would it do us? Before, maybe, but now …"

"We have no idea who Jacob Adler really is, or where he is," Sam said, "and nothing to go on. But we know what he wants, even if we don't know why." He reached up and ran his thumb down the knotted skin on the side of her head, where light, baby-fine hair had only just begun to cover the place where the bullet had dragged a narrow, angry path. "I hope he's given up. I hope he's far away. But there's no way to know. Which means you're in danger until he's caught, Cora."

His finger running across the scar made it twinge lightly, a reminder of just how dangerous Jacob Adler had been. Was. "You're in danger," Sam said. "You and anyone else he thinks might have anything to do with that damn necklace. And since nobody knows why he wants it so badly or where the hell it is, when's it going to end? When he screws up and gets caught? When he kills somebody else? When he decides to come back and make sure you don't have it after all? But if you found it and turned it over to the police, maybe they could use it to lure him in or something. If nothing else, it would get you out of the crosshairs, him knowing without a doubt that you don't have it because it's in an evidence locker somewhere."

She put her hand on his, where it rested against her head. "But I can't." She pulled his hand away, holding it for a moment before letting it go. "If I could have found it, Kimmy would still be alive."

Cora stepped inside, away from the windows of the diner and the drugstore across the street, out of sight of the law office and the dentist, the hodgepodge of square and rectangular windows in the stuffy little second and third floor apartments above them. They felt like eyes watching her.

Sam followed her in, shutting the street door behind them, closing them into the small foyer at the foot of the stairs. Rocky saw them come in and chuffed impatiently, eager for someone to let him at the food bowl on the other side of the door. "Do you think it might be past finding?" Sam asked.

"I do," Cora said. Sam leaned against the stair railing, looking up at the bare bulb in the fixture overhead. It flickered just slightly every few seconds. He pulled his sleeve down over his hand and reached up, turning it slightly until the bulb glowed without blinking. Sam: always fixing things, not able to rest until there was a solution. What did he do when he came across something that didn't have one?

39

" Jessica didn't tell you anything about what she found?" Cora asked for the third time. Sam shook his head, slowing the truck to wave to a man in overalls checking his mail, then continued up the dirt road.

"Nope. Like I said, she just called last night and said she found something interesting. I asked her what, and she said if she told me I'd blab to you and then I wouldn't be able to talk you into coming up to the house." Outside, a barn painted a red so bright it seemed alive in the midday sunshine flashed by, giving way to a field, the corn cut to nubbly stumps.

"Would you have blabbed?"

"Would you have come?"

Cora looked out the window. Not a chance. It would seem silly to Sam, but she was nervous heading toward Jessica's. With her, Sam's brother, and three boys, that meant five people and five people's worth of lost things, if not more, depending on who lived nearby. There might even be generations of things lying there, clamoring for Cora's attention. And it seemed to be worse when she was tired or stressed, and Cora was both. What little sleep she managed to snatch last night had been fitful, clouded with nightmares of Jacob Adler with a golden necklace like a lasso, trying to loop it around her neck, of Kimmy and Avery Benson cheering him on, running hand in hand behind them.

She'd awoken half blind, limbs tingling, like there was something nearby she desperately needed to find. Cora had lain there frozen until finally it faded away. Just the memory made her stomach squirm.

"Hey, you okay?" Sam reached out and grabbed her wrist gently. He kept it there until she nodded a moment later.

"Fine."

Sam gave her a sideways glance, then turned his eyes back to the road. The barn was far behind them now, a glowing red dot in the side mirror.

"You'll like Jess and Carder's boys," Sam said, slowing to let an oncoming car across a short, narrow bridge. He honked and waved as it went by, then took his turn. "They're like having a litter of puppies. Though once they get their hands on Rocky, you won't probably see any of them." Sam's eyes flicked to the back seat. The window was down, and Rocky's head was all the way out, his tongue lolling out the side of his mouth. The road canted left, into the cover of trees, and a dark shadow passed over the dog.

Cora managed a wan smile. It was easy for him to be relaxed. It was his family, and he wasn't likely to spend any of his day stumbling around blind. That would surely impress the kids. Yesterday was starting to seem like a fluke, everything returned now to the same senseless jumble of feelings it always had been.

"We're almost there," Sam said. "About half a mile."

They came out from under the cover of the trees, the day bright again, and made their way down a wide dirt road that rolled gently upward. "That's my second to oldest brother Denny's house." Sam pointed to a neat log cabin with a trampoline in the front yard and a fat yellow lab asleep on the front porch. Rocky woofed, getting a barrage of barks in return. "That's Winnie. Denny and MaryAnne have two boys. The house up there"—he pointed across the road to a driveway that wound around and out of sight. Cora could see just a bit of pointed roof poking up at the sky from behind a hill—"that's my mom and dad's house, the one I grew up in."

"You don't all live up here, do you?" Cora only ever had her mom and Kimmy. The three of them had been a little island. This was a whole continent.

"Not all of us. Clay and Virginia live on the other side of the hill past Carder and Jessica's, but Cash lives in Tunkhannock with his wife. They started out here but moved so their kids could go to the school district he teaches in. My other brother Kirk is in the navy. He's stationed in Guam right now, but he has a cabin here. Mom and Dad broke off a piece of land for each of us when we turned eighteen."

"You live up here too?" Cora looked around for another driveway or a house tucked between the hills and the fields where freshly cut timothy lay drying in snaking lines, waiting to be baled.

"On the other side of Jess and Carder's place." Sam pointed vaguely into the distance. "Here we are. Hold on."

There was a deep rut where the heavy rains had cut across the bottom of the driveway. They bounced up and down, Cora reaching a hand for the console between them and getting Sam's arm instead. "Sorry," he said, smiling over at her. They crested a small rise, and in front of them a neat split-level house with red shutters appeared, drowning in the center of a ring of chaos. There were bikes, soccer goals, a batting cage, and an endless number of balls of all shapes and sizes. Running through the chaos were two young boys.

When Sam stopped the truck in front of a set of redwood steps, the boys dropped the taped-up hockey sticks they were hitting balls with and came running.

"Uncle Sam, Uncle Sam," they yelled through the open window. They skidded to a halt when they saw Cora in the passenger seat. The older of the boys eyed her for a moment, then grinned mischievously. "Is this your girlfriend? Mom said you were bringing her up and not to act like hoodlums."

The boy waved at Cora, who found herself a little warmer than she'd been a moment ago. "Thomas," Sam said, "this is Cora. She's—"

"Is that your dog?" Thomas's head swiveled toward the back seat, where Rocky had chosen the perfect moment to poke his head out the window. "He's huge. Does he bite?"

"Only rude kids," Sam said. He started to open his door, when Rocky squeezed himself out the open window and leapt to the ground. Sam winced at the sound of dog nails scraping the paint on the way out. Cora felt bad about the paint but thrilled that Rocky hit the ground and took off to run circles around the two boys like he'd never taken a bullet to the shoulder.

"Saved by the dog," Sam said, coming around and opening her door.

"Thomas, Mason," Jessica bellowed out the screen door. "Pick up all these toys before your uncle and his friend get here or I swear to all that is holy I will …" She trailed off when she saw the truck in the drive and what probably looked like a black bear chasing her kids around the yard. "Of course, you're early. I was hoping to have time to do something about this dumpster fire before you showed up." She waved a hand around the yard. "Oh well, there goes passing for quality."

"Aw, Jess." Sam went up the steps, waving for Cora to follow. "You're married to my brother. There wasn't going to be any passing for quality."

A little shyly, Cora followed Sam inside. Fortunately, Jessica and Sam were chattering away happily, and it gave her a chance to hang back and take things in.

The inside of the house couldn't have been more different from the mayhem outside. It wasn't big; the living room the front door opened into was small and square, paneled in wood in an outdated, yellowy finish. But it was free of even a speck of dust, the wood oiled to a shine that picked up the sun through the lace-curtained windows and turned it a soft gold. The path across the living room was covered in a strip of clear plastic runner that reminded Cora of her Aunt Reva, the carpet on either side of it vacuumed into perfectly spaced swooshes.

"Come on in. Sit, sit." Jessica waved them into chairs at the kitchen table, the oak surface bare except for a neatly squared manila folder in the center. "Let me go threaten the boys' ability to sit so they get that yard picked up, then I'll show you what I found."

Jessica opened a door at the back of the kitchen. She stepped outside, and Cora could follow her progress along the side of the house toward the front, the top of her head and her bobbing ponytail just visible in front of the windows.

"Hard to believe she's got three boys running around here when everybody's home. Four, if you count my brother." Sam grinned at

Cora. "Which you should. You wouldn't know it from the yard, but Jessica runs a pretty tight ship."

Cora nodded. Sam went to look out the window over the sink, out the back toward the tree line. He turned when they heard Jessica come back in through the front. In the kitchen, she opened a cupboard, and there was a clink of glasses being taken down. "I was reading back through the stuff I found for Avery Benson, the stuff I showed you the other day, and something occurred to me. I did a little digging." Jessica put down the glasses and opened the fridge, turning back around with a pitcher of iced tea in each hand. "Sam, you get Splenda because you and every one of your brothers are working on a spare tire just like your dad's."

"I do not have a spare tire."

"I said working on it. But it's only a matter of time 'til somebody drops dead of a heart attack. You"—she gestured with one of the pitchers at Cora—"you can have real sugar. You could use a few pounds."

She turned to fill the glasses, and Sam rolled his eyes behind her back. Setting them on the table, she sat down next to Cora and pulled the folder over in front of her. "Okay, so here's what I found."

Jessica flipped the folder open.

"Jessica, what the hell? This is one sheet of paper printed out from Google."

Shrugging, Jessica picked up the paper. "So, sue me. I figured I'd never get you up here for something that could have been a text message. But it's still interesting. Listen." She stabbed a finger at the paper. "So, remember the article about the mine collapse, the one listing the names of the missing?"

Cora nodded. "The one Fiona Clennan wasn't on."

"That's the one," Jessica said. "Her mother wasn't on it either, because she was at the church. You know who else wasn't on there? Minnie Blackwell."

"Who?" Sam and Cora said in unison.

"Minnie Blackwell, as in the daughter of Fiona Clennan and Atticus Blackwell. The baby they had. Remember the birth announcement?"

"So?" Sam said. "I bet there were plenty of names missing from that list, especially kids."

"That's true, but I bet none of them have an obituary from nineteen seventy-eight." Jessica spun the sheet of paper around. "Take a look at this."

Sliding aside her glass, Cora pulled it closer and read aloud. *"Minnie Brisley, nee Blackwell, aged seventy, passed away peacefully at St. Ignatius Nursing Home on Wednesday, August the sixteenth, nineteen seventy-eight. She was preceded in death by her parents, Fiona and Atticus Blackwell, her husband, Richard Brisley and an infant son. Minnie Brisley is survived by her daughter, Penny (Brisley) Farraday of Germantown, Pennsylvania, and granddaughter Gina (Farraday) Marsden of Philadelphia. Funeral services will be held privately."*

"Do you think she really was their daughter?" Cora looked up at Jessica.

Jessica shrugged. "What are the chances there was another Fiona and Atticus Blackwell with a daughter born in nineteen oh eight? It has to be their daughter."

"You're right, Jess," Sam said. "This is one of those meetings that could have been an email. Or a text message. A really short one."

"Shut up and drink your tea, Sam, it's interesting."

"I wonder if—" Cora was cut off by a clatter at the front door, a noise that was half knocking, half someone letting themselves in without waiting for a reply.

"Jessie," a woman's voice called in. "Jessie, where are you? Charlie and I brought up some cookies for the boys. I brought some for Denny's boys too. MaryAnne said they were going to swing by. Is Sam here? I see his truck."

Cora turned to Sam, panic in her eyes.

"Come on, then," he whispered, grabbing her hand and pulling her out of her chair. "Let's make a run for it."

40

Sam pulled Cora toward the back door. Jessica rolled her eyes but opened it for them so they could slip out and down the back steps. "Quick," he said, after the door shut behind them, "let's get out of here before the whole pack descends."

They hurried across the backyard, toward the tree line where a footpath was cut through the thick stand of maples. They were running when they hit the trees, ducking out of sight when there came the sound of the back screen door opening. "Sam, where are you going?" a woman's voice called out. "Samuel Cooper, I saw you go out this door."

"My mom," Sam said in a laughing, exaggerated whisper. "Don't stop. If she gets her hooks in you, you're going to be spending the next ten hours looking at my baby pictures." Sam led Cora along the shaded path until they were out of sight and earshot. When they slowed to a walk, Sam kept hold of her hand.

"Where are we going?" Cora asked, the calluses on his palms rough against her skin.

"My place," he said.

"Wait, Rocky." Cora pulled against his hand, back the way they'd come. He tightened his grip and tugged her forward.

"He's fine. Let the boys wear him out a little. Let him wear *them* out. Jess will owe you one if they pass out over dinner later."

They walked up a gentle rise, her hand growing warm and damp in his. She was thinking about pulling away before Sam noticed, when he let go and pointed. "There it is. Not much to it, but it's nice and quiet."

It was an A-frame, more a cabin than a house. But it was trim and neat, the front covered with cedar shakes painted a gentle green that made it melt into the woods around it.

Inside it was tidy, and as rustic as she would have expected for a game warden. There were turkey fans and mounted horns on the wall—thankfully no taxidermied heads with their beady glass eyes— and a bear pelt on the floor in front of the couch. Sam flicked a switch, turning on the bulbs in a fixture made of deer antlers arranged in a circle. She raised an eyebrow, and he shrugged. "I find those things all day long on the game lands. I've got a pile about as big as you out back. I'm thinking about making these and selling them." Sam pulled open the door and let her out onto the deck. "Go on out. I'll be right back."

"You're right. It's so quiet," she said when Sam came out. He held out one of the bottles he had in each hand, and she took it, then turned to look across the clearing behind the house. It was more than quiet, really. It was peaceful in a way places rarely were for Cora; in her fingertips, in the corner of her eye, there was nothing. The feeling of lost things was the faintest hum, the feeling of electricity far away and low, like the rumble of a distant thunderstorm.

"Where are we?" she asked. "I feel all turned around. Usually, I've a good sense of where I am, but here ..."

Sam took a drink from his beer and pointed over his head, behind them. "That's north. Not much that way besides my family's places until you get down off the mountain into Canton." He swiveled his arm. "West is Pine Gap. We came up that side of the mountain. That way—" He stuck his arm out the opposite direction, across Cora, brushing her chest. She saw him redden as he twitched it away. "Sorry. That way is section twelve of the game lands. Section twenty is beyond that."

Cora took a second to orient herself. "Then the lake is there somewhere." She pointed dead ahead, across the green disc of yard, toward the belt of pines. "And Blackwell Cemetery has to be over there somewhere."

He nodded. "Maybe a mile to the lake, a little less to the cemetery.

Not that you'd want to go to either from this direction. Nothing but woods."

She stared ahead into the dense green forest. "No matter where I go, seems like I always circle around and find myself at that place."

"Well, finding is what you do, right?"

"Right," she said, unenthusiastically.

"Have you thought about it anymore? Or practiced?" Sam gave her a hopeful look. Cora turned away. He put a hand on her shoulder, but she slipped out from under it. "What is it?"

"Being able to find my bracelet, it doesn't mean anything."

"I don't know, it seemed like—"

"Sam. I can't." The words came out with a sharp edge to them. She didn't turn around, didn't move to face him. Eventually she heard the groan of a chair as he sat down.

She hadn't meant to bark at him, but he didn't understand. Cora *had* tried. After he dropped her off, she'd repeated the experiment down in the empty pawnshop, tossing her bracelet, eyes closed, feeling it pull. When that got too easy, she'd moved on, out to the sidewalk, recruiting Rocky to help. She looped it around his collar and sent him off, told him to hide. Cora found she could feel it when he was out of sight, almost see him with it when he loped around the corner onto Union Street.

Finding it got easier every time, though once she had a breathless moment, when the dog had gone nearly to her old street and the feeling had faded away completely. It clearly still had a range. But she could do it, had been able to find something with intention, not once, not twice, but a dozen times. And the side effects had lessened with repetition. The blur in her eyes was no worse than blinking away a tear, the tingle a gentle pull when she was focused on something *she* was missing, something *she* needed. It hadn't been just a fluke. Cora had felt triumphant, thrilled with the development. But then …

"Cora, if it doesn't work, it doesn't work." She heard him set down his bottle and get up from his chair. "There's nothing wrong with that. I shouldn't have even hauled you out to that field and made you try. It's just me not being able to leave well enough alone." He took her by the hand and pulled her around to face him. Cora swiped at the hot tears running down her cheeks.

"Don't cry, Cora. It's nothing. Who cares if you can't make it work for you? Don't be upset. If it doesn't—"

"It does," she choked out. "It does work. I *can* control it."

His eyebrows furrowed. "Isn't that a good thing?"

She shook her head, felt a stray tear fall from her chin. "One of the last things Kimmy said to me was that I used it as an excuse. Now I know she was right." Cora pulled her hand free and wiped her eyes with her sleeve. "I've been crippled by this my whole life. I just accepted that it was who I was. I felt sorry for myself. I can't even stand myself, thinking about it. Sam, I never really tried." Cora let her arms fall limply to her sides, all the anger bled out of her. "Then, in one day—not even a day—in a couple hours, I managed to get a handle on it. In a week, a month, who knows? Maybe I can figure out how to make it all work. Do you know what that means?"

She looked up at him, eyes blurry with tears. He shook his head. "It means I had a choice. I didn't have to find the things I've found. I didn't have to go into that cemetery and find Avery Benson. I got my sister killed, because I never tried. I just accepted I couldn't control what was happening to me, and all this time, that was bullshit. Because of that, my sister is dead."

Cora looked out into the band of trees, at the dark ring around the lighter green of the grass. The changing angle of the sun shifted the shadows, making the view less a bowl of soft green and more menacing. The trunks of the trees with the black spaces between were like teeth, a wide hungry mouth waiting to swallow her. "Do you see? If I can control it now, I could have controlled it then. That makes me culpable. It makes me responsible."

"Cora, no," Sam said. He grabbed her by the shoulders and gave her a gentle shake. "That's not true and you know it. Jacob Adler killed your sister. Kimmy just ended up in his path. You ended up in his path. That doesn't make it your fault."

"I wish I could believe that, Sam."

"You should. It's the truth." He let go of her arms and pulled the sides of her sweater together. She shuddered at the warmth against the chill fall breeze swirling around them. "Cora, when they find him, and they find out why he did it, why he was after Avery Benson, you'll see it had nothing to do with you and that there wasn't anything you could have done to change it."

"*When* they find him," she said flatly. "You mean *if* they find him. I thought it was ridiculous, that I might be able to find things on command. I used to joke about it. But now, I'd give anything to get Jacob Adler close enough to get a bead on. If I thought he'd fall for it, I'd take out a billboard yelling I've got his damn necklace and to come and get it. Just to get him close enough to ..." Cora trailed off, went still. Was that such a bad idea?

"Cora?" Sam's hands went back to her shoulders.

"Sam, why not?" Cora said, running through the possibility in her head. "I could lure him here. If he's still looking for the necklace, and I did a fake listing or something, put it up on eBay or the lost and found. He'd come back and get close enough for me to sense and then—"

"Absolutely not. What the hell, Cora. No." Sam's words came out short and sharp, fierce in a way she'd never heard before. His hands tightened on the lapels of her sweater, and he pulled her closer with it. "Are you crazy? You want to invite a murderer back into town on the off chance you'll be able to see him coming with the card trick you learned yesterday? No way."

"Sam, I—"

"No. End of story. You'll get yourself killed. This is not a game. Jacob Adler murdered Avery Benson with his bare hands. He murdered your sister, Cora. He almost killed you. Do you want to risk your life again on the chance you might be able to sense him coming?"

"I just thought—"

"Cora, no."

"Let me go, Sam." She tried to twist out of his grip, but he held on. "What do you care?" She'd been cold a moment ago, but anger was starting to burn in the middle of her, a flush rising up her neck, angry tears forming in her eyes. She refused to look at him, tried to pull away, until she felt his hand on her chin, pushing it up, making her face him.

"What do I care?" he said. "If anything happened to you, I …" He trailed off, looking at her instead. He took his hand from her chin and used his thumb to wipe a tear away from her cheek. "Cora, promise me you won't do anything to make him come back here. It would never work anyway. Think about it. A man smart enough to avoid every camera in town and not leave a fingerprint isn't going to fall for something like that without any proof. And it's unnecessary, anyway. So, promise me you won't. Cora, promise me."

He stared at her intently as he spoke, one hand against her cheek, the other holding her there, keeping her from turning away. She didn't want to promise, but if he leaned in and kissed her, she realized she would.

Sam leaned forward, his lips brushing hers, hesitantly at first, like he expected her to pull away. When she didn't, when she parted her lips, let herself be pulled against him, against the warm hardness of his chest, his kisses grew more intense. For a perfect moment the feeling overthrew everything else, the only thrumming the feeling of her heart pounding inside her chest, the only electricity where her skin touched his. Too soon he pulled away, leaned back to look at her.

"Cora, promise me."

"I promise."

41

"You sure you don't want to come with me? Might be fun." Sam waited for Cora to unlock the door and step inside the apartment's foyer.

"Absolutely one hundred percent, no," she said. "I didn't go to high school sporting events when I was in high school. I'm definitely not going to start now." Even if he could have promised her there wouldn't be a single missing thing around for ten square miles, even if she had total control over her ability, she still would have said no. Cora didn't like crowds, and she imagined there would be a lot of Coopers in this one. Cora definitely wasn't ready to face that.

"I could skip it," he said. "It's not like there won't be another one next week." Sam leaned against the door frame. "I know Rocky is dying to spend some quality time with me." The dog snuffled in irritation at the top of the stairs, making it clear he couldn't care less about anything but dinner.

"No, you should go. Jessica would give you hell if you don't. I'd hate to be responsible for that. I'm just going to feed Rocky and walk him quick. Then I'm going to go to bed."

Sam looked like he was going to say something else. If he offered again to stay, she might take him up on it. But then what? Cora's face went warm. Then he looked at his watch. "I guess I'd better, then." He looked up at Cora, uncertain smile on his face. "Tomorrow … are you busy?"

Cora snorted. "Terribly."

"Dinner, maybe?" Sam asked. She nodded. He reached out and

pulled her close, hands tight around her waist. She wasn't sure where things were going. Or if they were going, but it was nice to not feel like a fool every time he came close, wondering if she was reading things completely wrong.

She pulled away reluctantly when Rocky yipped impatiently. "Fine, dog. I hear you."

Sam paused in the doorway. "Lock it, right?" She nodded. Then he was gone.

"Thanks a bunch," Cora said, letting Rocky into the apartment. She closed and locked the door, filled his food bowl, then sank down onto the squat, sprung couch, the old vinyl cushions letting out a squeak and a sigh. "You could have gone another couple minutes without a meal, you know." Rocky picked his nose up from his already empty bowl and looked at her. "Oh, come on, you know I don't mean it. Get over here."

Rocky came and put his front legs on the cushion beside her, then leaned over and butted her in the chest with his head. "I said I didn't mean it." He hopped back down and trotted over to the door, then stood on his hind legs and snatched his leash from the hook.

"Yes, yes, you are in charge. You saved my life, and now you are the master. I see you're ready for your walk, milord."

Pulling on a jacket, Cora jammed the leash in her pocket. Outside, the faint, far-off clink of plates behind the glass windows of the Divine Diner and the sound of the jukebox down at P.J.'s floated in the air, fading away as she neared the blinking light before the turn onto Union. There was the ever-present feeling of lost things, a buzz and hum and a fuzz in her peripheral vision, but it was faint and indistinct. Cora couldn't put it all away; she had a feeling that it would always be there, even if she could learn to manage the worst of it. But now, when Rocky turned the corner ahead of her, she thought she could feel him there, out of sight but within her ability to find. She *was* finding a balance with it, she thought. It was a terrible see-saw feeling, that knowledge. That after all these years she might be able to control her demons, manage what she'd always believed unmanageable. But if she'd done it sooner, tried harder, tried at all, everything would be different.

When she turned the corner, Rocky was waiting for her. He stayed by her side as they walked the dark stretch of road toward her old street. The air was cold and crisp, but Cora was too busy sorting through the jumble inside her head to give it much notice. She thought about Sam and the light, warm happiness attached to the memory of the afternoon. It probably didn't mean anything. Maybe it had even been calculated, to elicit a promise from Cora. But her sister would have liked the development in any case, had maybe even anticipated it. Kimmy. The thought was heavy, wiping the film of happiness from the day, dragging it away with the fading light.

When she turned onto her old street, her thoughts turned to Jacob Adler. What poison lived inside a person that allowed them to kill and then kill again without a moment's thought? Was it bred into the bone? Was it made? Who was he? *Where* was he?

Rocky trotted ahead, down the familiar crumbling sidewalk. There was still a watercolor line of orange daylight over the rooftops, but it was dark in the blue and white trailer where Marla Tiddles slept a glazed, intoxicated sleep. Mr. Debusher's house was dark as well, where the old man kept old man's hours, alone in a bed where one side had been cold and empty for a decade. Darkest of all was the empty hole where Cora's house had stood.

It was a flat stretch of dirt now, filled in, smoothed over, black as a pool of ink in the failing light. Gone forever, and for what? A deranged man's fantasy? A piece of jewelry, a deadly necklace on a long gold chain, probably lost forever?

Abruptly, Cora's vision went blurry. *So much for control and balance,* she thought. *So much for working around it.* The tingle in her extremities was a warm flush threatening to turn into a painful burn. In a practiced motion, Cora swiveled her head until her vision cleared. When it settled into a tunnel to her right, she saw Rocky, and behind him, the torn-up space where the remnants of her fence had been removed to make way for the heavy equipment that had leveled the remains of her house.

She closed her eyes, took a deep breath, and then opened them. A few steps took her to the corner of the yard where Rocky buried his treasures. The dog followed her to sniff at the ground in front of Cora when she crouched down over the dirt. "What did you bury here, buddy, that's giving me grief all of a sudden?" Maybe something belonging to one of the neighbors, something they were remembering in their dreams so that it called for Cora to find it. "Are Mr. Debusher's dentures in here, huh? Or maybe it's you," she said to the dog. "Are you missing some old chew toy?"

Rocky cocked his head, then went to circle the yard, nosing around the newly flattened space. Nothing of interest to him here. But Cora could still feel it, a hot, insistent pull beneath her. She shook out her numb fingers and sank them into the dirt.

It was packed down and heavy with clay. Cora had to dig into it with both hands. She could feel it tearing away at her fingernails. The first layer she scraped away turned up a knot of old rope. She threw it aside. Next came a man's work glove. Then one of her sneakers, toe chewed away. "I knew you took that," she grumbled. But none of the objects quenched the burning feeling or cleared the fog that descended if she turned her eyes away from the growing hole. She clawed away another handful of dirt, and all at once, everything fell away. Cora shivered, suddenly freezing.

It felt soft, rotten at first, and she cringed away from it. She reached into the hole again and gingerly pulled the sodden bundle from the ground. It was heavy, brown and lumpen, like an apple gone soft, only the core still solid.

Rocky came over, suddenly interested, eyeing the object in her hand.

"No, Rocky." He nipped it away, carrying it in his teeth. "Put it down."

She recognized it then, seeing him standing stiff legged, the brown object between his teeth. A burl or tree nut or bit of wood. She hadn't been able to get him to drop it before. Neither had Sam, nor his deputy, when Rocky picked it up in the cemetery the day she'd found Avery Benson's body.

Her stomach twisted, cold and tight, a fist squeezing her from the inside. "Rocky. Drop it," she whispered. He let it go, and it fell to the ground.

Cora groped a hand forward for it. From being under the ground, from all the rain and the water used to extinguish the fire, the fabric was rotten. It fell apart in her hands when she pulled open the mouth of the stained velvet jewelry pouch. The contents slithered out onto the ground.

Gleaming dully in the last of the day's light was a long, heavy chain of gold links fixed to a square pendant with a double border of rubies and diamond around a pane of glass that protected a bit of braided hair.

42

She laid it out, nudged the chain into a circle with her sleeve. It was
long enough to snake around the edge of the small table in the apartment. It was long enough to loop two or three times around a woman's
slender neck with enough left over to be gathered up by strong, angry
hands and pulled tightly, the links heavy enough to withstand the
force it took to choke away Fiona Clennan's life.

Cora leaned back in the chair and stared at it. The chain passed
through a round gold bail from which hung the heavy, square pendant.
Ruby cabochons made up the outside border, dark as drops of blood in
the weak light of the bulb overhead. Inside this outer border was a row
of round diamonds big as pencil erasers. They were set tightly around
the square face of the pendant. She would have mistaken it for fine
wire or silk thread, the intricately braided panel, if she hadn't known
the spun gold strands were Atticus Blackwell's hair, sealed under the
bit of clouded glass as a gift for his young bride.

Sliding the phone from her pocket, Cora dialed. Sam picked up after
the second ring. "Hello." She could hear the crowd in the background,
cheering, yelling, the distant blat of a tuba. "Cora, hello." There was a
clanking of feet against aluminum. A moment later, the noise subsided.
"You still there?"

"I'm here. Listen, I—" Her first thought once she was back in the
apartment and safe behind the locked door had been to call him. But
now that she had, something occurred to her.

"Hello. You there?"

"Yeah, sorry."

"Is everything okay?" There was a roar in the background, muffled cheering. "Is something wrong. Do you want me to—"

"No, no, sorry. I just called to tell you I'm in for the night. That's all."

There was a moment of quiet. "Good. I'm glad you called. Listen, this will be over in another half hour. Do you want me to stop by? I can grab something on the way back. Late dinner, six-pack maybe."

Cora examined the necklace laid out in front of her. She reached out and pulled down the window shade, closing it and herself away from the world. "I'm actually pretty tired. I'm going to go to bed. I'll see you tomorrow. Good night, Sam." She ended the call before he could say anything else. Then she held down the button, turning the phone off.

She didn't like touching it, the necklace. Though it had been more than a hundred years since it had taken Fiona Clennan's life, it seemed like a poisonous thing, and Cora didn't want it against her skin. Pulling her shirt sleeve down over her fingers, she picked up the pendant with her cuff. Tipping it back and forth, she examined the sparkling cut diamonds, the bulbous faces of the polished rubies, the basket-woven face of braided hair. Holding it in her hand, Cora had an idea this necklace was as much to blame for drawing her to the cemetery as Avery Benson's body, before Rocky carried it down and buried it where all of them had walked past it a hundred times.

If she told Sam she'd found the necklace, he would call the police. Cora had no doubt about that. That's what a reasonable person would do. They would call the police, who would come and collect it as evidence. But what would *they* do with it?

Would they be willing to use it to try to lure Jacob Adler in? Doubtful. Would it be bagged and tagged and locked away forever? Would it be quietly released to Avery Benson's next of kin, to Reggie, who would destroy it? What seemed most likely was that it would never see the light of day again. And neither would Jacob Adler. With nothing to draw him out, he would go on living, unpunished. Maybe go on killing.

Not an hour ago, Cora had made a promise. She'd sworn, her lips against Sam's, that she wouldn't do anything to bring Jacob there. Sitting here, the necklace spread out in front of her, she felt the promise bending, beginning to crack.

Why had she promised anyway? Because Sam was afraid she'd get hurt. Cora found she didn't care if *she* got hurt. And Sam, Rocky, everyone would be safer if Jacob Adler was behind bars.

Cora got up from the table. Rocky started to follow her, but she shoved him back into the apartment with her knee. "I'll be right back, boy. I'm just going downstairs."

The lockbox under the register opened with Harold's fingerprints or the little barrel key on the ring with the rest of the store keys he'd left with Cora for safekeeping. She opened the box and reached in, carefully pulling out the handgun he kept there for protection. She didn't have to thumb forward the lever and drop the clip to know it was full. The weight in her hand told her plenty. She carefully pulled the slide back to make sure there wasn't one in the chamber, then locked the box back up. Stopping only to borrow Harold's laptop from the office, Cora headed back upstairs.

Cora turned her phone back on just long enough to take a picture of the necklace laid out on her table, then turned it back off. She opened the laptop and began to type.

43

Cora knew she was dreaming. The light above her was too golden, the ground below her too tremulous to be real. And the colors were too bright. Avery Benson's hair was redder than it had been in life, redder even than the rubies around the border of the necklace, as crimson and saturated as if the strands had been dyed with blood. She was alive again, which was another sure sign this was a dream; her eyes were wide open, the same shade of seawater green as Jacob Adler's. Avery had Kimmy's hand clasped in hers. Seeing her sister, alive and smiling, Cora's heart was squeezed by an invisible fist. It seemed a heart could feel pain even in a dream.

They swung their hands back and forth like sisters, Kimmy and Avery, whispering to each other, sharing secrets. Cora leaned closer, but she couldn't hear what they were saying, because they spoke behind the ripples of some shimmering membrane that deadened the sound and caused their figures to waver and bend like children in a funhouse mirror.

Finally, they noticed Cora and waved to her. *Come through, come through.* Their lips shaped the words in unison. Cora stepped toward them, and all at once the world shifted on its axis. Instead of standing in front of them, she was looking down to where they floated just under the surface of the water. Behind them Cora could see the faint, shadowy outlines of a sunken town. Again, they beckoned for her to come, come with them, come to Blackwell. There wasn't any need to feel so alone. There were so many people there, under the lake.

She shook her head. She couldn't. It was too cold. Too dark. Cora was afraid. When she tried to step back, Kimmy reached for her. Her sister's hand broke through the surface of the lake, shedding its skin as it passed through, fingernails and flesh sloughing away as they met the air, until it was a skeleton's hand grabbing Cora's ankle. They pulled her under, Kimmy and Avery Benson, both of them fleshless now, raw figures of matted hair and articulated bone. The water filled Cora's lungs, icy and foul and black.

Cora bolted upright, choking. Rocky lifted his head from his paws to examine her, watching her gasp for breath with one black marble eye from the other side of the bed.

When her heart had stopped hammering, she picked up the phone and flipped it over, staring at the blank, powered-off screen. It had seemed like the only way forward, to use the necklace to flush Jacob Adler out. Even in the light of day, Cora didn't think it was a *terrible* plan, but it was possible she should have spent a little more time working out the details. And not telling Sam, promising him and then lying to him; that part was a mistake. She would have to tell him.

Rocky paced the small apartment restlessly with his leash in his mouth while she got dressed, knocking the underside of the table with his back and rattling the laptop. "Come on, boy, we'll take a walk and then we'll go find Sam."

Cora pulled on a coat and a knit cap and threw the strap of her new bag over her shoulder, then fussed with it, cursing the stiff, unfamiliar fabric. Running her hand through the contents, her fingers brushed the handgun she'd taken from Harold's safe.

Halfway out the door, she stopped. The necklace lay where she'd left it last night, spread out on the table. She opened the flap of her bag again and nudged it off the edge of the table, letting it slither inside.

Stepping out onto the sidewalk, Cora shivered and buttoned her jacket up under her neck. Rocky stayed glued to her leg as they made their way toward the west end of the street where a busy night at the diner had forced her to park. He paced anxiously when she stopped in front of one of the planters of dead petunias that lined Church Street and pushed aside the rotting plants to pull out a man's wallet. It had been calling out to her weakly and she'd gone to it almost without realizing what she was doing. Her mind was too busy elsewhere to even register the pull toward the wallet. Cora had been focused on examining every face on the street. It was like when she was a child and had stared at each person that passed by, looking for a bit of herself, wondering if one of them was the parent that abandoned her, a sibling she'd never know, looking for the right hair color or eyes or the right nose. Except now, in every face she was searching for Jacob Adler.

She pulled out the phone and powered it on while Rocky clambered into the truck. Her call to Sam went immediately to voicemail.

Cora drove slowly out of town, trying Sam once more and getting his voicemail again. When she reached the turn onto Southside Road she paused in the empty intersection, staring down the road ahead. What if she just kept going? Cora had never been away from home. Now, there wasn't a home to be away from. She could keep driving. For once in her life, she had more than enough money. It was a cruel joke that it had come from losing things rather than finding them. The insurance from losing the house. All the money in the bank waiting for a check that would never be cashed because she'd lost Kimmy.

There was a flash in the rearview mirror, a vehicle approaching in the distance. Cora toed the gas pedal and eased across the intersection, babying the engine that would protest loudly if she pushed it up to speed too quickly. The car was coming up fast, not stopping at the intersection, only slowing slightly, then shooting across. She goosed the truck further, earning a loud grumble and a little speed in return. The car was still coming, flying up behind her. As it drew closer, she saw it was a large SUV, painted green and tan.

"Shit," she gasped, driving her foot to the floor. Rocky scrabbled for purchase as the truck lurched forward. "It can't be."

The truck struggled to build up speed, gaining a little, but even pushed to the limit, it would never outpace the SUV. How was it possible? It was too soon. How was Jacob Adler already behind her, following her?

She reached blindly for her phone, fumbled it, sent it skittering across the seat and to the floor beside her feet. She took one hand off the wheel and reached for it, but a blast from the SUV's horn jerked her upright again.

It was close now, just feet behind her. The sun reflecting off the SUV's windshield was blinding, obscuring her vision. She looked ahead, but there was nothing but a straight tunnel of road pinned between high rows of corn on each side. There wasn't a turn for miles, not one that led to people and safety. All that was behind her. If she tried to stop and turn around, she'd be crushed from behind or caught trying to get the clumsy truck pointed the other direction. No matter what she did, he would be on her the minute she let off the gas.

He was so close now, on her bumper, sun shining off his windshield and hiding his figure behind the wheel. His horn screamed again, making her jump and jerk the wheel, swerving across the center line. She pumped the already buried gas pedal, but it did no good. The SUV rode her bumper, the horn sounding out.

Cora took one white-knuckled hand off the wheel and fumbled for her bag, feeling for the gun. She pulled it into her lap. "Rocky, no, get down." The dog had turned, looking out the back at the vehicle behind them with a strange coolness. She wished she could summon up something like it. All Cora felt was wild, unrelenting terror. The horn behind her screamed a long, unbroken scream.

44

Her heart was pounding so hard and fast as she silently urged on the struggling truck that the sound of rushing blood inside her head drowned out everything else. She didn't hear the phone ringing but saw it flashing beside the foot she had jammed onto the gas pedal. Sam's name scrolled across the screen.

She took one hand off the wheel and reached, fumbling it. Glancing back at the road, she reached again and came up with the phone. "Sam! Sam, help! He's behind me. Jacob is here, he's—"

"Cora, it's me," Sam shouted. "Slow down. It's me. I'm behind you."

"No, it's him. It's Avery Benson's car. He's—"

"I swear to you, it's me. Slow down."

The vehicle behind her slowed, creating some distance between them. At the same time, the sun receded and the blinding glare fell away from the windshield. Cora slammed on the brakes and the truck shuddered to a halt, grinding into the gravel on the side of the road.

"What the hell, Cora?" Sam was out of his green and tan Game Commission SUV and at her window in an instant. She turned to slide out, still holding on to the steering wheel to steady herself. She was so relieved to see Sam and not Jacob Adler in Avery Benson's stolen vehicle that her knees didn't want to work.

"Sam," she managed to get out, holding on to the wheel a moment longer before taking a step forward. "I thought it was him. I thought it was Jacob. Sam, I tried to call you. Your phone has been off all—"

"It wasn't off. I've been out in section twelve, with no service. Then

I get back in range and see this." He shoved his phone in front of her face. It took her a moment to focus on the tiny print on the moving screen. The listing for the necklace on the lost and found site.

"Cora, what were you thinking?" His face was hard and tight with anger. "Did you think I wouldn't see this?" He waved the phone angrily in front of her face. "You *know* every one of these postings comes across my desk."

She shrank back toward the truck, finding Rocky standing in the open door behind her. He was rigid and alert, rumbling against her, on edge from the tone of Sam's voice. He let out a low snarl.

"You wouldn't dare," Sam said, though he took a step back, in case Rocky did dare. When he spoke again, his tone was still angry but more measured.

"Cora, you promised me." He glared at her, and she swallowed guiltily, looking across the road to avoid his eyes. "You *promised* me. Where the hell did you get it, anyway? Were you lying about the necklace too? Damn it, Cora, he killed two people for this. Your sister. He tried to kill you. Do you think he won't kill you now that he knows you found it? Or did you have this all along?"

"Do you really think that?" she shot back, finding her voice, and finding it angry. "Do you really think I would have let him kill my sister to keep a piece of stupid jewelry? I found it last night. Rocky had carried it home from the cemetery. You know that piece of wood he wouldn't give up? Well, it wasn't a piece of wood. It was the necklace. He buried it in the yard. It was there this whole time."

She fumbled around in her bag, pulling out the necklace on its long chain. She shoved it at Sam. He gripped it in his palm, staring at it in disbelief. Then he shoved it into his coat pocket with disgust.

"You promised me, Cora." Sam leaned forward, ignoring Rocky's growl. She didn't think he'd really bite Sam, but she didn't tell him to back off, either. "You promised me, and then you went ahead and did it anyway. This isn't some game, Cora. This isn't a movie." He grabbed the frame of the open door beside her head, tendons strained across his large fist. "This was a stupid, stupid move. Stupid and dangerous."

"Dangerous," she snarled. "Who does it put in danger? Me? I don't care. And anyway, did you read the listing? I didn't put that it was me. I used an email I made last night. There's nothing else. If Jacob finds it and makes contact, then I'll set up a meeting and call the police. It's a good plan." She leaned back, raising her chin. It had sounded like a good enough plan in her head last night, though she couldn't deny it sounded a little thin this morning.

"It's a great plan if you assume Jacob Adler is a sane person," Sam shot back. "A guy that murdered two people for the damn thing isn't going to bother sending an email and setting up a meeting, because he's not going to believe for a second that it isn't you. This screams that you're trying to bait him, and he's going to come straight here and try to take it."

"Let him," Cora said, crossing her arms over her chest. "It's done. Maybe it was hasty, but it's done. I'll call the police and tell them what I did, and they can pick him up." She turned to get back into the truck. When she moved, Sam saw the gun sitting on the seat between Rocky's feet.

His arm shot past her, and he had it almost before she could even register the movement. He checked the chamber and dropped the magazine, then held one part in each hand, staring at her. "Are you crazy?" he said, a vein pulsing in his forehead. "Are you trying to get yourself killed? Do you even have any idea how to use this?"

She shrugged. "Safety off, business end at the other guy."

"This is not funny!" he barked at her. Rocky started forward, and Cora caught him by the collar.

"Easy, Rocky. Unless he keeps calling me crazy."

"I did no such thing. But you sure are acting like it. You can't just take matters into your own hands, run around with a gun. Is this even your gun? Do you know how many unregistered, unlicensed weapons I take off people every day?" She shrugged. She didn't care. "Add another one to my God damned day." He shoved the magazine in one coat pocket and the gun in the other.

"Hey"—she reached forward—"give it back." He stepped backward.

Fine. She'd go rummage around the pawnshop and see if Harold had another one.

"Get in the truck. You're coming with me to my place where it's safer, and then we're calling the police."

"What? Why?" Cora shook her head.

"Because you broke your promise and went right ahead and put a target on your back. Because if you get in that truck and let me get you somewhere safe, then maybe I won't mention this." He nodded downward, where the butt of the gun was sticking out of his coat pocket.

"You wouldn't. Anyway, calm down." Cora was calm. Calmer, at least, now that her heart wasn't beating out of her chest. "Sam, listen, I should have told you. I screwed up and I'm sorry. I found the necklace and all I could think about was how it was the only way to make him pay for what he's done. I'll take the listings down. They've only been up for a couple hours anyway."

"Do it. Right now."

One look at his face and it was clear that he meant right now while I'm glaring at you, not right now after you go home and open up the laptop. Cora found her phone and opened the browser. It took a couple moments of squinting at the screen, but she finished and shoved the phone back into the truck. "There. You happy?"

"Happy? I'm not happy. Jesus, Cora, I'm so mad at you." His words said he was angry, but the look on his face had changed to something different. Something that looked more like sadness or disappointment and made her feel worse than the anger. He took off his hat and ran a hand through his hair. "Cora, get in the truck. I'll be right behind you. Go directly to the apartment, pack a bag for you and Rocky for a couple days. I'll take you to my place and we can talk to the police and arrange for some protection. Sorting this out is going to make a lot of people's lives more difficult, you know, not just yours."

"That's ridiculous, Sam. I'm not going to hole up somewhere and—"

"Yes, you are." His words were clipped. The anger was back. She looked at the tight line of his lips and couldn't believe they were the same ones that had been warm and soft just the day before. "You are, and don't bother arguing with me. If you force my hand, I'll take this gun you don't have a permit or carry license for right to the state barracks and kill two birds with one stone. If I have to, I'll swear on my mother's life you threatened me with it. I may only be a game warden, but that's still an officer of the law." A wry smile twisted his tight lips. "I bet they'll keep you nice and safe while you wait for charges. Maybe that's not such a bad idea."

"You wouldn't," she said, eyes narrowed. "Rocky, bite him. You can't arrest a dog for assaulting an *officer of the law*." Rocky growled at the sound of his name.

"Go for it," Sam said, his eyes flicking toward the dog. "I don't care if I have to go through him to pick you up and toss you in that truck, you're going. Do you understand me?"

Cora looked at him, then back at Rocky. "Sit, Rocky." He relaxed and plopped down on his haunches, letting out a woof that sounded relieved that guard dog time was over. She looked back up at Sam, who was staring at her expectantly. After a long moment, she nodded.

She climbed back into her truck and made a painfully slow three-point turn. On the way back to Pine Gap, Cora thought she could feel Sam glaring at her through the back window. Rocky whined next to her, probably queasy after the pell-mell car chase. "Not much farther, buddy. Just around the corner." He only needed to make it back to the apartment. If he threw up in Sam's work vehicle on the way to his house after that, it would serve Sam right.

The thought of the cabin made her flush. Half the heat in her cheeks was regret. He might have been kissing her there the day before, but she'd done a good job putting a stop to that. Cora was sorrier than she cared to admit about breaking her promise.

At the edge of town her vision clouded unexpectedly and her hands twitched on the wheel, causing the truck to swerve over the center line and narrowly miss a badly painted SUV coming in the opposite direction. Her phone rang a second later.

"What was that?" Sam said brusquely.

"Nothing."

"Okay. Park in front of the pawnshop. Go up and pack. I'll wait outside." He ended the call without another word. She dropped the phone into her bag, irritated. The little wave of gray that had crossed her vision at the turn, the slight burn in the fingertips that had caused her to swerve was strange, the way it flared up and then faded, gone by the time the phone rang, but by the time she was halfway down Church Street, the feeling had settled into its usual in-town dull roar, and the sudden odd surge was forgotten.

She didn't look back as Sam pulled up to park behind her. Cora got out and slammed the truck door, then went up to the apartment. "Ski resort or beach vacation?" she asked Rocky, grabbing a shopping bag from under the counter and shoving a pair of pajamas into it. "Don't forget the lingerie." She grimaced, throwing a couple pair of practical cotton Fruit of the Looms in. Not that anyone was likely to see them but her. She crammed a sweater and a pair of jeans on top and went in search of her toothbrush.

Locking the door behind her, bag of clothes over her wrist, tub of dogfood under the other, she opened the back door of Sam's vehicle for Rocky, then tossed her armload in after him. While she got in silently and buckled her seatbelt, Sam slid out of his jacket and threw it into the back seat, then looked over at her and nodded. "Ready?"

"Yes. Let's go."

They rode in tense silence until the town was behind them and the road began to incline toward Blackwell Mountain. She snuck a look sideways at Sam. His jaw was set in a clenched, hard line. "There isn't *really* much chance Jacob saw what I put up online about the necklace," she said meekly. "You don't *really* think there's a reason to be this worried, do you?" She hazarded another glance over. At first, he didn't respond. When he finally turned toward her, his face was softer than it had been a moment ago.

"I don't know, Cora. Maybe not. But it wouldn't have hurt you to pick up the phone." In the back seat Rocky whined. "See, even the dog knows that."

"Sam, go slow. He's been in the car a lot today. And not Sunday driving."

Sam paused just before the dirt crossroad. A left turn would swing up and away toward Sam's house. Straight ahead would take them farther in and eventually bring them to Blackwell Lake. Remembering last night's dream, Cora shivered.

A second later her vision grayed out again, a sudden blankness followed by a hot burn in her fingers. She flexed them uncomfortably.

"Damn carsick dog," Sam muttered, not noticing the glassy look in Cora's eyes next to him. "Sorry if it's cold, but I'm going to roll down the windows, just in case." Sam rolled slowly toward the crossroad, unbuckling his seatbelt to reach for the coat he'd taken off earlier, shrugging it on. "If I bring this back with a back seat full of mess I—"

Neither of them saw it coming until the last second. Only Rocky gave a small warning yip before the speeding car slammed into them like a battering ram.

45

The smell made her nostrils flare. Fetid and musty, and underneath the layers of uncleanliness, the ghost of a man's cologne, something sharp and peppery. Cora's eyes flew open, but she couldn't see anything, her vision blocked by whatever her face was bouncing against. She turned her head, the movement sending an arrow of pain through her body. She could see the ground rolling beneath her now, and one of her hands dangling limply below her, the arm it was attached to filled with a sickening hot pain. She kicked out viciously with her legs, not sure which end was up. Then she was falling. Cora landed in a broken pile on the ground.

"Enough of that. But perfect timing."

She rolled painfully onto her back and turned her head toward the voice. Cora blinked her eyes, but she knew who it was even before her double vision cleared. She skittered backward, pushing herself away with her feet and her one working arm. Crushed shells sliced through her pants and into the palm of her hand.

"Oh, no. I don't think so." He reached down and grabbed her by the ankles, hauling her forward again. She let out a shriek of pain as her broken, useless arm dragged behind her. Lying on her back, gasping for air, she looked up into Jacob Adler's eyes.

They were Jacob's eyes, but that was the only part of him she recognized. He was nothing like the man who had impressed and seduced her with his elegant dress and manners. The formerly close-cut hair was uncombed and matted. The trim beard was gone, revealing a deep, puckered scar that ran from his left ear to his chin like a malformed cleft.

The shirt he was wearing was wrinkled, the fabric limp and hanging slack from his shoulders from being worn too many times without washing. His pants, once neat and crisp, had lost their sharp creases down the front and showed shiny at the knees, hanging too long over his scuffed black shoes.

He saw Cora examining him. "So sorry if I'm not meeting your oh-so-high standards," he said. "The money Avery had on her only went so far, you know, especially since I had to blow so much of it getting into your pants. Thanks a bunch for running right to the bank with that cash, by the way. I'd planned on taking that back. And it's not like I could use her credit cards or sell her stuff. Cops would have been on me in a second. And of course"—he reached down and hauled Cora to her feet, jerking her painfully when she tried to struggle away—"and of course I hadn't planned on it having to last very long, after Avery was dead and I had the necklace."

"Where's Sam?"

Jacob let go of her arm and she stepped backward away from him. Her foot caught on the edge of a piece of wood. The crushed shell, the wooden dock. Blackwell Lake.

"Ranger Rick shot through the windshield like a rocket. He's a green smear on a tree. You dumb rednecks need to wear your seatbelts. The dog is smarter than either of you. At least he learned from his mistake and had the good sense to run away."

Sam unbuckling his seatbelt and reaching behind to put his jacket back on. The car slamming into them. The terrible pain and then nothing. The broken memories flashed in front of her eyes and Cora choked back vomit at the thought of Sam thrown through the glass. Jacob could be lying. He had to be. She had to go find him, find Rocky, get help.

She tried to edge sideways, away from the dock, looking for lights or movement anywhere around her. It was dark here, the sky thick with choking black clouds, but not one of the many windows were lit.

"Don't bother." Jacob took a step sideways to block her path. "There's no one here. Closed up tight as a tick for the season. Except for the old Benson place. I've had to break into that place twice now. Not quite as plush this time around, though." He shook his head. "Still, good to be back at the old family homestead."

In her head, all the pieces had been there; the eerie green eyes that had come down the branches of the Blackwell family tree, so striking on Atticus Blackwell they were mentioned in his wedding announcement, to his daughter Minnie Blackwell, and down to her descendants.

"Atticus Blackwell. His daughter. You're ..."

He clapped his hands mockingly. "Finally put that together, did you? I'm a chip off the old block, aren't I. Now that we have that out of the way ..." He reached a hand behind his back and pulled out a knife. An ugly black knife, handle small enough to be swallowed up in his big hand. The same knife that had taken her sister's life. "Time to tidy all this up."

When she had opened her eyes and seen Jacob Adler towering over her, maniacal gleam in his eyes, Cora had been terrified. Watching him tick the knife back and forth in his hand, the black blade bobbing back and forth and back and forth, knowing what he had done with it, her terror was strangely quieted, tempered enough by her rage that it allowed her to think. She eyed the blade with removal, watched the sharp raw edge move. If he reached out right now and drew it across her throat the way he had Kimmy's, he would get away with it. He might never pay for what he'd done. That couldn't be allowed to happen.

"Tell me why you want it so much," she whispered. She needed to buy herself some time to figure out how badly hurt she was. The side of her head felt numb and dead, the place where he had shot her torn open again, blood running down her neck and congealing, thick as molasses on her skin. Her right arm was useless, something in it damaged, likely broken in the accident. Everything hurt, from her head to her feet, the toes tingling their endless tingle. Even now, things that were lost called to her. "Why do you want it, Jacob? Or whoever you are."

He sighed a mocking sigh. "Seriously. This isn't a movie, Cora. In the real world, the bad guy doesn't stand around spitting out his life story."

"That's fine. Nobody wants to hear your sob story. And I'm sure it's a sob story." Cora's anger had made her words sharp, and she spat them out harshly. There was almost laughter in them, and she saw Jacob flinch, then recover. He reached out his hand, pointed the tip of the knife at Cora. She had no choice but to take a step back onto the dock. The water on either side of her was black as pitch, like a bottomless pit of crude oil. "No, wait, that's not true. I know who might want to hear it. A jury maybe. And then your cellmate. You can whisper it in his ear in the shower."

"Shut up, bitch," Jacob spat out. With his next menacing step forward, Cora took one back. "I just want what's mine. We've waited long enough. My family has done nothing but suffer because Atticus Blackwell refused to acknowledge his daughter. She lost everything, trying to get what was hers while his new family, they took everything."

"You're insane, you realize that." Cora eyed the water on either side of her, traced the parts of the bank she could see from the corner of her eye for something, someone. There was nothing except clouds in her vision and the pain in her body. She shook her head gently, to clear the haze, fixing her eyes on Jacob, who stood at the edge of the dock with his ugly knife held in front of him like a sword. "You're insane and you're a murderer. You're not getting anything but a couple life sentences."

"I'm not going to jail." He shook his head. For a moment there was someone else behind the icy green eyes, someone fearful. He gave the slightest shudder, then the evil glare returned. "I've been. I won't be going back."

"You've already been? Big surprise. What happened? They catch you feeling up the neighbor kids? Or are you the 'torture the family dog and bury it in the backyard' type. I bet that's it."

"Shut up!" Jacob swiped at her with the knife. She leaned backward, felt the whistle of the blade. "You know nothing. I did it for my family. Until me, they all failed. I figured out how to prove who we were. I broke into the Bensons' house to get the bitch's DNA. She attacked *me*. I wouldn't have had to kill her, but she wouldn't give up."

"You killed Avery Benson's mother," Cora gasped.

"All I needed was a piece of fucking hair. Her toothbrush. Anything. Anything to prove I shared Atticus Blackwell's blood. But she ruined it. I spent ten years in jail for that stupid bitch. My grandmother died while I was in there. Until the day she died, she never let me forget what was owed to us. What was taken from us. She never got to see things put right. But now, there's no one left to get in my way. I have the proof, and now, it's all going to be mine."

"How?" The question came out unbidden, the answer coming into her head almost at the same time she spoke. "The necklace. Atticus Blackwell's hair."

"Cora," Jacob said with a mocking smile. "And here I am thinking you're a complete burnout. Yes, Atticus Blackwell's hair. Avery's wouldn't have done me a damn bit of good. She wasn't even a fucking Blackwell, not really. Not a drop of Blackwell blood. Yet she inherited all of it. And she was going to give it all away."

She risked a step backward while Jacob ranted, sneaking a glance behind her. A few inches of wood, then nothing but depthless, cold, black.

"Can you believe that? She had it all, and she was going to give every last cent away. She was going to give half of it to any unwashed hick relatives of the people who died in Blackwell she could find and the rest to this shithole town. Even the necklace. She had the balls to look me in the eye and tell me it was worth more broken up and sold if it could bring somebody out of poverty. What about my fucking poverty? Those were her last words, you know, before I cracked her skull like an egg and you showed up and stole the necklace she tossed, thinking she could keep it from me."

"Her last words?" Cora said, taking a step backward. "Here's some last words, asshole. You're a murderer and you're going to see the inside of a jail cell. But you'll never, ever see the necklace."

Cora turned and ran the few short steps to the edge of the dock. Then she dove headlong into Blackwell Lake.

46

When Cora's head slid under the oily black water, it felt strangely warm after the chill air. She stayed under as long as she could, kicking and paddling with her one good arm, trying to gain as much distance from the dock as possible without resurfacing. When her breath ran out and her head broke the surface, she knew how deceptive the feeling of warmth was. The water might not be as cold as the early November air, but it was far colder than she could survive in for very long.

"Cute, Cora. Real cute." Jacob stood at the edge of the dock. She trod water and fumbled her way out of her heavy sweater, grunting in pain as she worked it off her broken arm. She kicked off her shoes as well, letting them slide one by one down into the inky depths. "What was the point of that, Cora? You're just delaying the inevitable." She kicked with her feet, moving herself farther away from the dock, but not far enough that she couldn't see the evil smile on Jacob's face. "Thanks, by the way. You're doing me a favor."

"I'm not going to tell you where it is, Jacob. Go while you have the chance. Someone will find the cars, and then they'll find us."

"Fat chance. This place is a God damned black hole. I would honestly kill myself if I had to live here like you do. I thought I was going to die from boredom watching you this whole time. It was honestly getting to be a race between you finally getting greedy enough to sell the necklace and me killing myself rather than spend another minute hiding in this hick town."

The times she'd felt eyes on her, felt something draw close then fade away, the strange moments of gray in her vision and fire in her limbs. Had that been him, watching her? "You've been here the whole time?" Cora spit out a mouthful of water. She was tiring fast, trying to kick backward toward the opposite bank without taking her eyes off Jacob.

"Where else would I go? Besides, I borrowed some money against my future inheritance from the kind of people who don't take kindly to not being paid back. I didn't have much choice but to wait for you to cough up the necklace. I knew you had it."

"I didn't have it." Cora opened her mouth to speak, inhaling a mouthful of water. In the decades since the foul coal slurry had rushed down the mountain and into the town, the poisonous sludge had settled out, but what filled her mouth felt as thick and oily as if the lake had been made yesterday. Cora choked and coughed, her head momentarily slipping under.

"Damn it." She heard Jacob's voice when she reemerged. It was getting harder and harder to make her legs kick as she tried to push herself across the lake. "Thought you were done for there." She saw Jacob shake his head in amusement. "Here's hoping."

"If I drown"—Cora spat out a mouthful of water—"you'll never know where the necklace is."

His laughter floated eerily across the surface of the water. "Sweetheart, I didn't bring you up here to torture you into telling me where it is, as much fun as that would have been. I've been watching you for weeks. If you had half a brain, you would have seen me, driving Avery Benson's car all spray painted like that piece of shit you drive. I've got alerts on all your usual online haunts, so I knew the second you thought you could get away with selling my property. All I had to do was keep track of you. You know, Cora"—he turned and walked off the dock, began circling the lake—"you really need to get a life. You don't go anywhere. And since you don't have it on you"—he waited to see if she would change her course, then stepped out onto the next dock, following her progress toward the far bank—"believe me, I checked, then it has to be at the pawnshop."

Her legs were moving feebly as Cora swam slowly forward, turning clumsily every few feet to keep Jacob in her sights. She couldn't feel her feet, but strangely, she could feel the tremor of lost things where her legs should have been, like disembodied, phantom limbs. With her own sensations being stolen by the cold, her strange abilities were taking their place. The call of lost things was strong enough now that it ran from head to toe, an eely electrical feeling inside her icy limbs. Her vision was occluded, a layer of gray film in front of her eyes, except when she turned to stroke toward the opposite bank. It was like a single warm point telling her to keep moving, toward the shore.

"It's not there," Cora said. "It's not at the—" The sky overhead broke, with a deafening crash of thunder and a bolt of lightning that lit up the sky and outlined the mocking smile on Jacob's face.

"Cora, you're missing the point. Must be hard, going through life being so clueless. I didn't pull you out of the car for information." He slid the knife into his pocket and reached behind him. She couldn't see it very clearly, but she didn't need to, to know it was a gun. "I can't believe I'm having to say this again, but I don't need you, now that you blew it and showed your hand. I need you to disappear. I need to be rid of you. Say hello to great-grandpa for me."

There was a sharp report and a splash to her left. Cora ducked under the water to avoid the second, closer bullet she knew would follow. She opened her eyes but there was only blackness, her sense of direction lost in the weightlessness of the water. Cora tried to kick, but she didn't know if she was kicking for the surface or pushing herself deeper into the lake.

She stopped struggling. Out of the darkness, shapes began to emerge. Cora saw a world form beneath her. Ghostly objects swirled and phantom people walked around the shadowy outline of a town. As she began to sink, it all became clearer. Rooftops and streets and a church with a silently swaying bell. And people, hundreds of people, all looking up at her, waiting for her to drift down and join them.

The urge to open her mouth and breathe in was so strong her lips parted slightly, and black water ran through her teeth. It would be easy enough, to let herself keep falling, join everything that was lost and waiting at the bottom of Blackwell Lake. It would be like drifting gently to sleep into a dream already fully formed before she even closed her eyes. Cora closed her eyes.

In the blackness there was a single point of light. It was stronger than the call of everything below, hotter than the electricity in her frozen hands and feet. Somewhere above, there was something greater that needed her to find it. It demanded that she find it. The undeniable pull claimed what little strength Cora had left and used it to make her feet kick, to make her good arm pull up and up.

Her head broke the surface in time with a deafening crack of thunder. She heard another bullet strike the water, or so she thought. It might have been one of the drops of rain that were hammering the surface of the lake. Jacob was still on the opposite dock, arm out, hand kicking back as he fired.

It was harder and harder to keep her head above the surface of the water. She was so cold now she only knew her legs were moving because she was getting closer to the bank. Cora was near enough now she could see tendrils of grass floating up like ghostly hair around her.

"Damn it, just fucking die," she heard him scream across the water. Another bullet struck, closer. It must have been his last, because he threw the gun into the water in a fit of rage and walked off the dock, picking up speed as he ran around the edge of the lake toward her.

47

The drops of rain came down hard as hail and just as cold when Cora hauled herself up over the rocky edge of the bank and onto the shore. The sky had gone black with the storm, but a sudden flash of lightning lit the sky and illuminated the figure of Jacob Adler charging around the edge of the lake toward her. She had pulled herself out of the water just shy of the southern end of the lake, far from where she'd jumped from the dock outside Avery Benson's chalet. She'd put nine or ten of the identical docks between herself and Jacob, but it wasn't enough distance to keep her safe for long.

Clutching her useless arm to her chest, Cora crossed the thin border of grass and then the path, the razor edges of the gleaming white pieces of shell slicing into her bare feet. She was sheltered from the worst of the downpour for a moment while she darted up the stairs of the closest chalet. She yanked desperately at the door, but it was no use. It was locked, as every other door would be now that the resort was closed for the season. Even if she could break a window and force her way in before Jacob reached her, where would she hide? What could she find to defend herself with?

There wasn't time. He was closer now, running down the path that lit up bright white with each flash of lightning. Cora stumbled back down the steps. She darted around the building and into the woods.

Crashing through the belt of underbrush, thorns and brambles tore at her bare skin, but Cora was so cold they felt like the brush of feathers. She tripped on frozen feet, her broken arm colliding with a tree branch. A scream of pain escaped before Cora could bite it back.

"That's a good girl. Keep making noise so I can hear you. Or better yet, just stay right there, Cora. I'll come help you. Into the next world."

She took off again, away from his voice, pushing blindly through the trees. It was so dark she'd gotten turned around already. Even if she was sure what direction she was headed, where should she go? The road could be empty for hours, days even, if the storm beating so severely on the trees above her brought a windfall across the narrow lane anywhere down the line. There was Sam's, and Jessica's just beyond it, but how far was that? A mile? Two? And she only knew roughly where they lay. She'd never make it.

"Come on, Cora. Don't be like that." He was closer than she anticipated, easily following her, maybe by her tracks, maybe by the sound of her heart, which was beating so hard it sounded like a drum to Cora. And he was making much better time, not shoeless and moving woodenly from the cold. "Do you really want to live like this, anyway?" His voice was taunting, falling into the seductive, slippery cadence it held when Cora first met him. "I mean, what have you got left, anyway? Look what you have to live with. You stole from me, that should be your biggest regret. You hopped into bed with a murderer. Thank God you passed out before I had to fuck you. Your sister is dead, which is your fault as much as mine, probably more. Oh, and your new boyfriend is wrapped around a pine tree somewhere." Jacob laughed loudly. "Seriously, I couldn't have planned that one better if I tried."

She crept forward, more quietly now. Under the canopy of the forest, the ground was soft, pine needle covered, and she felt carefully for each step. She also felt the unexplainable pull that had coaxed her across the lake and out of the water. With nowhere else safe to go, Cora followed it, letting it guide her forward.

Please God, let it be a weapon. Axe, gun, chainsaw, anything. Please don't let it be another watch or a compass or an old shoe. Please, for once, let this be something I need.

Whatever was leading her ahead, it was leading her away from Jacob.

She paused for a moment to listen. She couldn't make out anything but the branches above, wind-whipped and shivering in the storm.

Slipping from tree to tree, Cora bit back a cry when a sharp stick pierced her foot. She reached down and pulled it free, up through the flesh next to her big toe, swallowing a scream. When she heard the snap of a branch behind her, she ran, limping on her injured foot, holding her broken arm to her chest. She was beyond feeling the cold. All she had left was desperation and the small heat and light of whatever was pulling her forward. It didn't blind her, didn't hobble her. She would have been dead if it had. It pulled her steadily and surely forward, like the bracelet wrapped around the wrist of her broken arm had.

"I hear you, Cora. Enough of this. When I catch you, I'm going to gut you like a fish. Then, just for fun, I'm going to go find that dog of yours. The last thing he's going to eat is your entrails, sweetheart."

She wheeled to a halt when all at once she was out from under the cover of the trees. The rain fell like a barrage of bullets, striking open ground, fallen trees, and tilted marble headstones. A flash of lightning lit the sky over Blackwell Cemetery.

48

There was no way to hide her footprints over the bare ground of the cemetery, each bare foot leaving a clear, bloody indentation. The rain was slowing and the thick cover of clouds clearing, a mercy for her ability to see, but it would give her no help in erasing her tracks, and the faint light made her visible in the open space. For a moment she considered ducking back into the trees, but a glance behind her at the yawning, hungry darkness beneath them kept her from turning.

There was a flash of movement in the tree line, and Cora threw herself down behind a pair of headstones pinned under a fallen tree and froze. When Jacob's figure didn't emerge from the darkness, she collapsed into a pile behind her temporary blind.

She knew where she was. She had a better idea where Sam's place was. But she also knew that she would never make it. No matter how hard she tried to keep it still, her broken arm sent waves of pain that blackened her vision and turned her stomach each time she moved. The injured foot was leaking blood at an alarming rate, a puddle already accumulated around it where she lay. And she was too cold. Soaking wet, without shoes, in nothing but the thin cotton tank top she'd worn under her sweater, her body temperature had reached a dangerous low. Cora wasn't cold. She was beyond being cold. She was dying from the cold. She was on the ground, and now, she was finding it impossible to get up.

Cora thought about just sitting there. It might take him a while, and she might be too far gone when he did, but Jacob would find her.

Why fight it any longer? What was the point? She closed her eyes, the lids sinking heavily. They were the only part of her body that seemed to be doing what she wanted.

Everything else was gone, but the pull was still there. Her skin was a frozen shell, but on the inside, tendrils of warmth were threading through her veins. They wouldn't let her rest, even now, when she was so near the end. Because she couldn't make herself stop, Cora pushed painfully to her knees. She rested her head against the gravestone in front of her, against the swirling blackness the pain in her arm brought, until the heat surged in her chest, her legs pushing her, her frozen, bloody feet moving of their own accord. Cora didn't bother looking behind her, to see if Jacob Adler had reached the cemetery, though if he hadn't, he surely would. She took an unsteady step forward. Her vision shrank to a tunnel, and she took another, then another. She slogged across the cemetery, pulled along like a puppet on a string, toward the lower edge of the cemetery, where the ground started to roll down and away. Then, it all disappeared.

It had gotten her up off the ground, her ability to find leading her to something. Now that she had arrived, it left her. She had never felt so cold or so completely empty. There was nothing she could see, nothing but a single gravestone beside her and the shadow of the sun trapped behind the storm's gray clouds, as weak and unable to push through as she was. The hand she held out in front of her to feel her way looked like it had been carved from stone, like a cemetery angel. She took one last step forward.

A hand snaked out and grabbed her ankle.

Her mouth opened to scream but no sound came out. She tried to pull away, but with her good foot ensnared by the hand that had reached out from behind the gravestone, her pierced foot buckled under her weight. She hit the ground on her side, slamming her broken arm in the process. She kicked futilely against the burning hand clamped around her ankle.

"Cora," the voice said in a cracked, painful whisper. "Cora, it's me."

"Sam?" Cora stopped struggling, pushing herself up and moving to him. He was leaning up against the headstone, legs splayed out in front of him. She could see black lines of blood snaking down from his hairline. "Sam, I thought you were dead. Thank God. Jacob said—"

"I woke up under a tree with the dog licking my face."

"Rocky? Where is he?"

Sam shook his head. "As soon as I managed to get up, he ran off. I figured he'd go to you. I tried to follow him, but he was going too fast." Rocky was okay and far away from Jacob. That was something at least, a small relief. "There was no service, and nobody came by. I tried to make it to my place, but this was as far..." His words came out in hitches, like the effort of drawing breath was too much. "I think my ribs, my ankle. Broken. Where is he?"

Cora pulled herself beside him, pressed herself against him. "Not far," she whispered.

Sam shook his head. "This is bad. I can't go any farther. And you." He reached out a hand to touch her arm. One of his fingers was broken so badly it hung backward over the top of his hand. "You're hurt. And too cold."

He hitched himself forward and somehow slid off his jacket, pushing it toward her.

"No, Sam."

"You're going to argue with me now?" She slid her arms into the jacket, the bit of warmth left over from his body like a small miracle. "You have to go," Sam said. "Keep going. My house isn't that far. You can make it there and then to my brother's. They'll get help. They'll protect you. If I can slow him down I will, to give you more time."

"No, Sam. Not a chance. I'm not going anywhere."

"You're right, Cora." Jacob's voice sounded out of the gray. He stepped out of the trees, filthy and wild eyed, clasping the black-bladed knife in his fist. "You aren't going anywhere."

244

49

Cora pushed to her feet, trying to put herself in front of Sam. Swaying unsteadily, she heard the gasps of pain as he struggled to his feet behind her. "Run, Jacob. He called the police. They're on their way. You can make it if you go."

"Nice try, Cora. Really." He stood wide-legged in front of them. Cora shuffled backward, into Sam, who grabbed her arm for balance. "You're a good liar. I'll give you that. But I learn from my mistakes. If Deputy Dipshit here had gotten a call out, he wouldn't be propped up on a headstone bleeding all over his nice little uniform. I'm guessing you couldn't get a signal"—Jacob looked up into the sky and screamed—"because this place is the asshole of the universe."

Cora used the moment his head was turned to nudge Sam aside, trying to maneuver him so he wasn't pinned between her and the headstone.

"Go for it." Jacob's head dropped down and he stared at Cora. "You won't get far. He won't get anywhere." He ran the tip of the knife across his finger, testing the blade. "But I'm a nice guy."

"A nice guy? You're a psychopath," Cora spat out.

"That might hurt if it wasn't coming from some loose piece of white trash like you. Killing you is barely a crime. What's your life worth, anyway?"

Cora felt herself quaking with cold and rage, shaking so badly the sides of Sam's heavy jacket slapped against her legs. "Maybe nothing, Jacob. But my sister, her life was worth something. Avery Benson's was worth something. Her mother's. And me, at least I have the potential to amount to something." She could see she had Jacob's attention; his eyes fixed on her while he smiled a sick, cruel smile. Sam had his hand on her waist, trying to pull her behind him. With her useable hand, she pushed his down, toward the side of his jacket.

"That's the saddest thing I ever heard." Jacob sneered at her. "And potential requires a future. Which you are severely short on. Enough of this." He lunged forward, swiping wildly with the knife. Cora flung herself backward, pushing Sam aside as she tried to avoid Jacob's blade. She felt it like a whisper across the side of her face as she tumbled over the headstone and onto the ground behind it.

"I couldn't have planned this better." Jacob circled around to where she was trying futilely to roll over and get to her feet. She made it as far as her knees, then collapsed backward. "I mean, this is the second person I've killed on this same grave." Cora groped a hand blindly behind her, reaching for Sam. All she found was the name carved into the headstone's marble face. Fiona Clennan Blackwell. "Wraps things up nicely. Say—"

"Looking for this?"

From where she lay against Fiona Clennan's grave, Cora couldn't see what Sam was holding. She didn't need to. She'd guided Sam's hand to the heavy pocket of his jacket. The maniacal gleam in Jacob's eyes was more than enough to confirm that Sam had pulled the necklace from the pocket.

"Are you two insane?" Jacob pushed Cora aside with his foot. "You're seriously making this easier for me. Now I don't even have to go rummage through your yard sale shit to find it." He laughed, swiping his hand across his forehead, sending a shower of rain and sweat flying. "Hand it over."

"Come and get it, asshole." Sam was swaying unsteadily a few feet away. Fiona Clennan's necklace swung back and forth on its long chain, flashing a dull gold and red. There was nothing else in his hands. She reached down to the jacket pocket, sliding her good hand inside. Her fingers wrapped around the rough metal grip of Harold's gun, the one Sam had broken down and taken away from her in what felt like another lifetime. The problem was, she couldn't make her other arm work properly. While Jacob stepped over the headstone toward Sam, Cora struggled to get her hand into the opposite pocket for the magazine. She started to put the gun down, slide the jacket from her shoulders so she could retrieve the magazine and load the gun with her good hand, but there no time. Jacob was on Sam.

"I'll shoot, Jacob. Don't touch him."

Jacob whirled around to face the gun Cora was pointing at his head. He looked her up and down, then looked back over his shoulder at Sam, who looked tensed, ready to try to fight back but so unsteady on his feet he wouldn't last a moment. She stared at Jacob, willing herself not to twitch, willing him to believe the weapon in her hands was loaded.

Maybe he didn't believe it. Maybe he read her mind. Or maybe he was just crazy. But after one short moment, Jacob Adler stepped back over the tombstone. She willed Sam to go while he had the chance. Instead, he crumpled to the ground.

"Do it, bitch. Pull the trigger."

Cora stepped backward, stumbled, then found her feet and retreated another step. "Stop, Jacob. This is your last chance."

He didn't stop. He smiled and reached out with his knife, pointing it at her, pressing it against the barrel of the gun. "I didn't think so. I—"

Click.

She pulled the trigger; the firing pin encountered nothing. She let the gun fall to her side. Cora had played every card she had and failed. She wanted Sam to live. She wanted to live. But she wasn't going to give the man who killed her sister the satisfaction of watching her beg. She stared into the glass-green eyes. He was a man who had known who he was his entire life and had murdered and stolen and lied for that legacy. Cora had spent her entire life not knowing who she was until now.

"Do it then." She didn't flinch when he swung back his hand.

It never came back to cross her exposed neck. A black streak flashed in front of her instead.

Cora let the jacket slide to the ground, then went down on her knees on top of it, fumbling the magazine from the pocket. She jammed it into the gun and racked the slide awkwardly with one hand, biting back a cry of pain, then pulled herself back to her feet.

Rocky had Jacob's arm locked in his jaws, jerking it viciously, the knife clenched in Jacob's fist waving back and forth. Jacob tried to throw an arm around the dog's neck. He hooked his hand into Rocky's collar and pulled, choking him, trying to loosen the dog's grip.

"Jacob, let go of the knife," she yelled over Rocky's guttural snarls and Jacob's cries of pain. He twisted his hand into Rocky's collar, cutting off his windpipe.

Cora fired a shot into the ground next to them. "Jacob, let go of the dog. Drop the knife." A second later, Jacob's hands fell empty. Cora stepped over and kicked the knife away. "Rocky. Good Rocky. Go to Sam." As soon as the dog was clear, Cora trained the gun at Jacob Adler's head.

50

"**D**o it," Jacob said through jagged breaths, lying on his back, the barrel of the gun centered between his eyes. "Get it over with."

Cora felt Sam come up beside her, grab her shoulder for balance. "If you did, no one would ever question it. It was self-defense. No one would ever know otherwise."

Her hand shook. Her finger tensed. Out of the corner of her eye she saw Rocky's ears perk forward and she looked over her shoulder.

"I would know. And you would know." She took her finger off the trigger. "And they would know." There were figures approaching from the west side of the cemetery. Cora held the gun out to Sam. "Can you? Don't let him move." He nodded and took it from her. He took a step back and leaned against Fiona Clennan's tombstone without taking the barrel off Jacob for a moment.

"If you let me go, I'll give you half." Jacob started to roll over. Rocky snarled low in his throat.

"Shut up," Sam said.

Cora sank down to the ground and threw her good arm around the dog. "You're in charge from now on, okay? Like for good. I'm the pet now."

"Holy shit." Jessica's voice cut through the air. "What the hell happened to you guys?" She pointed at Jacob Adler. "And who the hell is that?" A group of men and women came up behind them. "Can you believe this shit, Carder?"

Cora looked over the small crowd, all armed, all the men looking a lot like Sam. She turned to Jessica.

"How did you find us?"

She rolled her eyes. "The dog. He showed up outside my house running like the devil was after him. It would be nice if you could teach him how to talk or scratch letters in the dirt or something. He wouldn't stop barking until he thought there was enough of us and we were armed and dangerous. We followed him until he took off. By then, we figured this was the only place he could be heading."

Sam had been helped to his feet. A number of rifles were trained on Jacob Adler, who had finally fallen silent. Even he knew it was over.

"Come on. They'll make sure he doesn't go anywhere until we can get back to civilization and call the staties. But you better get warmed up. It's too fucking cold to be soaking wet and tits out like this."

Cora almost laughed at something so normal as Jessica swearing like a sailor. She let herself be helped to her feet. But when Jessica tried to pull her away, she tugged her arm free and went over to Sam. "Where is it?" she asked. Sam nodded to the ground by his feet. Cora knelt and picked it up, then walked back to Jacob.

She let the pendant drop on its chain. It swung in front of him, his eyes following it back and forth. "Take a good look. Because you'll never see it again." She jerked the chain upward and caught the pendant in her hand. "Goodbye, Jacob."

51

"Hell of a place for a first date," Sam said, walking carefully with his cane, a cold wind blowing his hair up in a golden cloud around his head. There was a border of ice like a fine lace collar around the edge of the lake. It would tat itself farther and farther in, until the lake was covered, everything beneath it hidden in the darkness below.

"You're not counting Jell-O and applesauce in the hospital? I mean, with those backless hospital gowns, it was like skipping right to third base."

Sam laughed, throwing his head back. The sound echoed around them, sending a pair of mourning doves winging away in fright and bringing Rocky from where he'd been nosing around the edge of the water. "Whatever date this is, it's a hell of a choice. I get to pick next time."

"Deal." Cora nodded and smiled. A gust of wind blew down off the mountain, spinning snowflakes in tornadic spirals across the surface of the water. Sam reached over and put an arm carefully around her, avoiding the plaster cast that covered her arm from wrist to shoulder and pulling her close to him against the chill. She was warm enough in her heavy sweater, but she didn't protest, leaning into him.

"I take it you didn't come up for a swim."

She rolled her eyes. "Very funny. Once was enough. I know I told you about jumping in and swimming to get away from Jacob, but I never told you about when I went under." Another cold gust of wind scudded across the water, whipping up ripples that broke the mirror surface of the lake. "I could feel them all, Sam." She looked over at him. "I was running out of air, I was losing consciousness, but for a moment, I could see them all. I think I can still feel them, all those lost people, right now."

"All those people then, Cora," Sam said softly. "The people now, you can feel them, but that won't bring them back."

"I know," Cora said. "I'll never stop wondering if I could have saved Kimmy. But wondering doesn't change the past."

"But you can change the future."

"You're such a dork." Cora laughed and tucked herself more firmly out of the wind under his arm. Rocky sniffed around her boots, then plopped onto his belly on the dock in front of them. "But you know what, somebody's future is getting changed. Reggie Benson is honoring his daughter's wishes. Every cent of the Blackwell fortune is being donated to charity. A big chunk of that is earmarked for Pine Gap, because of the few people that survived, most of them went there."

"And there are no more Blackwells to lay claim to it."

She hadn't pulled the trigger and ended Jacob's life. She knelt to rub Rocky's head and to hide her face. What Sam didn't know was that when Jacob was lying on the ground before her, the man who murdered her sister in front of her, in her sights, Cora had started to pull that trigger. If help had come any later...

"I ..." Cora swallowed and stood back up, turning to Sam. "I wanted to kill him, Sam."

He studied her for a moment with dark, serious eyes, then nodded. "But you didn't. And he's dead now anyway. He brought that on himself."

She turned back to look out over the lake. After all he'd done, Jacob was dead. His bad debts to dangerous men had caught up with him before he served a day of his life sentence.

"It's colder than a brass bra out, you know. What did you want to come here for?"

"A brass bra?" Cora said. "You got that one from Jessica."

Sam shook his head. "You don't want to hear what she thinks it's colder than. But you can ask her at lunch. If you can get a word in edgewise. My mom's coming, and once she gets her hooks into you, you're toast. Sure you don't want to get in the car, head for the Mexican border?"

"Tempting," Cora said. "But I doubt Rocky would like the heat, so I guess I'll tough it out. I just want to do one thing quick, then we can go."

Cora smiled and reached into her pocket. She pulled out the long gold chain, and finally, Fiona Clennan Blackwell's pendant.

"Whew." Sam whistled.

She nodded, holding it up to the light. The rubies and diamonds flashed, throwing white fireworks and blood-red shards across the dock. She let it fall to the wood. Cora brought her boot down on the pendant.

Picking it back up, she carefully pried away the broken glass and fished out the little plait of hair. Shredding it between her thumb and forefinger, Cora watched the strands of gold carried away on the wind, scattered across the surface of the lake.

She took the necklace and swung it around and around by its long chain. Cora let go, and their heads turned, following it as it flew across the sky. It struck the water with a gentle plop and sank out of sight.

"It's gone, for good. It's beyond even my ability now. Some things should never be found."

I hope you enjoyed The Body at Blackwell Lake. If you did, kindly take a moment to visit amazon.com and leave a review.

Blackwell Lake, Blackwell Cemetery and Pine Gap are all products of my imagination. But they were inspired by some very real places in Pennsylvania, namely the real coal and lumber ghost towns of Laquin and Barclay. Blackwell Cemetery is a blatant rip-off Barclay Cemetery, a very real place, and one many claim is inhabited by some very real ghosts. Ghosts or not, if you ever visit Northeastern Pennsylvania and feel like braving narrow rutted lanes, potholes and miles without cellphone service, take an hour to walk amongst the tombstone of Barclay Cemetery. Brush last year's leaves and forest moss from the tilting headstones and read the names of long-dead miners and their families. Walk along the foundations of the old houses and the lost town's church. But don't stay too late, unless you're very brave, or very interested in seeing for yourself if the dead in abandoned cemeteries rest easy, or if they pace restlessly, like the dead beneath the waters of Blackwell Lake.

ABOUT THE AUTHOR

I'm not a big fan of attention. Thank goodness the 'About the Author' page is something many readers skip. If you're one of those cover-to-cover few that take the time to read the writer's life story, here are a few words to keep you from feeling ripped off.

A.M. Caplan was born and raised in the same part of Northeastern Pennsylvania in which most of her books are set. She doesn't have any cats yet, but she's young enough that her crazy cat lady future may still be realized. Intrigued? Probably not. I don't blame you.

You can find the author at **amcaplan.com**.

Also by A.M. Caplan

Echoes
Reverberation
Dead Quiet

Printed in Great Britain
by Amazon

44921505R00152